# Tradition

## (The Marrow of Tradition)

### Charles W. Chesnutt

Published by

**THE X PRESS, 55 BROADWAY MARKET, LONDON E8 4PH.**

TEL: 081 985 0797

Distributed by Turnaround, 27 Horsell Road, London N5 1XL
Tel: 071 609 7836

Printed by BPC Paperbacks Ltd, Aylesbury, Bucks.

ISBN 1-874509-12-3

# Introduction

A white ex-acquaintance told me proudly about how she had instigated an insurance fraud by walking into her local police station and claiming she had been mugged by a black guy. "I knew that if I said it was a black guy they would believe me immediately," she said.

Recently we have seen infamous cases in the United States where white men have murdered their pregnant wives and children and blamed black assailants. The police have been quick to assume a lynch mob mentality in their pursuit of these non-existent black criminals. This 'blame it on a black man' tradition goes as far back as slavery. Charles W. Chesnutt uses it as the basis of his novel *The Marrow of Tradition (1901)*, in which he confronts the origins and effects of white supremacist politics, which by the turn of the century had taken control of most of the South.

*Tradition* is set in the Deep South after the Civil War and Emancipation, in the town of Wellington, North Carolina, where the best doctors and teachers are black and the desperate white community struggle to retain any of the vestiges of 'white supremacy' which they enjoyed during slavery.

Captain McBane and his fellow townsman Major Carteret, live to make sure that there will always be at least one class of people beneath their social group. "These damned niggers", curses Major Carteret, who longs for a return to the days when his family owned thousands of slaves and basks in the glorification of 'white blood', and black repression. Pitched against them is a burgeoning black middle class led by the brilliant Dr. Miller, who has overcome all the obstacles in his way to climb to the top of his profession.

They clash when white supremacists, driven by envy at the increasing success of the new black middle classes, plot to start a race riot. (The infamous Wilmington Massacre of November 1898 — when violent means were used to impose white supremacy on a North Carolina town which Chesnutt often visited in his youth — seems to have been the basis of the fictional account in *Tradition*).

As the story unfolds, we discover that social intermingling in the Deep South has produced liaisons which cross the racial front lines of society-at-large. But while the black population are willing to accept their mixed ancestry, the whites will do anything to conceal theirs.

*Tradition* threads together the lives of two families. The Carterets represent the post-Civil War southern aristocracy. Dr Miller and his wife, Janet, embody the new order. The relationship between these two families is complicated by the fact that Olivia Carteret is the half-sister of Janet Miller, and however much Olivia would like to hide the fact, their lives are inextricably bound together.

*Tradition* is a classic family saga — shot through with laughter, tears and suspense — which richly deserves its place in the black literary hall of fame.

DOTUN ADEBAYO
November 1994

# ABOUT THE AUTHOR

Charles Waddell Chesnutt was born in Cleveland, Ohio, in 1858 the son of a grocery store owner.

He grew up in Fayetteville, North Carolina, where he received his formal education at a school founded by the Freedmen's Bureau.

Chesnutt started working as a schoolteacher from the age of fourteen and eventually became the principal of the State Colored Normal School in Fayetteville. He returned to Cleveland in 1884 to pursue a career in writing, through which he hoped to earn a better living and to fight racism.

His first published work, *The Goophered Grapevine (1887)*, was a short story written in dialect. He continued writing short stories which were eventually published in two collections, *The Conjure Woman(1899)* and *The Wife of His Youth and Other Stories of the Color Line (1899)*.

These collections sold well and were soon followed by his debut novel, *The House Behind the Cedars (1900)*, then by *The Marrow of Tradition (1901)* and *The Colonel's Dream (1905)*.

In 1928, Charles W. Chesnutt was awarded the NAACP's Spingarn Medal, for distinguished literary achievement. He died in 1932.

# I

# At Break of Day

"STAY HERE BESIDE HER, MAJOR. I SHALL NOT BE needed for an hour yet. Meanwhile I'll go downstairs and snatch a bit of sleep, or talk to old Jane."

The night was hot and sultry. Though the windows of the chamber were wide open and the muslin curtains looped back, not a breath of air was stirring. Only the shrill chirp of the birds and the muffled croaking of the frogs in some distant marsh broke the night silence. The heavy scent of magnolia, overpowering even the strong smell of drugs in the sickroom, suggested death and funeral wreaths, sorrow and tears, the long journey home, the last sleep. The major shivered with apprehension as the slender hand which he held in his own contracted nervously and in a spasm of pain clutched his fingers with a vice-like grip.

Major Carteret, dressed in brown linen, had thrown off his coat. The stifling heat, in spite of the palm-leaf fan, was scarcely less oppressive than his own thoughts. Long ago, while yet a mere boy in years, he had come home to find his family, one of the oldest and proudest in the state, hopelessly impoverished by the war—their ancestral home swallowed up in the common ruin. His elder brother had sacrificed his life on the bloody altar of the lost cause and his father, broken and chagrined, died not many years later, leaving the major the last of his line. He had tried in various pursuits to gain a foothold in the new life, but with indifferent success until he won the hand of Olivia Merkell, whom he had seen grow from a small girl to glorious womanhood. With her money he had founded the Morning Chronicle, which he had made the most influential

1

paper in the State. The fine old house in which they lived was hers. In this very room she had first drawn the breath of life; it had been their nuptial chamber; and here, too, within a few hours, she might die, for it seemed impossible that one could long endure such frightful agony and live.

One cloud alone had marred the otherwise perfect serenity of their happiness. Olivia was childless. To have children to perpetuate the name of which he was so proud, to write it still higher on the roll of honor, had been his dearest hope. A few months ago this dead hope had revived and altered the whole aspect of their lives. But as time went on, his wife's age had begun to tell upon her, until even Dr. Price, the most cheerful and optimistic of physicians, had warned him, while hoping for the best, to be prepared for the worst. Mrs. Carteret had only this day suffered from a nervous shock, which, it was feared, had hastened by several weeks the expected event.

Dr. Price went downstairs to the library, where a dim light was burning. An old black woman, dressed in a gingham frock, with a red bandana handkerchief coiled around her head, was seated by an open window. She rose and curtsied as the doctor entered and dropped into a willow rocking-chair near her own.

"How did this happen, Jane?" he asked in a subdued voice, "You ought to have taken better care of your mistress."

"Now look a-here, Doctor Price," returned the old woman in a whisper, "you don't wanna come talkin' none of yo' foolishness 'bout my not takin' care of Miss 'Livy. She never would 'a' said such a thing! Seven of eight months ago, when she sent for me, I says to her, says I:—

" 'Lawd, Lawd, honey! You don't tell me dat after all these long weary years of waitin' the good Lawd is done heard yo' prayer an' is gwine to send you the chile you been wantin' so long an' so bad? Bless his holy name! Will I come an' nurse yo' baby? Why, honey, I nursed you, an' nursed yo' mammy thru her las' sickness, an' laid her out when she died. I wouldn't let nobody else nurse yo' baby; an' mo'over, I'm gwine to come an' nurse you too. You're young side of me, Miss 'Livy, but you're awfully ole to be having yo' first' baby, an' you'll need

2

somebody roun', honey, what knows all 'bout the family, an' their ways an' their weaknesses, an' I don't know who that'd be if it weren't me.'

" 'Deed, Mammy Jane,' says she, 'there ain't nobody else I'd have but you. You can come as soon as you wanna an' stay as long as you mean to.'

"An here I is, an' here I'm gwine to stay. For Miss 'Livy is my ole mistress' daughter, an' my ole mistress was good to me, an' they ain't none of her folks gwine to suffer if ole Jane can help it."

"Your loyalty does you credit, Jane," observed the doctor; "but what happened to Mrs. Carteret to-day. Did the horse run away, or did she see something that frightened her?"

"No, suh, the hoss didn't git scared, but Miss 'Livy did see somethin', or somebody; an' it weren't no fault of mine nor hers neither—it goes further back, suh, further dan dis day. Does you 'member the time when my ole mistress, Miss 'Livy upstairs' mammy, died? No? Well, I'll tell you all about it.

"When my ole mistress, Miss 'Liz'beth Merkell took sick for the las' time, her sister Polly come to the house to help nurse her. Miss 'Livy was about six years ole then, the sweetes' little angel you ever laid eyes on; an' on her dyin' bed Miss 'Liz'beth ax' Miss Polly for to stay here an' take care of her chile, an' Miss Polly she promise'. She was a widow for the second time, an' didn't have no chillun, an' could jes' as well come as not.

"But there was trouble after the funeral, an' it happen' right here in dis library. Mars Sam was sitting by the table, when Miss Polly come downstairs, slow an' solemn, all in black.

" 'Well, Samuel,' says she, 'now dat we've done all we can for poor 'Liz'beth, it only 'mains for us to consider Olivia's future.'

"Mars Sam nodded his head, but didn't say nothin'.

" 'I don't need to tell you,' says she, 'dat I am willin' to carry out the wishes of my dead sister, an' sacrifice my own comfort, an' make myself yo' housekeeper an' yo' child's nurse. It was her dyin' wish, an' on it I will act', if it is also yours.'

"Mars Sam didn't want Miss Polly to come, suh; for he

3

didn't like her. He was scared of Miss Polly."

"I don't wonder," yawned the doctor, "if she was anything like she is now."

"Worse, suh, for she was younger, an' stronger. She always would have her say, no matter 'bout what, an' her own way. She had already been in the house for a week, an' Mars Sam knew if she once come to stay, she'd be the mistress of everybody in it an' him too. But what could he do but say yes?

" 'Then it is understood, is it,' says Miss Polly, when he had spoke, 'dat I am to take charge of the house?'

" 'All right, Polly,' says Mars Sam, wid a deep sigh. 'You won' fin' much to do, for Julia is a good housekeeper, an' can tend to most everything, under yo' directions.'

"Miss Polly stiffen' up like a ramrod. 'Samuel,' says she, 'when I assumes charge of yo' house, there ain't gwine to be no 'vided 'sponsibility; an' as for dis Julia, me an' her couldn't git 'long together nohow. If I stays, Julia goes.'

"When Mars Sam heard dat, he picked up his courage. Miss Polly had showed her hand too plain. My mistress hadn't got cold yet, an' Miss Polly, who'd been a widow for two years dis las' time, was already figurin' on takin' her place for good.

" 'My dear Polly,' says Mars Sam, quite determined, 'I couldn't possibly send Julia away. Fact is, I couldn't git 'long widout Julia. She's been runnin' dis house like clockwork befo' you come, an' I likes her ways. My dear, 'Liz'beth set a heap of store by Julia, an' I'm gwine to keep her for 'Liz'beth's sake.'

"Miss Polly's eyes flashed fire. 'Ah,' says she, 'I see—I see! You prefer her housekeepin' to mine, indeed! Dat is a fine way of talk to a lady! An' a heap of respec' you is got for the memory of my poor dead sister!'

"Mars Sam was willin' for her to imagine what she please', jes' so long as she kept out of his house an' let him alone.

" 'No, Polly,' says he, gittin' bolder as she got madder, 'there ain't no use talkin'. Nothin' would make me part wid Julia.'

"Miss Polly roared an'hollered, but Mars Sam held on. Miss Polly wouldn't give in neither, an' so she finally went away.

They made some kind of arrangement afterwards, an' Miss Polly took Miss 'Livy to her own house. Mars Sam paid her board an' 'lowed Miss Polly somethin' for takin' care of her."

"And Julia stayed?"

"Julia stayed, suh, an' a couple of years later her chile was born, right here in dis house."

"But you said," observed the doctor, "that Mrs. Ochiltree was in error about Julia."

"Yes, suh, so she was, when my ole mistress died. But dis was two years after—an' what has to be has to be. Julia had a easy time; she had a black gal to wait on her, a buggy to ride in, an' everything she wanted. Everybody s'posed Mars Sam would give her a house an' lot, or leave her somethin' in his will. But he died suddenly and didn't leave no will, an' Miss Polly got herself 'pointed guardian to young Miss 'Livy, an' drive Julia an' her young un out of the house, an' lived here in dis house wid Miss 'Livy till Miss 'Livy married Major Carteret."

"And what became of Julia?" asked Dr. Price.

Such relations, the doctor knew very well, had been all too common in the old slavery days and not a few of them had been projected into the new era. Sins, like snakes, die hard. The habits and customs of a people were not to be changed in a day, nor by the stroke of a pen.

"Well," resumed Jane, "everybody s'posed, after what had happen', dat Julia'd keep on livin' easy, for she was young an' good-lookin'. But she didn't. She tried to make a livin' sewin', but Miss Polly wouldn't let the bes' white folks hire her. Then she took up washin', but didn't do no better at dat; an' by an' by she got so discourage' dat she married a shifty yaller man, an' died of consumption soon after—an' was 'bout as well off, for dis man couldn't hardly feed her nohow."

"And the child?"

"One of the Northern white lady teachers at the mission school took a likin' to little Janet, an' put her thru school, an' sent her to the North for study to be a school teacher. When she come back, 'stead of teachin' she married ole Adam Miller's

5

son."

"The rich stevedore's son, Dr. Miller?"

"Yes, suh, dat's the man—you knows him. Dis boy was jes' gwine away for to study to be a doctor, an' he married dis Janet, an' took her 'way wid him. They went off to Europe, or Irope, or Orope, or somewhere or another, 'way off yonder, an' come back here las' year an' started dis here hospital an' school for to train the black gals for nurses."

"He's a very good doctor, Jane and is doing a useful work. But you haven't yet told me what brought on Mrs. Carteret's trouble."

"I'm jes' comin' to dat dis minute, suh. Dis Janet, what's Miss 'Livy's half-sister, is as much like her as if they was twins. Folks sometimes takes 'em for one another—I s'pose it tickles Janet almost to death, but it do make Miss 'Livy rippin'. An' then 'way back yonder jes' after the war, when the ole Carteret mansion had to be sol', Adam Miller bought it, an' dis Janet an' her husban' is been livin' in it ever since ole Adam died, 'bout a year ago; an' dat makes the major mad, 'cause he don't wanna see cullud folks livin' in the ole family mansion what he was born in. An' mo'over, an' dat 's the worst of all, whiles Miss 'Livy ain't had no chillun befo', dis sister of hers is got a fine-lookin' little yaller boy, what favors the family so dat if Miss 'Livy'd see the chile anywhere, it'd almost break her heart for to think 'bout her not having no chillun herself. So today, when Miss 'Livy was out ridin' an' met dis Janet wid her boy, she jes' had a fit of hysterics right there in the buggy. She was almost home, an' William got her here, an' you know the res'."

Major Carteret, from the stairs, called the doctor anxiously.

"You had better come along up now, Jane," said the doctor.

For two long hours they fought back the grim spectre that stood by the bedside. The child was born at dawn. Both mother and child, the doctor said, would live.

"Bless its little heart!" exclaimed Mammy Jane, as she held up the tiny mite. "It's the very spit an' image of its pappy!"

The doctor smiled. The major laughed aloud. Jane's witticism was a welcome diversion from the strain of the last few hours.

"Be that as it may," said Dr. Price cheerfully, "and I'll not dispute it, the child is a very fine boy—a very fine boy, indeed! Take care of it, major," he added with a touch of solemnity, "for your wife can never bear another."

With the child's first cry a refreshing breeze from the distant ocean cooled the hot air of the chamber; the heavy odor of the magnolia, gave place to the scent of rose and lilac and honeysuckle. The birds in the garden were singing lustily.

All these sweet and pleasant things found an echo in the major's heart. He stood by the window and looking toward the rising sun, breathed a silent prayer of thanksgiving. All nature seemed to rejoice in sympathy with his happiness at the fruition of this long-deferred hope and to predict for this wonderful child a bright and glorious future.

Old Mammy Jane, however, was not entirely at ease concerning the child. She had discovered, under its left ear, a small mole, which led her to fear that the child was born for bad luck.

Not wishing to be considered as a prophet of evil, Jane kept her own counsel in regard to this significant discovery. But later, after the child was several days old, she filled a small vial with water in which the infant had been washed and took it to a certain wise old black woman, who lived on the farther edge of the town and was well known to be versed in witchcraft and conjuration. The conjure woman added to the contents of the bottle a bit of calamus root and one of the conical vertebrae from the skeleton of a black cat, with several other mysterious ingredients, the nature of which she did not disclose. Following instructions given her, Aunt Jane buried the bottle in Carteret's back yard, one night during the full moon, as a good-luck charm to ward off evil from the little grandson of her dear mistress, long since dead and gone to heaven.

7

# II

# The Christening Party

THEY NAMED THE CARTERET BABY THEODORE Felix. Theodore was a family name and had been borne by the eldest son for several generations. Having thus given the child two beautiful names, replete with religious and sentimental significance, they called him—"Dodie."

The baby was christened some six weeks after its birth. Old Mammy Jane, who had been brought up in the church, but who, like some better informed people in all ages, found religion not inconsistent with a strong vein of superstition, felt her fears for the baby's future much relieved when the rector had made the sign of the cross and sprinkled little Dodie with the water from the carved marble font. Upon this special occasion Mammy Jane had been provided with a seat downstairs among the white people, to her own satisfaction and to the envy of a small colored attendance in the gallery.

On the following Monday evening the major gave a christening party. Owing to Mrs. Carteret's still delicate health, only a small number of intimate friends and family were invited to attend. These were the rector; old Mrs. Polly Ochiltree, the godmother; old Mr. Delamere, a distant relative and also one of the sponsors; and his grandson, Tom Delamere. The major had also invited Lee Ellis, his young city editor, for whom he had a great liking. These, with the family itself, which consisted of the major, his wife and his half-sister, Clara Pemberton, a young woman of about eighteen, made up the eight persons for whom covers were laid.

Ellis was the first to arrive, a tall, loose-limbed young man, with a slightly freckled face, hair verging on auburn, a firm chin and honest gray eyes. He was left alone for a few minutes in the parlor, a spacious, high-ceilinged room, with large windows and fitted up in excellent taste, with stately reminiscences of a past generation. The walls were hung with figured paper. The ceiling was whitewashed and decorated in the middle with a plaster centre-piece, from which hung a massive chandelier sparkling with prismatic rays from a hundred crystal pendants. The furniture was old and in keeping with the room.

At seven o'clock a carriage drove up, from which alighted an elderly gentleman, with white hair and mustache and bowed somewhat with years. Short of breath and painfully weak in the legs, he was assisted from the carriage by a colored man, apparently about forty years old, to whom short side-whiskers and spectacles imparted an air of sobriety. This attendant gave his arm respectfully to the old gentleman, who leaned upon it heavily, but with as little appearance of dependence as possible. The servant, assuming a similar unconsciousness of the weight resting upon his arm, assisted the old gentleman carefully up the steps.

"I'm all right now, Sandy," whispered the gentleman as soon as his feet were planted firmly on the piazza. "You may come back for me at nine o'clock."

Having taken his hand from his servant's arm, he advanced to meet a lady who stood in the door awaiting him, a tall, elderly woman, gaunt and angular of frame, with a mottled face and high cheekbones partially covered by bands of hair entirely too black and abundant for a person of her age.

"Perhaps you'd better not send your man away, Mr. Delamere," observed the lady, in a high shrill voice, which grated upon the old gentleman's ears. "You might need him before nine o'clock. One never knows what may happen after one has had the second stroke. And moreover, our butler has fallen down the back steps—negroes are so careless!—and sprained his ankle so that he can't stand. I'd like to have Sandy stay and wait on the table in Peter's place, if you don't mind."

"I thank you, Mrs. Ochiltree, for your solicitude," replied

9

Mr. Delamere, with a shade of annoyance in his voice, "but my health is very good just at present and I do not anticipate any catastrophe which will require my servant's presence before I am ready to go home. But I have no doubt, madam," he continued, with a courteous inclination, "that Sandy will be pleased to serve you, if you desire it, to the best of his poor knowledge."

"I shall be honored, ma'am," assented Sandy, with a deep bow, "only I'm 'feared I ain't rightly dressed for to wait on table. I was only goin' to prayer meetin', an' so I didn't put on my bes' clothes. If Miss Ochiltree ain't gwine to need me for the nex' fifteen minutes, I can ride back home in the carriage an' dress myself suitable for the occasion, suh."

"If you think you'll wait on the table any better," said Mrs. Ochiltree, "you may go along and change your clothes; but hurry back, for it is seven now and dinner will soon be served."

Sandy retired with a bow. While descending the steps to the carriage, which had waited for him, he came face to face with a young man just entering the house.

"Am I in time for dinner, Sandy?" asked the newcomer.

"Yes, Mister Tom. Dinner won't be ready till I git back, which won't be for fifteen minutes or so yet."

Throwing away his cigarette, the young man crossed the piazza with a light step and entered the house with the air of one thoroughly at home. The lights in the parlor had been lit and Ellis, who sat talking to Major Carteret when the newcomer entered, covered him with a jealous glance.

Slender and of medium height, with a small head of almost perfect contour, a symmetrical face, dark almost to swarthiness, black eyes, which moved somewhat restlessly, curly hair of raven tint, a slight mustache, small hands and feet and fashionable attire, Tom Delamere, was easily the handsomest young man in Wellington.

He gave his hand to the major, nodded curtly to Ellis, saluted his grandfather respectfully and inquired for the ladies.

"Olivia is dressing for dinner," replied the major; "Mrs. Ochiltree is in the kitchen, struggling with the servants. Clara—

Ah, here she comes now!"

Ellis, was already looking toward the hall and was the first to see her. Clad in an evening gown of simple white, to the close-fitting corsage of which she had fastened a bunch of pink roses, she was to Ellis a dazzling apparition. To him she was the embodiment of symmetry, her voice sweet music, her movements the perfection of grace; and it scarcely needed a lover's imagination to read in her fair countenance a pure heart and a high spirit. There were suggestive depths of tenderness, too, in the curl of her lip, the droop of her long lashes, the glance of her blue eyes—depths that Ellis had long since divined, though he had never yet explored them. She gave Ellis a friendly nod as she came in, but for the smile with which she greeted Delamere, Ellis would have given all that he possessed.

"You are the last one, Tom," she said reproachfully. "Mr. Ellis has been here half an hour."

Delamere threw a glance at Ellis which was not exactly friendly.

"The rector is not here," answered Tom triumphantly. "You see I am not the last."

"The rector," replied Clara, "was called out of town at six o'clock this evening, to visit a dying man and so cannot be here. You are the last, Tom and Mr. Ellis was the first."

Delamere gave a plausible excuse which won Clara's pardon and another enchanting smile, which pierced Ellis like a dagger. He knew very well that Delamere's excuse was a lie. Ellis himself had been ready as early as six o'clock, but judging this to be too early, had stopped in at the Clarendon Club for half an hour, to look over the magazines. While coming out he had glanced into the cardroom, where he had seen his rival deep in a game of cards, from which Delamere had evidently not been able to tear himself until the last moment.

The two young people walked over to a window on the opposite side of the large room, where they stood talking to one another in low tones. The major had left the room for a moment. Old Mr. Delamere, who was watching his grandson and Clara with an indulgent smile, proceeded to rub salt into

Ellis' wounds.

"They make a handsome couple," he observed. "I remember well when her mother, an ideally beautiful woman of an excellent family, married Daniel Pemberton, who was not of so good a family, but had made money. The major, disapproved of the match; he considered that his mother, although a widow and nearly forty, was marrying beneath her. But he has been a good brother to Clara and a careful guardian of her estate. Ah, young gentleman, you cannot appreciate, what it means, to one standing on the brink of eternity, to feel sure that he will live on in his children and his children's children!"

Ellis was appreciating at that moment what it meant, to see the girl whom he loved absorbed completely in another man. She had looked at him only once since Tom Delamere had entered the room and then merely to use him as a spur with which to prick his favored rival.

"Yes, sir," he returned mechanically, "Miss Clara is a beautiful young lady."

"And Tom is a good boy—a fine boy," returned the old gentleman. "I am very well pleased with Tom and shall be entirely happy when I see them married."

Ellis could not echo this sentiment. The very thought of this marriage made him miserable. He had always understood that the engagement was merely tentative, a sort of family understanding. Ellis saw Delamere with the eye of a jealous rival and judged him mercilessly. He did not at all believe that Tom Delamere would make a fit husband for Clara Pemberton; but his opinion would have had no weight—he could hardly have expressed it without showing his own interest. Moreover, there was no element of the sneak in Lee Ellis' make-up. The very fact that he might profit by the other's discomfiture left Delamere secure, so far as he could be affected by anything that Ellis might say. But Ellis did not shrink from a fair fight and though in this one the odds were heavily against him, yet so long as this engagement remained indefinite, so long, indeed, as the object of his love was still unwed, he would not cease to hope. Such a sacrifice as this marriage dearly belonged in the

12

catalogue of impossibilities. Ellis had not lived long enough to learn that impossibilities are merely things of which we have not learned, or which we do not wish to happen.

Sandy returned at the end of a quarter of an hour and dinner was announced. Mr. Delamere led the way to the dining-room with Mrs. Ochiltree. Tom followed with Clara. The major went to the head of the stairs and came down with Mrs. Carteret upon his arm, her beauty rendered more delicate by the pallor of her countenance and more complete by the happiness with which it glowed. Ellis went in alone. In the rector's since it was practically a family party which sat down, with the exception of Ellis, who, as we have seen, would willingly have placed himself in the same category.

The table was tastefully decorated with flowers, which grew about the house in lavish profusion. In warm climates nature adorns herself with true feminine vanity.

"What a beautiful table!" exclaimed Tom, before they were seated.

"The decorations are mine," said Clara proudly. "I cut the flowers and arranged them all myself."

"Which accounts for the admirable effect," rejoined Tom with a bow, before Ellis, to whom the same thought had occurred, was able to express himself. He had always counted himself the least envious of men, but for this occasion he coveted Tom Delamere's readiness.

"The beauty of the flowers," observed old Mr. Delamere, with sententious gallantry, "is reflected upon all around them. It is a handsome company."

Mrs. Ochiltree beamed upon the table with a dry smile.

"I don't perceive any effect that it has upon you or me," she said. "And as for the young people, 'Handsome is as handsome does.' If Tom here, for instance, were as good as he looks—"

"You flatter me, Aunt Polly," Tom broke in hastily, anticipating the crack of the whip; he was familiar with his aunt's conversational idiosyncrasies.

"If you are as good as you look," continued the old lady, with an indulgent smile, "some one has been slandering you."

"Thanks, Aunt Polly! Now you don't flatter me."

"There is Mr. Ellis," Mrs. Ochiltree went on, "who is not half so good-looking, but is steady as a clock, I dare say."

"Now, Aunt Polly," interposed Mrs. Carteret, "let the gentlemen alone."

"She doesn't mean half what she says," continued Mrs. Carteret apologetically, "and only talks that way to people whom she likes."

Tom threw Mrs. Carteret a grateful glance. He had been apprehensive, with the sensitiveness of youth, lest his old great-aunt should make a fool of him before Clara's family. Nor had he relished the comparison with Ellis, who was out of place, anyway, in this family party. He had never liked the fellow, who was too much of a plodder and a prig to make a suitable associate for a whole-souled, generous-hearted young gentleman. He tolerated him as a visitor at Carteret's and as a member of the Clarendon Club, but that was all.

"Mrs. Ochiltree has a characteristic way of disguising her feelings," observed old Mr. Delamere, with a touch of sarcasm.

Ellis had merely flushed and felt uncomfortable at the reference to himself. The compliment to his character hardly offset the reflection upon his looks. He knew he was not exactly handsome, but it was not pleasant to have the fact emphasized in the presence of the girl he loved; he would like at least fair play and judgment upon the subject left to the young lady.

Mrs. Ochiltree was quietly enjoying herself. In early life she had been accustomed to impale fools on epigrams, like flies on pins, to see them wriggle. But with advancing years she had lost the faculty of nice discrimination—it was pleasant to see her victims squirm, whether they were fools or friends. Even one's friends, she argued, were not always wise and were sometimes the better for being told the truth. At her niece's table she felt at liberty to speak her mind. She had long ago outgrown the period where ambition or passion, or its partners, envy and hatred, were springs of action in her life and simply retained a mild enjoyment in the exercise of an old habit, with no active malice whatever. The ruling passion grew

14

stronger as the restraining faculties decreased in vigor.

A diversion was created at this point by the appearance of old Mammy Jane, dressed in a calico frock, with clean white neckerchief and apron, carrying the wonderful baby in honor of whose naming this feast had been given. Though only six weeks old, the little Theodore had grown rapidly and Mammy Jane declared was already quite large for his age and displayed signs of an unusually precocious intelligence. He was passed around the table and duly admired. Clara thought his hair was fine. Ellis inquired about his teeth. Tom put his finger in the baby's fist to test his grip. Old Mr. Delamere was unable to decide as yet whether he favored most his father or his mother. The object of these attentions endured them patiently for several minutes and then protested with a vocal vigor which led to his being taken promptly back upstairs. Whatever fate might be in store for him, he manifested no sign of weak lungs.

"Sandy," said Mrs. Carteret when the baby had retired, "pass that tray standing upon the side table, so that we may all see the presents."

Mr. Delamere had brought a silver spoon and Tom a napkin ring. Ellis had sent a silver watch; it was a little premature, he admitted, but the boy would grow to it and could use it to play with in the mean time. Mrs. Ochiltree's present was an old and yellow ivory rattle, with a handle which the child could bite while teething and a knob screwed on at the end to prevent the handle from slipping through the baby's hand.

"I saw that in your cedar chest, Aunt Polly," said Clara, "when I was a little girl and you used to pull the chest out from under your bed to get me a dime."

"You kept the rattle in the right-hand corner of the chest," said Tom, "in the box with the red silk purse, from which you took the gold piece you gave me every Christmas. '

A smile shone on Mrs. Ochiltree's severe features at this appreciation, like a ray of sunlight on a snowbank.

"Aunt Polly's chest is like the widow's curse," said Mrs. Carteret, "which was never empty."

"Or Fortunatus' purse, which was always full," added old

Mr. Delamere, who read the Latin poets and whose allusions were apt to be classical rather than scriptural.

"It will last me while I live," said Mrs. Ochiltree, adding cautiously, "but there'll not be a great deal left. It won't take much to support an old woman for twenty years."

Mr. Delamere's man Sandy waited upon the table with the decorum of a trained butler and a gravity all his own. He had changed his suit of plain gray for a long blue coat with brass buttons, which dated back to the fashion of a former generation, with which he wore a pair of plaid trousers of strikingly modern cut and pattern. With his whiskers, his spectacles and his solemn air of responsibility, he would have presented, to one unfamiliar with the negro type, an amusingly impressive appearance. But there was nothing incongruous about Sandy to this company, except to Tom Delamere, who possessed a keen eye for contrasts and always regarded Sandy, in that particular rig, as a very comical darkey.

"Is it quite prudent, Mrs. Ochiltree," suggested the major at a moment when Sandy, having set down the tray, had left the room for a little while, "to mention, in the presence of the servants, that you keep money in the house?"

"I beg your pardon, major," observed old Mr. Delamere, with a touch of stiffness. "The only servant in hearing of the conversation has been my own; and Sandy is as honest as any man in Wellington."

"You mean, sir," replied Carteret, with a smile, "as honest as any negro in Wellington."

"I make no exceptions, major," returned the old gentleman, with emphasis. "I would trust Sandy with my life—he saved it once at the risk of his own."

"No doubt," mused the major, "the negro is capable of a certain doglike fidelity—I make the comparison in a kindly sense—a certain personal devotion which is admirable in itself and fits him eminently for a servile career. I should imagine, however, that one could more safely trust his life with a negro than his portable property. "

"Very clever, major! I read your paper and know that your

feeling is hostile toward the negro, but"—

The major made a gesture of dissent, but remained courteously silent until Mr. Delamere had finished.

"For my part," the old gentleman went on, "I think they have done very well, considering what they started from and their limited opportunities. There was Adam Miller, for instance, who left a comfortable estate. His son George carries on the business and the younger boy, William, is a good doctor and stands well with his profession. His hospital is a good thing and if my estate were clear, I should like to do something for it."

"You are mistaken, sir, in imagining me hostile to the negro," explained Carteret. "On the contrary, I am friendly to his best interests. I give him employment; I pay taxes for schools to educate him and for courthouses and jails to keep him in order. I merely object to being governed by an inferior and servile race."

Mrs. Carteret's face wore a tired expression. This question was her husband's hobby and therefore her own nightmare. Moreover, she had her personal grievance against the negro race and the names mentioned by old Mr. Delamere had brought it vividly before her mind. She had no desire to mar the harmony of the occasion by the discussion of a distasteful subject.

Mr. Delamere, glancing at his hostess, read something of this thought and refused the challenge to further argument.

"I do not believe, major," he said, "that Olivia relishes the topic. I merely wish to say that Sandy is an exception to any rule which you may formulate in derogation of the negro. Sandy is a gentleman in ebony!"

Tom could scarcely preserve his gravity at this characterization of old Sandy, with his ridiculous air of importance, his long blue coat and his loud plaid trousers. That suit would make a great costume for a masquerade. He would borrow it some time—there was nothing in the world like it.

"Well, Mr. Delamere," returned the major good-humoredly, "no doubt Sandy is an exceptionally good negro—he might

17

well be, for he has had the benefit of your example all his life—and we know that he is a faithful servant. But nevertheless, if I were Mrs. Ochiltree, I should put my money in the bank. Not all negroes are as honest as Sandy and an elderly lady might not prove a match for a burly black burglar."

"Thank you, major," retorted Mrs. Ochiltree, "I'm not yet too old to take care of myself. That cedar chest has been my bank for forty years and I shall not change my habits at my age."

At this moment Sandy reentered the room. Carteret made a warning gesture, which Mrs. Ochiltree chose not to notice.

"I've proved a match for two husbands and am not afraid of any man that walks the earth, black or white, by day or night. I have a revolver and know how to use it. Whoever attempts to rob me will do so at his peril."

After dinner Clara played the piano and sang duets with Tom Delamere. At nine o'clock Mr. Delamere's carriage came for him and he went away accompanied by Sandy. Under cover of the darkness the old gentleman leaned on his servant's arm with frank dependence and Sandy lifted him into the carriage with every mark of devotion.

Ellis had already excused himself to go to the office and look over the late proofs for the morning paper. Tom remained a few minutes longer than his grandfather and upon taking his leave went round to the Clarendon Club, where he spent an hour or two in the card-room with a couple of congenial friends. Luck seemed to favor him and he went home at midnight with a comfortable balance of winnings. He was fond of excitement and found a great deal of it in cards. To lose was only less exciting than to win. Of late he had developed into a very successful player—so successful, indeed, that several members of the club generally found excuses to avoid participating in a game where he made one.

# III

# The Editor at Work

TO GO BACK A LITTLE. . . FOR SEVERAL DAYS AFTER
his child's birth Major Carteret's chief interest in life had been
confined to his house. He did not love Olivia the less, for
maternity had crowned her wifehood with an added glory and
now all the old pride of race, class and family welled up anew
and swelled and quickened the current of his life.

Upon the major's first appearance at the office, which took
place the second day after the child's birth, he opened a box of
cigars in honor of the event. The word had been passed around
by Ellis and the whole office force, including reporters,
compositors and press men, came in to congratulate the major
and smoke at his expense. Even Jerry, the colored porter—
Mammy Jane's grandson and therefore a protege of the
family—presented himself among the rest, or rather, after the
rest. The major shook hands with them all except Jerry, though
he acknowledged the porter's congratulations with a kind nod
and put a good cigar into his outstretched palm, for which
Jerry thanked him without manifesting any consciousness of
the omission. He was quite aware that under ordinary
circumstances the major would not have shaken hands with
white working men, to say nothing of negroes; and he had
merely hoped that in the pleasurable distraction of the moment
the major might also overlook the distinction of color. Mr. Ellis
had once shaken hands with Jerry—but Mr. Ellis' Quaker
father had never owned any slaves and he could not be
expected to have as much pride as one of the best families who
had possessed land and negroes for time out of mind.

Having finished this pleasant ceremony, the major turned to

19

his desk. The first subject he took up was one bearing upon the future of his son. Quite obviously the career of a Carteret must not be left to chance, but planned and worked out with a sense of the value of good blood.

There lay upon his desk a letter from a well-known promoter, offering the major an investment which promised large returns. The Morning Chronicle provided him an ample income. The money available for this investment was part of his wife's patrimony. It was invested in a local cotton mill, which was paying ten per cent, but this was a beggarly return compared with the immense profits promised by the offered investment—profits which would enable his son, upon reaching manhood, to take a place in the world commensurate with the dignity of his ancestors, one of whom, only a few generations removed, had owned an estate of ninety thousand acres of land and six thousand slaves.

This letter having been disposed of by an answer accepting the offer, the major took up his pen to write an editorial. Public affairs in the state were not going to his satisfaction. At the last state election his own party, after an almost unbroken rule of twenty years, had been defeated by the so-called "Fusion" ticket, a combination of Republicans and Populists. A clean sweep had been made of the offices in the state, which were now filled by new men. Many of the smaller places had gone to colored men, their people having voted almost solidly for the Fusion ticket. In spite of the fact that the population of Wellington was two thirds colored, this state of things was gall and wormwood to the defeated party, of which the Morning Chronicle was the acknowledged organ. Major Carteret shared this feeling. Only this very morning, while passing the city hall, on his way to the office he had seen the steps of that noble building disfigured by a fringe of job-hunting negroes, like a string of buzzards sitting on a rail.

Taking for this theme the unfitness of the negro to participate in government—an unfitness due to his limited education, his lack of experience, his criminal tendencies and more especially to his hopeless mental and physical inferiority to the white race—the major had demonstrated, it seemed to him clearly enough, that the ballot in the hands of the negro was a menace to the commonwealth. He had argued, with entire conviction, that the white and black races could never attain social and political harmony by commingling their blood; he had proved by several historical parallels that no two unassimilable races could ever live together except in the relation of superior and inferior and he was just dipping his gold pen into the ink to indite his conclusions, when Jerry, the porter, announced two visitors.

"General Belmont an' Cap'n McBane to see you, suh."

"Show them in, Jerry."

The man who entered first upon this invitation was a dapper little gentleman with light-blue eyes and a Vandyke beard. He wore a frock coat, patent leather shoes and a Panama hat.

"How do you do, Captain McBane," Carteret said, turning to the second visitor.

The individual thus addressed was strikingly different in appearance from his companion. His broad shoulders, burly form, square jaw and heavy chin betokened strength, energy and unscrupulousness. With the exception of a small, bristling mustache, his face was clean shaven, with here and there a speck of dried blood due to a carelessly or unskillfully handled razor. A single deep-set gray eye was shadowed by a beetling brow, over which a crop of coarse black hair, slightly streaked with gray, fell almost low enough to mingle with his black, bushy eyebrows. His coat had not been brushed for several days, if one might judge from the accumulation of dandruff upon the collar and his shirt-front, in the middle of which blazed a showy diamond, was plentifully stained with tobacco juice. He wore a large slouch hat, which, upon entering the office, he removed and held in his hand.

The major pushed a button, which rang a bell in the hall, summoning the colored porter to his presence.

"Jerry," said the editor when his servant appeared, "bring a couple of chairs for these gentlemen."

21

While they stood waiting, the visitors congratulated the major on the birth of his child, which had been announced in the Morning Chronicle.

"And now that you have a son, major," remarked the gentleman first described, as he lit one of the major's cigars, "you'll be all the more interested in doing something to make this town fit to live in, which is what we came up to talk about. Things are in an awful condition! A negro justice of the peace has opened an office on Market Street and only yesterday summoned a white man to appear before him. Negro lawyers get most of the business in the criminal court. Last evening a group of young white ladies, going quietly along the street arm-in-arm, were forced off the sidewalk by a crowd of negro girls. Coming down the street just now, I saw a spectacle of social equality and negro domination that made my blood boil with indignation—a white and a black convict, chained together, crossing the city in charge of a negro officer! We cannot stand that sort of thing, Carteret—it is the last straw! Something must be done and that quickly!"

The major thrilled with responsive emotion. The matter was not only in his own thoughts, but it was the spontaneous revulsion of white men against the rule of an inferior race.

General Belmont, the smaller of the two, was a man of good family, a lawyer by profession and took an active part in state and local politics. Aristocratic by birth and instinct and a former owner of slaves, his conception of the obligations and rights of his caste was nevertheless somewhat lower than that of the narrower but more sincere Carteret who believed in the divine right of white men and gentlemen, as his ancestors had believed in.

Captain George McBane had sprung from the poor white class, to which, even more than to the slaves, the abolition of slavery had opened the door of opportunity. No longer overshadowed by a slave-holding caste, some of this class had rapidly pushed themselves forward. Some had made honorable records. Others, foremost in negro-baiting and election frauds, had done the dirty work of politics, as their fathers had done that of slavery, seeking their reward at first in minor offices—for which men of gentler breeding did not care—until their ambition began to reach out for higher honors.

Of this class McBane—whose captaincy, by the way, was merely a polite fiction—had been one of the most successful. He had held, until recently, as the reward of questionable political services, a contract with the State for its convict labor, from which in a few years he had realized a fortune. But the methods which made his contract profitable had not commended themselves to humane people and charges of cruelty and worse had been preferred against him. He was rich enough to escape serious consequences from the investigation which followed, but when the Fusion ticket carried the state he lost his contract and the system of convict labor was abolished. Since then McBane had devoted himself to politics: he was ambitious for greater wealth, for office and for social recognition.

At sight, therefore, of these two men, with whose careers and characters he was entirely familiar, Carteret felt sweep over his mind the conviction that now was the time and these the instruments with which to undertake the redemption of the state from the evil fate which had befallen it.

Jerry, the porter, who had gone downstairs to the counting-room to find two whole chairs, now entered with one in each hand. He set a chair for the general, who gave him an amiable nod, to which Jerry responded with a bow and a scrape. Captain McBane made no acknowledgment, but fixed Jerry so fiercely with his single eye that upon placing the chair Jerry made his escape from the room as rapidly as possible.

"I don't like dat Cap'n McBane," he muttered, upon reaching the hall. "They says he got dat eye knock' out tryin' to whip a cullud 'oman, when he was a boy, an' dat he ain't never had no use for niggers since—'cep'n' for what he could make outta 'em wid his convic' labor contracts. His daddy was a' overseer befo' him, an' it come natural for him to be a nigger-driver. I don't want dat one eye of his restin' on me no longer 'n I can help, an' I don't know how I'm gwine to like dis job if

23

he 's gwine to be comin' roun' here. He ain't nothin' but poor white trash nohow; but Lawd! Lawd! look at the money he 's got— livin' at the hotel, wearin' diamonds, an' socializin' wid the bes' quality of dis town! 'Pears to me the bottom rail is gittin' mighty close to the top. Well, I s'pose it all comes from being white. I wish to God I was white!"

Jerry sat waiting in the hall, his ear to the door and was able to catch what was going on within. He could hear the major, now and then, use the word "negro," and McBane's deep voice was quite audible when he referred to "the damned niggers," while the general's suave tones now and then pronounced the word "niggro." Something serious was on foot, involving his own race,. The bell rang again.

"Jerry," said the major, "wait on Captain McBane."

"Yes, suh," responded Jerry, turning toward the captain, whose eye he carefully avoided meeting directly.

"Take that half a dollar, boy an' go 'cross the street and get me three whiskies. Bring back the change and make haste."

The captain tossed the half dollar at Jerry, who, looking to one side, of course missed it. He picked the money up, however and backed out of the room. Jerry did not like Captain McBane, to begin with and it was dear that the captain was no gentleman, or he would not have thrown the money at him. Jerry might have overlooked this discourtesy had it not been coupled with the remark about the change, which seemed to him in very poor taste.

Returning in a few minutes with three glasses on a tray, he passed them round, handed Captain McBane his change and retired to the hall.

"Gentlemen," exclaimed the captain, lifting his glass, "I propose a toast: 'No nigger domination.' "

"Amen!" said the others and three glasses were solemnly drained.

"Major," observed the general, smacking his lips, "I should like to use Jerry for a moment, if you will permit me."

Jerry appeared promptly at the sound of the bell. He had remained conveniently near—calls of this sort were apt to come

24

in sequence.

"Jerry," said the general, handing Jerry half a dollar, "go over to Mr. Brown's—I get my liquor there—and tell them to send me three glasses of my special mixture. And, Jerry—you may keep the change!"

"Thank y', General, thank y', marster," replied Jerry, with unctuous gratitude, bending almost double as he backed out of the room.

"Dat's a gentleman, a real ole-time gentleman," he said to himself when he had closed the door. "But there's somethin' gwine on in there! 'No nigger damnation!' I'm sho' there ain't no nigger I knows what wants damnation, but if dat one-eyed Cap'n McBane got anything to do wid it, it don't mean no good for the niggers—damnation'd be better for 'em than dat Cap'n McBane! He look at a nigger like he could jes' eat him alive."

"In this nectar of the gods, gentlemen," said the general when Jerry had returned with the glasses, "I drink with you to 'White Supremacy!' "

"White Supremacy everywhere!" added McBane.

"Now and forever!" concluded Carteret solemnly.

When the visitors, half an hour later, had taken their departure, Carteret, turned to his desk and finished, his famous editorial in which he sounded the bell of a new crusade.

At noon, when the editor, having laid down his pen, was leaving the office, he passed Jerry in the hall without a word or a nod. The major wore a rapt look, which Jerry observed with a vague uneasiness.

"He looks jes' like he was walkin' in his sleep," muttered Jerry uneasily. "There's somethin' up, sho 's you born! 'No nigger damnation!' Anybody'd 'low they was all gwine to heaven; but I knows better! When a group of white folks gits to talkin' 'bout the niggers like dem in yonder, it's mo' likely they're gwine to ketch somethin' else dan heaven! I got to keep my eyes open an' keep up wid what's happenin'. If there's gwine to be another flood 'roun' here, I wants to Be in the ark wid the white folks—I may have to be another Ham, an' start the cullud race all over again."

25

# IV

# Theodore Felix

THE YOUNG HEIR OF THE CARTERETS AT SIX months old was, according to Mammy Jane, the largest, finest, smartest and altogether most remarkable baby that had ever lived in Wellington.

"You really mean that about Dodie, do you, Mammy Jane?" asked the delighted mother, who never tired of hearing her own opinion confirmed concerning this wonderful child, which had come to her like an angel from heaven.

"Does I mean it!" exclaimed Mammy Jane, with a tone and an expression which spoke volumes of reproach. "Now, Miss 'Livy, what is I ever uttered or said or spoke or done dat would make you s'pose I could tell you a lie 'bout yo' own chile?"

"No, Mammy Jane, I'm sure you wouldn't."

" 'Deed, ma'am, I'm tellin' you the Lawd's truth. I never saw a baby wid such fine hair for his age, nor such blue eyes, nor such a grip, nor such a heft. Why, dat chile mus' weigh 'bout twenty-for' pounds, an' he not but six months ole. Does dat gal what does the nursing' whiles I'm gone tend to dis chile right, Miss 'Livy?"

"She does fairly well, Mammy Jane, but I could hardly expect her to love the baby as you do. There's no one like you, Mammy Jane."

" 'Deed there ain't, honey; you is talkin' the gospel truth now! None of these young folks ain't got the trainin' my ole mistress give me."

The nurse came in shortly afterwards, a neat-looking brown girl, dressed in a clean calico gown, with a nurse's cap and apron.

26

"Look a-here, gal," said Mammy Jane sternly, "I wants you to understand dat you got to take good care of dis chile; I nursed his mammy there, an' his gran'mammy befo' him, an' you got a privilege dat most likely you don't 'preciate. I wants you to 'member, in yo' incomings an' outgoings, dat I got my eye on you, an' am gwine to see dat you does yo' work right."

"Do you need me for anything, ma'am?" asked the young nurse, who had stood before Mrs. Carteret, giving Mammy Jane a mere passing glance and listening impassively to her harangue. The nurse belonged to the younger generation of colored people. She had graduated from the mission school and had received some instruction in Dr. Miller's class for nurses. Standing, like most young people of her race, on the border line between two irreconcilable states of life, she had neither the picturesqueness of the slave, nor the unconscious dignity of those whom freedom has been the immemorial birthright; she was in what might be called the chip-on-the-shoulder stage, through which races as well as individuals must pass in climbing the ladder of life—not an interesting, at least not an agreeable stage, but an inevitable one and for that reason entitled to a paragraph in a story of Southern life, which, with its as yet imperfect blending of old with new, of race with race, of slavery with freedom, is like no other life under the sun.

Had this old woman, who had no authority over her, been a little more polite, or a little less offensive, the nurse might have returned her a pleasant answer. These old-time negroes, she said to herself, made her sick with their slavering over the white folks, who, she supposed, favored them and made much of them because they had once belonged to them—much the same reason why they fondled their cats and dogs. For her own part, they gave her nothing but her wages and small wages at that and she owed them nothing more than equivalent service. It was purely a matter of business; she sold her time for their money. There was no question of love between them.

Receiving a negative answer from Mrs. Carteret, she left the room without a word, ignoring Mammy Jane completely and

27

leaving that venerable relic of antebellum times gasping in helpless astonishment.

"Well, I nevah!" she ejaculated, as soon as she could get her breath, "if dat ain't the beatinis' performance I ever saw or heard of! These young niggers ain't got the manners they was born wid! I don't know what they're comin' to, when they ain't got no mo' respec' for ole age—I don't know—I don't know!"

"Now what are you croaking about, Jane?" asked Major Carteret, who came into the room and took the child into his arms.

Mammy Jane hobbled to her feet and bobbed a curtsy. She was never lacking in respect to white people of proper quality; but Major Carteret, the quintessence of aristocracy, called out all her reserves of deference. The major was always kind and considerate to these old family retainers, brought up in the feudal atmosphere now so rapidly passing away. Mammy Jane loved Mrs. Carteret; toward the major she entertained a feeling bordering upon awe.

"Well, Jane," returned the major sadly, when the old nurse had related her grievance, "the old times have vanished, the old ties have been ruptured. The old relations of dependence and loyal obedience on the part of the colored people, the responsibility of protection and kindness upon that of the whites, have passed away forever. The young negroes are too self-assertive. Education is spoiling them, Jane; they have been badly taught. They are not content with their station in life. Some time they will overstep the mark. The white people are patient, but there is a limit to their endurance."

"Dat's what I tells these young niggers," groaned Mammy Jane, with a portentous shake of her turbaned head, "when I hears 'em gwine on wid their foolishness; but they don't mind me. They 'lows they knows mo' than I does, 'cause they been learnt to look in a book. But, pshuh! my ole mistress showed me mo' than dem niggers'll learn in a thousand years! I's fetch' my grandson' Jerry up to be humble, an' keep in 'is place. An' I tells these other niggers dat if they 'd do the same, an' not crowd the white folks they'd git enough to eat, an' live out their days in peace an' comfort. But they don't mind me— they don't mind me!"

"If all the colored people were like you and Jerry, Jane," rejoined the major kindly, "there would never be any trouble. You have friends upon whom, in time of need, you can rely implicitly for protection and succor. You served your mistress faithfully before the war; you remained by her when the other negroes were running hither and thither like sheep without a shepherd; and you have transferred your allegiance to my wife and her child. We think a great deal of you, Jane."

"Yes, indeed, Mammy Jane," assented Mrs. Carteret, with sincere affection, glancing with moist eyes from the child in her husband's arms to the old nurse, whose dark face was glowing with happiness at these expressions of appreciation, "you shall never want so long as we have anything. We would share our last crust with you."

"Thank y', Miss 'Livy," said Jane with reciprocal emotion, "I knows who my friends is, an' I ain't gwine to let nothin' worry me. But for the Lawd's sake, Mars Philip, gimme dat chile, an' lemme pat him on the back, of he'll choke hisself to death!"

The old nurse had been the first to observe that little Dodie, for some reason, was gasping for breath. Catching the child from the major's arms, she patted it on the back and shook it gently. After a moment of this treatment, the child ceased to gasp, but still breathed heavily, with a strange, whistling noise.

"Oh, my child!" exclaimed the mother, in great alarm, taking the baby in her arms, "what can be the matter with him, Mammy Jane?"

"For the Lawd's sake, ma'am, I don't know, 'less he's swallowed somethin'; an' he ain't had nothin' in his hands but the rattle Miss Polly give him."

Mrs. Carteret caught up the ivory rattle, which hung suspended by a ribbon from the baby's neck.

"He has swallowed the little piece off the end of the handle," she cried, turning pale with fear, "and it has lodged in his throat. Telephone Dr. Price to come immediately, Philip, before my baby chokes to death! Oh, my baby, my precious

29

baby!"

An anxious half hour passed, during which the child lay quiet, except for its labored breathing. The suspense was relieved by the arrival of Dr. Price, who examined the child carefully.

"It's a curious accident," he announced at the close of his inspection. "So far as I can discover, the piece of ivory has been drawn into the trachea, or windpipe and has lodged in the mouth of the right bronchus. I'll try to get it out without an operation, but I can't guarantee the result."

At the end of another half hour Dr. Price announced his inability to remove the obstruction without resorting to more serious measures.

"I do not see," he declared, "how an operation can be avoided."

"Will it be dangerous?" inquired the major anxiously, while Mrs. Carteret shivered at the thought.

"It will be necessary to cut into his throat from the outside. All such operations are more or less dangerous, especially on small children. If this were some other child, I might undertake the operation unassisted; but I know how you value this one, major and I should prefer to share the responsibility with a specialist."

"Is there one in town?" asked the major.

"No, but we can get one from out of town."

"Send for the best one in the country," said the major, "who can be got here in time. Spare no expense, Dr. Price. We value this child above any earthly thing."

"The best is the safest," replied Dr. Price. "I will send for Dr. Burns, of Philadelphia, the best surgeon in that line in America. If he can start at once, he can reach here in sixteen or eighteen hours and the case can wait even longer, if inflammation does not set in."

The message was dispatched forthwith. By rare good fortune the eminent specialist was able to start within an hour or two after the receipt of Dr. Price's telegram. Meanwhile the baby remained restless and uneasy, the doctor spending most of his time by its side. Mrs. Carteret, who had never been quite strong since the child's birth, was a prey to the most agonizing apprehensions.

Mammy Jane, not wishing to add to her mistress' distress, was secretly oppressed by forebodings which she was unable to shake off. The child was born for bad luck. The mole under its ear, just at the point where the hangman's knot would strike, had foreshadowed dire misfortune. She had already observed several little things which had rendered her vaguely anxious.

For instance, upon one occasion, on entering the room where the baby had been left alone, asleep in his crib, she had met a strange cat hurrying from the nursery and, upon examining closely the pillow upon which the child lay, had found a depression which had undoubtedly been due to the weight of the cat's body. The child was restless and uneasy and Jane had ever since believed that the cat had been sucking little Dodie's breath, with what might have been fatal results had she not appeared just in the nick of time.

This untimely accident of the rattle, a fatality for which no one could be held responsible, had confirmed the unlucky omen. Jane's duties in the nursery did not permit her to visit her friend the conjure woman; but she did find time to go out in the back yard at dusk and to dig up the charm which she had planted there. It had protected the child so far; but perhaps its potency had become exhausted. She picked up the bottle, shook it vigorously and then laid it back, with the other side up. Refilling the hole, she made a cross over the top with the thumb of her left hand and walked three times around it.

What this strange symbolism meant, or whence it derived its origin, Jane did not know. The cross was there and the Trinity, though Jane was scarcely conscious of these, at this moment, as religious emblems. But she hoped, on general principles, that this performance would strengthen the charm and restore little Dodie's luck. It certainly had its moral effect upon Jane's own mind, for she was able to sleep better and contrived to impress Mrs. Carteret with her own hopefulness.

31

# V

# A Journey Southward

AS THE SOUTH-BOUND TRAIN WAS LEAVING THE
station at Philadelphia, a gentleman took his seat in the single
sleeping-car attached to the train and proceeded to make
himself comfortable.

"How do you do, Dr. Burns?"

The gentleman looked up with an air of surprise, which
gave place to an expression of cordial recognition.

"Why, it's Miller!" he exclaimed, rising and giving the other
his hand, "William Miller—Dr. Miller, of course. Sit down,
Miller— I'm delighted to see you looking so well and so
prosperous."

"I deserve no credit for either, sir," returned the other, as he
took the proffered seat, "for I inherited both health and
prosperity. It is a fortunate chance that permits me to meet
you."

The first man was white and the second black, or, more
correctly speaking, a light brown. The white man was perhaps
fifty years of age and the other not more than thirty, They were
both tall and sturdy, both well dressed, the white man with
perhaps a little more distinction; both seemed from their faces
and their manners to be men of culture and accustomed to the
society of cultivated people. In past years they had been
teacher and pupil. Dr. Alvin Burns was professor in the famous
medical college where Miller had attended lectures. The
professor had taken an interest in his only colored pupil, to
whom he had been attracted by his earnestness of purpose, his
evident talent and his excellent manners and fine physique. It
was in part due to Dr. Burns' friendship that Miller had won a

scholarship which had enabled him, without drawing too heavily upon his father's resources, to spend in Europe, studying in the hospitals of Paris and Vienna, the two most delightful years of his life.

Miller's father, Adam Miller, had been a thrifty colored man, the son of a slave, who, had bought himself with money which he had earned and saved, over and above what he had paid his master for his time. Adam Miller had inherited his father's thrift, as well as his trade, which was that of a stevedore, or contractor for the loading and unloading of vessels at the port of Wellington. After the civil war, he had made money. His savings, shrewdly invested, he had brought up his eldest son to the trade; the other he had given an education, in the proud hope that his children or his grandchildren might be gentlemen in the town where their ancestors had once been slaves.

Upon his father's death, shortly after Dr. Miller's return from Europe and a year or two before the date at which this story opens, he had promptly spent part of his inheritance in founding a hospital, to which was to be added a training school for nurses and in time perhaps a medical college and a school of pharmacy. He had been strongly tempted to leave the South and seek a home for his family and a career for himself in the freer North, where race antagonism was less keen, or at least less oppressive, or in Europe, where he had never found his color work to his disadvantage. But his people had needed him and he had wished to help them and had sought by means of this institution to contribute to their uplifting. As he now informed Dr. Burns, he was returning from New York, where he had been to purchase equipment for his new hospital, which would soon be ready for the reception of patients.

"How much I can accomplish I do not know," said Miller, "but I'll do what I can. There are nine million of us and it will take a great deal of learning of all kinds to leaven that lump."

"It is a great problem, the future of your race," returned the other, "a tremendously interesting problem. It is a serial story which we are all reading and which grows in vital interest with each successive installment. It is not only your problem, but ours. Your race must come up or drag ours down."

"We shall come up," declared Miller; "slowly and painfully, perhaps, but we shall win our way. If our race had made as much progress everywhere as they have made in Wellington, the problem would be well on the way toward solution."

"Wellington?" exclaimed Dr. Burns. "That's where I'm going. A Dr. Price, of Wellington, has sent for me to perform an operation on a child's throat. Do you know Dr. Price?"

"Quite well," replied Miller, "he is a friend of mine."

"So much the better. I shall want you to assist me. I read in the Medical Gazette, an account of a very interesting operation of yours. I felt proud to number you among my pupils. I must certainly have you with me in this one."

"I shall be delighted, sir," returned Miller, "if it is agreeable to all concerned."

Several hours were passed in pleasant conversation while the train sped rapidly southward. They were already far down in Virginia and had stopped at a station beyond Richmond, when the conductor entered the car.

"All passengers," he announced, "will please transfer to the day coaches ahead. The sleeper has a hot box and must be switched off here."

Dr. Burns and Miller obeyed the order, the former leading the way into the coach immediately in front of the sleeping-car.

"Let's sit here, Miller," he said, having selected a seat near the rear of the car and deposited his suitcase in a rack. "It's on the shady side."

Miller stood a moment hesitatingly, but finally took the seat indicated and a few minutes later the journey was again resumed.

When the train conductor made his round after leaving the station, he paused at the seat occupied by the two doctors, glanced interrogatively at Miller and then spoke to Dr. Burns, who sat in the end of the seat nearest the aisle.

"This man is with you?" he asked, indicating Miller with a slight side movement of his head and a keen glance in his

34

direction.

"Certainly," replied Dr. Burns curtly and with some surprise. "don't you see that he is?"

The conductor passed on. Miller paid no apparent attention to this little interlude, though no syllable had escaped him. He resumed the conversation where it had been broken off, but nevertheless followed with his eyes the conductor, who stopped at a seat near the forward end of the car and engaged in conversation with a man whom Miller had not hitherto noticed.

As this passenger turned his head and looked back toward Miller, the latter saw a broad-shouldered, burly white man and recognized in his square-cut jaw, his coarse, firm mouth and the single gray eye with which he swept Miller for an instant with a scornful glance, a well-known character of Wellington, with whom the reader has already made acquaintance in these pages. Captain McBane wore a frock coat and a slouch hat; several buttons of his vest were unbuttoned and his solitaire diamond blazed in his soiled shirt-front like the headlight of a locomotive.

The conductor in his turn looked back at Miller and retraced his steps. Miller braced himself for what he feared was coming, though he had hoped, on account of his friend's presence, that it might be avoided.

"Excuse me, sir," said the conductor, addressing Dr. Burns, "but did I understand you to say that this man was your servant?"

"No, indeed!" replied Dr. Burns indignantly. "The gentleman is not my servant, nor anybody's servant, but is my friend. But, by the way, since we are on the subject, may I ask what affair it is of yours?"

"It's very much my affair," returned the conductor, somewhat nettled at this questioning of his authority. "I'm sorry to part friends, but the law of Virginia does not permit colored passengers to ride in the white cars. You'll have to go forward to the next coach," he added, addressing Miller this time.

35

"I have paid my fare on the sleeping-car, where the separate-car law does not apply," remonstrated Miller.

"I can't help that. You can doubtless get your money back from the sleeping-car company. But this is a day coach and is distinctly marked 'White,' as you must have seen before you sat down here. The sign is put there for that purpose."

He indicated a large card neatly framed and hung at the end of the car, containing the legend, "White," in letters about a foot long, painted in white upon a dark background, typical, one might suppose, of the distinction thereby indicated.

"You shall not stir a step, Miller," exclaimed Dr. Burns wrathfully. "This is an outrage upon a citizen of a free country. You shall stay right here."

"I'm sorry," returned the conductor, "but there's no use kicking. It's the law of Virginia and I am bound by it as well as you. I have already come near losing my place because of not enforcing it and I can take no more such chances."

"And my friend has his rights to maintain," returned Dr. Burns with determination. "There is a vital principle at stake in the matter."

"Really, sir," argued the conductor, who was a man of peace and not fond of controversy, "there's no use talking—he absolutely cannot ride in this car."

"How can you prevent it?" asked Dr. Burns, lapsing into the argumentative stage.

"The law gives me the right to remove him by force. I can call on the train crew to assist me, or on the other passengers. If I should choose to put him off the train entirely, in the middle of a swamp, he would have no redress—the law so provides. If I did not wish to use force, I could simply switch this car off at the next siding, transfer the white passengers to another and leave you and your friend in possession until you were arrested and fined or imprisoned."

"What he says is absolutely true, doctor," interposed Miller at this point. "It is the law and we are powerless to resist it. If we made any trouble, it would merely delay your journey and imperil a life at the other end. I'll go into the other car."

36

"You shall not go alone," said Dr. Burns stoutly, rising in his turn. "A place that is too good for you is not good enough for me. I will sit wherever you do."

"I'm sorry again," said the conductor, who calmly conscious of his power, could scarcely restrain an amused smile; "I dislike to interfere, but white passengers are not permitted to ride in the colored car."

"This is an outrage," declared Dr. Burns, "a damned outrage! You are curtailing the rights, not only of colored people, but of white men as well. I shall sit where I please!"

"I warn you, sir," rejoined the conductor, hardening again, "that the law will be enforced. The beauty of the system lies in its strict impartiality—it applies to both races alike."

"And is equally infamous in both cases," declared Dr. Burns. "I shall immediately take steps"—

"Never mind, doctor," interrupted Miller, soothingly, "it's only for a little while. I'll reach my destination just as surely in the other car and we can't help it, anyway. I'll see you again at Wellington."

Dr. Burns, finding resistance futile, at length acquiesced and made way for Miller to pass him.

The colored doctor took up his valise and crossed the platform to the car ahead. It was an old car, with faded upholstery, from which the stuffing projected here and there through torn places. Apparently the floor had not been swept for several days. The dust lay thick upon the window sills and the water-cooler, from which he essayed to get a drink, was filled with stale water which had made no recent acquaintance with ice. There was no other passenger in the car and Miller occupied himself in making a rough calculation of what it would cost the Southern railroads to haul a whole car for every colored passenger. It was expensive, to say the least; it would be cheaper and quite as considerate of their feelings, to make the negroes walk.

The car was conspicuously labeled at either end with large cards, similar to those in the other car, except that they bore the word "Colored" in black letters upon a white background. The author of this piece of legislation had contrived, with an ingenuity worthy of a better cause, that not merely should the passengers be separated by the color line, but that the reason for this division should be kept constantly in mind. Lest a white man should forget that he was white, these cars would keep him constantly admonished of the fact; should a colored person lose sight of his disability, these signs would remind him continually that between him and the rest of mankind not of his own color, there was by law a great gulf fixed.

Having composed himself, Miller had opened a newspaper and was deep in an editorial which set forth in glowing language the inestimable advantages which would follow to certain recently acquired islands by the introduction of American liberty, when the rear door of the car opened to give entrance to Captain George McBane, who took a seat near the door and lit a cigar. Miller knew him quite well by sight and by reputation and detested him as heartily. He represented the aggressive, offensive element among the white people of the New South, who made it hard for a negro to maintain his self-respect or to enjoy even the rights conceded to colored men by Southern laws. McBane had undoubtedly identified him to the conductor in the other car. Miller had no desire to thrust himself upon the society of white people, which, indeed, to one who had traveled so much and so far, was no novelty; but he very naturally resented being at this late day—the law had been in operation only a few months—branded and tagged and set apart from the rest of mankind upon the public highways, like an unclean thing. Nevertheless, he preferred even this to the exclusive society of Captain George McBane.

"Porter," he demanded of the colored train attache who passed through the car a moment later, "is this a smoking car for white men?"

"No, suh," replied the porter, "but they comes in here sometimes, when they ain't no cullud ladies on the car."

"Well, I have paid first-class fare and I object to that man's smoking in here. You tell him to go out!"

"I'll tell the conductor, suh," returned the porter in a low tone. "I'd jus' as soon talk to the devil as to that man."

The white man had spread himself over two seats and was smoking vigorously, from time to time spitting carelessly in the aisle, when the conductor entered the compartment.

"Captain," said Miller, "this car is plainly marked 'Colored.' I have paid first-class fare and I object to riding in a smoking car."

"All right," returned the conductor, frowning irritably. "I'll speak to him."

He walked over to the white passenger, with whom he was evidently acquainted, since he addressed him by name.

"Captain McBane," he said, "it's against the law for you to ride in the nigger car."

"Who are you talkin' to?" returned the other. "I'll ride where I damn please."

"Yes, sir, but the colored passenger objects. I'm afraid I'll have to ask you to go into the smoking-car."

"The hell you say!" rejoined McBane. "I'll leave this car when I get good and ready and that won't be till I've finished this cigar. See?"

He was as good as his word. The conductor escaped from the car before Miller had time for further expostulation. Finally McBane, having thrown the stump of his cigar into the aisle and added to the floor a finishing touch in the way of expectoration, rose and went back into the white car.

Left alone in his questionable glory, Miller buried himself again in his newspaper, from which he did not look up until the engine stopped at a tank station to take water.

As the train came to a standstill, a huge negro, covered thickly with dust, crawled off one of the rear trucks unobserved and ran round the rear end of the car to a watering-trough by a neighboring well. Moved either by extreme thirst or by the fear that his time might be too short to permit him to draw a bucket of water, he threw himself down by the trough, drank long and deep and plunging his head into the water, shook himself like a wet dog and crept furtively back to his dangerous perch.

Miller, who had seen this man from the car window, had noticed a very singular thing. As the dusty tramp passed the rear coach, he cast toward it a glance of intense ferocity. Up to that moment the man's face, which Miller had recognized under its grimy coating, had been that of an ordinarily good-natured, somewhat reckless, pleasure-loving negro, at present rather the worse for wear. The change that now came over it suggested a concentrated hatred almost uncanny in its murderousness. With awakened curiosity Miller followed the direction of the negro's glance and saw that it rested-upon a window where Captain McBane sat looking out. When Miller looked back, the negro had disappeared.

At the next station a Chinaman, of the ordinary laundry type, boarded the train and took his seat in the white car without objection. At another point a colored nurse found a place with her mistress.

"White people," said Miller to himself, who had seen these passengers from the window, "do not object to the negro as a servant. As the traditional negro—the servant— he is welcomed; as an equal, he is repudiated."

Miller was something of a philosopher. He had long ago had the conclusion forced upon him that an educated man of his race, in order to live comfortably in the United States, must be either a philosopher or a fool; and since he wished to be happy and was not exactly a fool, he had cultivated philosophy. By and by he saw a white man, with a dog, enter the rear coach. Miller wondered whether the dog would be allowed to ride with his master and if not, what disposition would be made of him. He was a handsome dog and Miller who was fond of animals, would not have objected to the company of a dog, as a dog. He was nevertheless conscious of a queer sensation when he saw the porter take the dog by the collar and start in his own direction and felt consciously relieved when the canine passenger was taken on past him into the baggage-car ahead. Miller's hand was hanging over the arm of his seat and the dog, an intelligent shepherd, licked it as he passed. Miller was not entirely sure that he would not have liked the porter to leave the dog there; he was a friendly dog and seemed inclined to be sociable.

Toward evening the train drew up at a station where quite a party of farm laborers, fresh from their daily toil, swarmed out from the conspicuously labeled colored waiting-room and into the car with Miller. They were a jolly, good-natured crowd and, free from the embarrassing presence of white people, proceeded to enjoy themselves after their own fashion. Here an amorous fellow sat with his arm around a buxom girl's waist. A musically inclined individual—his talents did not go far beyond inclination—produced a mouth-organ and struck up a tune, to which a limber-legged boy danced in the aisle. They were noisy, loquacious, happy, dirty and malodorous. For a while Miller was amused and pleased. They were his people and he felt a certain expansive warmth toward them in spite of their obvious shortcomings. By and by, however, the air became too close and he went out upon the platform. For the sake of the democratic ideal, which meant so much to his race, he might have endured the affliction. He could easily imagine that people of refinement, with the power in their hands, might be tempted to strain the democratic ideal in order to avoid such contact; but personally and apart from the mere matter of racial sympathy, these people were just as offensive to him as to the whites in the other end of the train. Surely, if a classification of passengers on trains was at all desirable, it might be made upon some more logical and considerate basis than a mere arbitrary, tactless and, by the very nature of things, brutal drawing of a color line. It was a veritable bed of Procrustes, this standard which the whites had set for the negroes. Those who grew above it must have their heads cut off, figuratively speaking—must be forced back to the level assigned to their race; those who fell beneath the standard set had their necks stretched, literally enough, as the ghastly record in the daily papers gave conclusive evidence.

Miller breathed more freely when the lively crowd got off at the next station, after a short ride. Moreover, he had a light heart, a conscience void of offense and was only thirty years

41

old. His philosophy had become somewhat jaded on this journey, but he pulled it together for a final effort. Was it not, after all, a wise provision of nature that had given to a race, destined to a long servitude and a slow emergence, a cheerfulness of spirit which enabled them to catch pleasure on the wing and endure with equanimity the ills that seemed inevitable? The ability to live and thrive under adverse circumstances is the surest guaranty of the future. The race which at the last shall inherit the earth—the residuary legacy of civilization—will be the race which remains longest upon it. The negro was here before the Anglo Saxon was evolved and his thick lips and heavy-lidded eyes looked out from the inscrutable face of the Sphinx across the sands of Egypt while yet the ancestors of those who now oppress him were living in caves, practicing human sacrifice and painting themselves with woad— and the negro is here yet.

" 'Blessed are the meek,' " quoted Miller at the end of these consoling reflections, " 'for they shall inherit the earth.' If this be true, the negro may yet come into his estate, for meekness seems to be set apart as his portion."

The journey came to an end just as the sun had sunk into the west.

Simultaneously with Miller's exit from the train, a great black figure crawled off the trucks of the rear car, on the side opposite the station platform. Stretching and shaking himself with a free gesture, the black man, seeing himself unobserved, moved somewhat stiffly round the end of the car to the station platform.

" 'For the Lawd!" he muttered, "if I hadn't had a charmed life, I'd 'a' never got here on dat ticket, an' dat's a fac'— it sho' am! I kind of 'lowed I was gone a dozen times, as it was. But I got my job to do in dis worl', an' I knows I ain't gwine to die 'til I've 'complished it. I jes' want one mo' look at dat man, an' then I'll have to git somethin' to eat; for two raw turnips in twelve hours is slim pickings for a man of my size!"

# VI

# Janet

AS THE TRAIN DREW UP AT THE STATION PLATFORM
Dr. Price came forward from the white waiting-room and stood
expectantly by the white coach. Miller came down the platform
in time to intercept Burns and to introduce him to Dr. Price.

"My carriage is in waiting," said Dr. Price.

"You are very kind, Doctor. Miller, will you dine with me?"

"Thank you, no," said Miller, "I am expected at home. My
wife and child are waiting for me in the buggy yonder."

"Oh, very well; of course you must go; but don't forget our
appointment. Let's see, Dr. Price, I can eat and get ready in half
an hour—that will make it"—

"I have asked several of the local physicians to come at eight
o'clock," said Dr. Price. "The case can safely wait until then."

"Very well, Miller, be on hand at eight. I shall expect you
without fail. Where shall he come, Dr. Price?"

"To the residence of Major Philip Carteret, on Vine Street."

"I have invited Dr. Miller to assist in the operation," Dr.
Burns continued, as they drove toward the hotel. "He was a
favorite pupil of mine and a credit to the profession. I presume
you saw his article in the Medical Gazette?"

"Yes and I assisted him in the case," returned Dr. Price. "He
is a capable man."

Miller's wife and child were waiting for him in fluttering
anticipation. He kissed them both as he climbed into the buggy.

"We came at four o'clock," said Mrs. Miller, a handsome
young woman, whose complexion, in the twilight, was not
distinguishable from that of a white person, "Then came back
at six and have been waiting ever since."

"Yes, papa," piped the child, a little boy of six or seven, who sat between them, "and I am very hungry."

Miller felt very much elated as he drove homeward through the twilight. By his side sat the two persons whom he loved best in all the world. His affairs were prosperous. The colored population of the city was large, but in the main poor and the white physicians were not unwilling to share this unprofitable practice with a colored doctor. He had built up a considerable practice among his own people; but except for some poor unfortunate whose pride had been lost in poverty or sin, no white patient had ever called upon him for treatment.

On the way homeward Miller told his wife of this appointment. She was greatly interested; she was herself a mother, with an only child. Moreover, there was a stronger impulse than mere humanity to draw her toward the stricken mother. Janet had a tender heart and could have loved this white sister, her sole living relative of whom she knew. All her life long she had yearned for a kind word, a nod, a smile, the least thing that imagination might have twisted into a recognition of the tie between them. But it had never come.

And yet Janet was not angry. She was of a forgiving temper; she could never bear malice. She was educated and appreciated to the full the social forces arrayed against any such recognition as she had dreamed of. Blood is thicker than water, but, if it flow too far from conventional channels, may turn to gall and wormwood. Nevertheless, when the heart speaks, reason falls into the background and Janet would have worshiped this sister, even afar off, had she received even the slightest encouragement. She had never acknowledged, even to her husband, from whom she concealed nothing else, her secret thoughts upon this lifelong sorrow. This silent grief was nature's penalty, or society's revenge, for whatever heritage of beauty or intellect or personal charm had come to her with her father's blood. For she had received no other inheritance. Her sister was rich by right of her birth; if Janet had been fortunate, her good fortune had not been due to any provision made for her by her white father.

44

# VII

# The Operation

DR. PRICE WAS NOT ENTIRELY AT EASE IN HIS MIND as the two doctors drove rapidly from the hotel to Major Carteret's. Himself a liberal man, from his point of view, he saw no reason why a colored doctor might not operate upon a white male child—there are fine distinctions in the application of the color line—but several other physicians had been invited, some of whom were men of old-fashioned notions, who might not relish such an innovation.

This, however, was but a small difficulty compared with what might be feared from Major Carteret himself. For he knew Carteret's unrelenting hostility to anything that savored of recognition of the negro as the equal of white men. It was traditional in Wellington that no colored person had ever entered the front door of the Carteret residence and that the luckless individual who once presented himself there upon alleged business and resented being ordered to the back door had been unceremoniously thrown over the piazza railing into a rather thorny clump of rose-bushes below. If Miller were going as a servant, to hold a basin or a sponge, there would be no difficulty; but as a surgeon—well, he wouldn't borrow trouble. Under the circumstances the major might yield a point.

But as they neared the house the major's unyielding disposition loomed up formidably. Perhaps if the matter were properly presented to Dr. Burns, he might consent to withdraw the invitation. It was not yet too late to send Miller a note.

"By the way, Dr. Burns," he said, "I'm very friendly to Dr. Miller and should personally like to have him with us tonight. But—I ought to have told you this before, but I couldn't very well do so, on such short notice, in Miller's presence—we are a conservative people and our local customs are not very flexible. We jog along in much the same old way our fathers did. I'm not at all sure that Major Carteret or the other gentlemen would consent to the presence of a negro doctor."

"I think you misjudge your own people," returned Dr. Burns, "they are broader than you think. We have our prejudices against the negro at the North, but we do not let them stand in the way of anything that we want. At any rate, it is too late now and I will accept the responsibility. If the question is raised, I will attend to it. When I am performing an operation I must be aut Caesar, aut nullus. "

Dr. Price was not reassured, but he had done his duty and felt the reward of virtue. If there should be trouble, he would not be responsible. Moreover, there was a large fee at stake and Dr. Burns was not likely to prove too obdurate.

They were soon at Carteret's, where they found assembled the several physicians invited by Dr. Price. These were successively introduced as Drs. Dudley, Hooper and Ashe, all of whom were gentlemen of good standing, socially and in their profession and considered it a high privilege to witness so delicate an operation at the hands of so eminent a member of their profession.

Major Carteret entered the room and was duly presented to the famous specialist. Carteret's anxious look lightened somewhat at sight of the array of talent present. It suggested, of course, the gravity of the impending event, but gave assurance of all the skill and care which science could afford.

Dr. Burns was shown to the nursery, from which he returned in five minutes.

"The case is ready," he announced. "Are the gentlemen all present?"

"I believe so," answered Dr. Price quickly.

Miller had not yet arrived. Perhaps, thought Dr. Price, a happy accident, or some imperative call, had detained him. This would be fortunate indeed. Dr. Burns' square jaw had a very determined look. It would be a pity if any acrimonious

46

discussion should arise on the eve of a delicate operation. If the clock on the mantel would only move faster, the question might never come up.

"I don't see Dr. Miller," observed Dr. Burns, looking around the room. "I asked him to come at eight. There are ten minutes yet."

Major Carteret looked up with a sudden frown.

"May I ask to whom you refer?" he inquired, in an ominous tone.

The other gentlemen showed signs of interest, not to say emotion. Dr. Price smiled quizzically.

"Dr. Miller, of your city. He was one of my favorite pupils. He is also a graduate of the Vienna hospitals and a surgeon of unusual skill. I have asked him to assist in the operation."

Every eye was turned toward Carteret, whose crimsoned face had set in a look of grim determination.

"The person to whom you refer is a negro, I believe?" he said.

"He is a colored man, certainly," returned Dr. Burns, "though one would never think of his color after knowing him well."

"I do not know, sir," returned Carteret, with an effort at self-control, "what the customs of Philadelphia or Vienna may be; but in the South we do not call negro doctors to attend white patients. I could not permit a negro to enter my house upon such an errand."

"I am here, sir," replied Dr. Burns with spirit, "to perform a certain operation. Since I assume the responsibility, the case must be under my entire control. Otherwise I cannot operate."

"Gentlemen," interposed Dr. Price, smoothly, "I beg of you both—this is a matter for calm discussion and any asperity is to be deplored. The life at stake here should not be imperiled by any consideration of minor importance."

"Your humanity does you credit, sir," retorted Dr. Burns. "But other matters, too, are important. I have invited this gentleman here. My professional honor is involved and I merely invoke my rights to maintain it. It is a matter of

47

principle, which ought not to give way to a mere prejudice."

"That also states the case for Major Carteret," rejoined Dr. Price, suavely. "He has certain principles— call them prejudices, if you like—certain inflexible rules of conduct by which he regulates his life. One of these, which he shares with us all in some degree, forbids the recognition of the negro as a social equal."

"I do not know what Miller's social value may be," replied Dr. Burns, stoutly, "or whether you gain or lose by your attitude toward him. I have invited him here in a strictly professional capacity, with which his color is not at all concerned."

"Dr. Burns does not quite appreciate Major Carteret's point of view," said Dr. Price. "This is not with him an unimportant matter, or a mere question of prejudice, or even of personal taste. It is a sacred principle, lying at the very root of our social order, involving the purity and prestige of our race. You Northern gentlemen do not quite appreciate our situation; if you lived here a year or two you would act as we do. Of course," he added, diplomatically, "if there were no alternative—if Dr. Burns were willing to put Dr. Miller's presence on the ground of imperative necessity"—

"I do nothing of the kind, sir," retorted Dr. Burns with some heat. "I have not come all the way from Philadelphia to undertake an operation which I cannot perform without the aid of some particular physician. I merely stand upon my professional rights."

Carteret was deeply agitated. The operation must not be deferred; his child's life might be endangered by delay. If the negro's presence were indispensable he would even submit to it, though in order to avoid so painful a necessity, he would rather humble himself to the Northern doctor. The latter course involved merely a personal sacrifice—the former a vital principle. Perhaps there was another way of escape. Miller's presence could not but be distasteful to Mrs. Carteret for other reasons. Miller's wife was the living evidence of a painful episode in Mrs. Carteret's family, which the doctor's presence would inevitably recall. Once before, Mrs. Carteret's life had been endangered by encountering, at a time of great nervous strain, this ill-born sister and her child. She was even now upon the verge of collapse at the prospect of her child's suffering and should be protected from the intrusion of any idea which might add to her distress.

"Dr. Burns," he said, with the suave courtesy which was part of his inheritance, "I beg your pardon for my heat and throw myself upon your magnanimity, as between white men"—

"I am a gentleman, sir, before I am a white man," interposed Dr. Burns, slightly mollified, however, by Carteret's change of manner.

"The terms should be synonymous," Carteret could not refrain from saying. "As between white men and gentlemen, I say to you, frankly, that there are vital, personal reasons, apart from Dr. Miller's color why his presence in this house would be distasteful. With this statement, sir, I throw myself upon your mercy. My child's life is worth more to me than any earthly thing and I must be governed by your decision."

Dr. Burns was plainly wavering. The clock moved with provoking slowness. Miller would be there in five minutes.

"May I speak with you privately a moment, doctor?" asked Dr. Price.

They withdrew from the room and were engaged in conversation for a few moments. Dr. Burns finally yielded.

"I shall nevertheless feel humiliated when I meet Miller again," he said, "but of course if there is a personal question involved, that alters the situation. Had it been merely a matter of color, I should have maintained my position. As things stand, I wash my hands of the whole affair, so far as Miller is concerned, like Pontius Pilate—yes, indeed, sir, I feel very much like that individual."

"I'll explain the matter to Miller," returned Dr. Price, amiably, "and make it all right with him. We Southern people understand the negroes better than you do, sir. Why should we not? They have been constantly under our interested observation for several hundred years. You feel this vastly more than Miller will. He knows the feeling of the white people and is accustomed to it. He wishes to live and do business here and is quite too shrewd to antagonize his neighbors or come where he is not wanted. He is in fact too much of a gentleman to do so."

"I shall leave the explanation to you entirely," rejoined Dr. Burns, as they reentered the other room.

Carteret led the way to the nursery, where the operation was to take place. Dr. Price lingered for a moment. Miller was not likely to be behind the hour, if he came at all and it would be well to head him off before the operation began.

Scarcely had the rest left the room when the doorbell sounded and a servant announced Dr. Miller.

Dr. Price stepped into the hall and met Miller face to face.

He had meant to state the situation to Miller frankly, but now that the moment had come he wavered. It had been easy to theorize about the negro; it was more difficult to look this man in the eyes—whom at this moment he felt to be as essentially a gentleman as himself—and tell him the humiliating truth.

Dr. Price did not like to lie, even to a negro. His claim of superiority to the colored doctor rested fundamentally upon the fact that he was white and Miller was not and as a gentleman, he would not care to have another gentleman, even a colored man, catch him in a lie.

"I'm sorry, Miller," he said with apparent regret, "but we were here ahead of time and the case took a turn which would admit of no delay, so the gentlemen went in. Dr. Burns is with the patient now and asked me to explain why we did not wait for you."

"I'm sorry too," returned Miller, regretfully, but nothing doubting. He was well aware that in such cases danger might attend upon delay. He had lost his chance, through no fault of his own or of any one else.

"I hope that all is well?" he said, hesitatingly, not sure whether he would be asked to remain.

50

"All is well, so far. Step round to my office in the morning, Miller, or come in when you're passing and I'll tell you the details."

This was tantamount to a dismissal, so Miller took his leave. Descending the doorsteps, he stood for a moment, undecided whether to return home or to go to the hotel and await the return of Dr. Burns, when he heard his name called from the house in a low tone.

"Oh, doctor!"

He stepped back toward the door, outside of which stood the colored servant who had just let him out.

"Dat's all a lie, doctor," he whispered, " 'bout the operation being already performed. They-all had jes' gone in the minute befo' you come—Doctor Price hadn't even got out of the room. They been quarrelling' 'bout you for the las' half hour. Major Carteret say he wouldn't have you, an' the Northern doctor say he wouldn't do nothin' widout you, an' Doctor Price he joined in on both sides, an' they had it hot an' heavy, nip an' took, till by an' by Major Carteret up an' say it weren't altogether yo' color he objected to, an' wid dat the Northern doctor give in. He's a fine man, suh, but they was too much for him!"

"Thank you, Sam, I'm much obliged," returned Miller mechanically. "One likes to know the truth."

In the ordinary course of events Miller would not have anticipated such an invitation and for that reason had appreciated it all the more. The rebuff came with a corresponding shock. He had the heart of a man, the sensibilities of a cultivated gentleman; the one was sore, the other deeply wounded.

Janet met him at the door. "How is the baby?" she asked excitedly.

"Dr. Price says he is doing well."

"What is the matter, Will and why are you back so soon?"

He would have spared her the story, but she was a woman and would have it. He was wounded, too and wanted sympathy, of which Janet was an exhaustless fountain. So he told her what had happened. She comforted him after the

51

manner of a loving woman and felt righteously indignant toward her sister's husband, who had thus been instrumental in the humiliation of her own. Her anger did not embrace her sister and yet she felt obscurely that their unacknowledged relationship had been the malignant force which had given her husband pain and defeated his honorable ambition.

When Dr. Price entered the nursery, Dr. Burns was leaning attentively over the operating table. The implements needed for the operation were all in readiness— the knives, the basin, the sponge, the materials for dressing the wound—all the ghastly paraphernalia of vivisection.

Mrs. Carteret had been banished to another room, where Clara vainly attempted to soothe her. Old Mammy Jane, still burdened by her fears, fervently prayed the good Lord to spare the life of the sweet little grandson of her dear old mistress.

Dr. Burns had placed his ear to the child's chest, which had been bared for the incision. Dr. Price stood ready to administer the anaesthetic. Little Dodie looked up with a faint expression of wonder, as if dimly conscious of some unusual event. The major shivered at the thought of what the child must undergo.

"There's a change in his breathing," said Dr. Burns, lifting his head. "The whistling noise is less pronounced and he breathes easier. The obstruction seems to have shifted."

Applying his ear again to the child's throat, he listened for a moment intently and then picking the baby up from the table, gave it a couple of sharp claps between the shoulders. Simultaneously a small object shot out from the child's mouth, struck Dr. Price in the neighborhood of his waistband and then rattled lightly against the floor. Whereupon the baby, as though conscious of his narrow escape, smiled and gurgled and reaching upward clutched the doctor's whiskers with his little hand, which, according to old Jane, had a stronger grip than any other infant's in Wellington.

# VIII

## The Campaign Drags

THE CAMPAIGN FOR WHITE SUPREMACY WAS dragging. Carteret had set out, in the columns of the Morning Chronicle, all the reasons why this movement, inaugurated by the three men who had met, six months before, at the office of the Chronicle, should be supported by the white public. Negro citizenship was a grotesque farce—Sambo and Dinah raised from the kitchen to the cabinet were a spectacle to make the gods laugh. The laws by which it had been sought to put the negroes on a level with the whites must be swept away in theory, as they had failed in fact. If it were impossible, without a further education of public opinion, to secure the repeal of the fifteenth amendment, it was at least the solemn duty of the state to endeavor, through its own constitution, to escape from the domination of a weak and incompetent electorate and confine the negro to that inferior condition for which nature had evidently designed him.

Until Carteret and his committee began their baleful campaign the people of the state were living in peace and harmony. The anti-negro legislation in more southern states, with large negro majorities, had awakened scarcely an echo in this state, with a population two thirds black. Even the triumph of the Fusion party had not been regarded as a race issue. To discuss means for counteracting this apathy, a meeting of the "Big Three," as they had begun to designate themselves jocularly, was held at the office of the "Morning Chronicle," on the next day but one after little Dodie's fortunate escape from the knife.

"It seems," said General Belmont, opening the discussion,

"as though we had undertaken more than we can carry through. It is clear that we must reckon on opposition, both at home and abroad. If we are to hope for success, we must extend the lines of our campaign. The North, as well as our own people, must be convinced that we have right upon our side."

McBane was tapping the floor impatiently with his foot during this harangue.

"I don't see the use," he interrupted, "of so much beating about the bush. We may as well be honest about this thing. We are going to put the niggers down because we want to and think we can; so why waste our time in mere pretense?"

"My dear captain," resumed the general, with biting suavity, "your frankness does you credit, but we cannot carry on politics in these degenerate times without a certain amount of diplomacy. In the good old days when your father was alive and perhaps nowadays in the discipline of convicts, direct and simple methods might be safely resorted to; but this is a modern age and we must profess a decent regard for the opinions of even that misguided portion of mankind which may not agree with us. This is the age of crowds and we must have the crowd with us."

The captain flushed at the allusion to his father's calling, at which he took more offense than at the mention of his own. He knew perfectly well that these old aristocrats, while reaping the profits of slavery, had despised the instruments by which they were attained—the poor white overseer only less than the black slave. McBane was rich; he lived in Wellington, but he had never been invited to the home of either General Belmont or Major Carteret, nor asked to join the club of which they were members. His face, therefore, wore a distinct scowl and his single eye glowed ominously. He would help those fellows carry the state for white supremacy and then he would have his innings—he would have more to say than they dreamed, as to who should fill the offices under the new deal. Men of no better birth or breeding than he had represented Southern states in Congress since the war. Why should he not run for governor, representative, whatever he chose? He had money enough to buy out half a dozen of these broken-down aristocrats and money was all-powerful.

"You see, captain," the general went on, looking McBane smilingly and unflinchingly in the eye, "we need white immigration—we need Northern capital. 'A good name is better than great riches,' and we must prove our cause a righteous one."

"We must be armed at all points," added Carteret, "and prepared for defense as well as for attack—we must make our campaign a national one."

"For instance," resumed the general, "you, Carteret, represent the Associated Press. Through your hands passes all the news of the state. What more powerful medium for the propagation of an idea? The man who would govern a nation by writing its songs was a blubbering idiot beside the fellow who can edit its news dispatches. The negroes are playing into our hands—every crime that one of them commits is reported by us. With the latitude they have had in this state they are growing more impudent and self-assertive every day. A yellow demagogue in New York made a speech only a few days ago, in which he deliberately and in cold blood, advised negroes to defend themselves to the death when attacked by white people! I remember well the time when it was death for a negro to strike a white man."

"It's death now, if he strikes the right one," interjected McBane, restored to better humor by this mention of a congenial subject.

The general smiled a fine smile. He had heard the story of how McBane had lost his other eye.

"The local negro paper is quite outspoken, too," continued the general, "if not impudent. We must keep track of that; it may furnish us some good campaign material."

"Yes," returned Carteret, "we must see to that. I threw a copy into the waste-basket this morning, without looking at it. Here it is now!"

# A White Man's 'Nigger'

CARTERET FISHED FROM THE DEPTHS OF THE wastebasket and handed to the general an eighteen by twenty-four sheet, poorly printed on cheap paper, with a "patent" inside, a number of advertisements of proprietary medicines, quack doctors and fortune-tellers and two or three columns of editorial and local news. Candor compels the admission that it was not an impressive sheet in any respect, except when regarded as the first local effort of a struggling people to make public expression of their life and aspirations. From this point of view it did not speak at all badly for a class to whom, a generation before, newspapers, books and learning had been forbidden fruit.

"It's an elegant specimen of journalism, isn't it?" laughed the general, airily. "Listen to this 'ad':—

" 'Kinky, curly hair made straight by one application of our specific. Our face bleach will turn the skin of a black or brown person four or five shades lighter and of a mulatto perfectly white. When you get the color you wish, stop using the preparation.'

"Just look at those heads!—'Before using' and 'After using.' We'd better hurry, or there'll be no negroes to disfranchise! If they don't stop till they get the color they desire and the stuff works according to contract, they'll all be white. Ah! what have we here? This looks as though it might be serious."

Opening the sheet the general read aloud an editorial article, to which Carteret listened intently, his indignation increasing in strength from the first word to the last, while McBane's face grew darkly purple with anger.

The article was a frank and bold discussion of lynching and its causes. It denied that most brutal lynchings were for the offense most often and generally charged as their justification and declared that, even of those seemingly traced to this cause, many were not for crimes at all, but for voluntary acts which might naturally be expected to follow from the miscegenation laws by which it was sought, in all the Southern States, to destroy liberty of contract and, for the purpose of maintaining a fanciful purity of race, to make crimes of marriages to which neither nature nor religion nor the laws of other states interposed any insurmountable barrier. Such an article in a Northern newspaper would have attracted no special attention and might merely have furnished food to an occasional reader for serious thought upon a subject not exactly agreeable; but coming from a colored man, in a Southern city it was an indictment of the laws and social system of the South that could not fail of creating a profound sensation.

"Infamous—infamous!" exclaimed Carteret, his voice trembling with emotion. "The paper should be suppressed immediately."

"The impudent nigger ought to be horsewhipped and run out of town," growled McBane.

"Gentlemen," said the general soothingly, after the first bit of indignation had subsided, "I believe we can find a more effective use for this article, which, by the way, will not bear too close analysis—there's some truth in it, at least there's an argument."

"That is not the point," interrupted Carteret.

"No," interjected McBane with an oath, "that ain't at all the point. Truth or not, no damn nigger has any right to say it."

"This story," said Carteret, "violates an unwritten law of the South. If we are to tolerate this race of weaklings among us, until they are eliminated by the stress of competition, it must be upon terms which we lay down. One of our conditions is violated by this article, in which our wisdom is assailed and our women made the subject of offensive comment. We must make known our disapproval."

57

"I say lynch the nigger, break up the press and burn down the newspaper office," McBane responded promptly.

"Gentlemen," interposed the general, "would you mind suspending the discussion for a moment, while I send Jerry across the street? I think I can then suggest a better plan."

Carteret rang the bell for Jerry, who answered promptly. He had been expecting such a call ever since the gentlemen had gone in.

"Jerry," said the general, "step across to Brown's and tell him to send me three Calhoun cocktails. Wait for them—here's the money."

"Yes, suh," replied Jerry, taking the proffered coin.

"And make haste, charcoal," added McBane, "for we're gettin' damn dry."

A momentary cloud of annoyance darkened Carteret's brow. McBane had always grated upon his aristocratic susceptibilities. The captain was an upstart, a product of the democratic idea operating upon the poor white man, the descendant of the indentured bond-servant and the socially unfit. He had wealth and energy, however and it was necessary to make use of him; but the example of such men was a strong incentive to Carteret in his campaign against the negro. It was distasteful enough to rub elbows with an illiterate and vulgar white man of no ancestry—the risk of similar contact with negroes was to be avoided at any cost. He could hardly expect McBane to be a gentleman, but when among men of that class he might at least try to imitate their manners. A gentleman did not order his own servants around offensively, to say nothing of another's.

The general had observed Carteret's annoyance and remarked pleasantly while they waited for the servant's return:—

"Jerry, now, is a very good negro. He's not one of your new negroes, who think themselves as good as white men and want to run the government. Jerry knows his place—he is respectful, humble, obedient and content with the face and place assigned to him by nature."

58

"Yes, he's one of the best of 'em," sneered McBane. "He'll call any man 'master' for a quarter, or 'God' for half a dollar; for a dollar he'll grovel at your feet and for a cast-off coat you can buy an option on his immortal soul—if he has one! I've handled niggers for ten years and I know 'em from the ground up. They're all alike— they're a scrub race, an affliction to the country and the quicker we're rid of 'em all the better."

Carteret had nothing to say by way of dissent. McBane's sentiments, in their last analysis, were much the same as his, though he would have expressed them less brutally.

"The negro," observed the general, daintily flicking the ash from his cigar, "is all right in his place and very useful to the community. We lived on his labor for quite a long time and lived very well. Nevertheless we are better off without slavery, for we can get more out of the free negro and with less responsibility. I really do not see how we could get along without the negroes. If they were all like Jerry, we'd have no trouble with them."

Having procured the drinks, Jerry, the momentary subject of the race discussion which goes on eternally in the South, was making his way back across the street, somewhat disturbed in mind.

"Oh Lawd!" he groaned, "I never troubles trouble till trouble troubles me; but when I got dem drinks befo', General Belmont gimme half a dollar an' tol' me to keep the change. Dis time he did n' say nothin' 'bout the change. I s'pose he jes' forgot about it, but what is a poor nigger gwine to do when he has to content wid white folks' forgetfulness? I don't see no way but to do some forgettin' myself. I'll jes' stan' outside the do' here till they gits so wrap' up in their talk dat they won't 'member nothin' else, an' then at the right minute I'll hand the glasses 'roun, an' most likely the General will forget all 'bout the change."

While Jerry stood outside, the conversation within was plainly audible and some inkling of its purport filtered through his mind.

"Now, gentlemen," the general was saying, "here's my

plan. That editorial in the negro newspaper is good campaign matter, but we should reserve it until it will be most effective. Suppose we just stick it in a pigeon-hole and let the editor— what's his name?"

"The nigger's name is Barber," replied McBane. "I'd like to have him for a month or two; he'd write no more editorials."

"Let Barber have all the rope he wants," resumed the general, "and he'll be sure to hang himself. In the mean time we will continue to work up public opinion and when the state campaign opens we'll print the editorial, with suitable comment, scatter it broadcast throughout the state, fire the Southern heart, organize the white people on the color line, have a little demonstration with red shirts and shotguns, scare the negroes into fits, win the state for white supremacy and teach our colored fellow citizens that we are tired of negro domination and have put an end to it forever. The Afro-American Banner will doubtless die about the same time."

"And so will the editor!" exclaimed McBane ferociously; "I'll see to that. But I wonder where that nigger is with them cocktails? I'm so thirsty I could swallow blue blazes."

"Here's yo' drinks, General," announced Jerry, entering with the glasses on a tray.

The gentlemen exchanged compliments and imbibed— McBane at a gulp, Carteret with more deliberation, leaving about half the contents of his glass.

The general drank slowly, with every sign of appreciation. "If the illustrious statesmen," he observed, "whose name this mixture bears, had done nothing more than invent it, his fame would still deserve to go thundering down the endless ages."

"It ain't bad liquor," assented McBane, smacking his lips.

Jerry received the empty glasses on the tray and left the room. He had scarcely gained the hall when the general called him back.

"O Lawd!" groaned Jerry, "he's gwine to ax me for the change. Yes, suh, yes, suh; comin', General, comin, suh!"

"You may keep the change, Jerry," said the general.

Jerry's face grew radiant at this announcement. "Yes, suh,

General; thank y', suh; much obliged, suh. I was jus' gwine to fetch it in, suh. Thank y', suh, truly, suh!"

Jerry backed and bowed himself out into the hall.

"Dat was a close shave," he muttered, as he swallowed the remaining contents of Major Carteret's glass. "I 'lowed dem twenty cents was gone dat time—an' where I was gwine to git the money to take my gal to the church festival to-night, the Lawd only knows!—'less'n I borrowed it off of Mr. Ellis, an' I owes him sixty cents already. But I wonder what dem white folks in there is up to? There's one thing sho'—they're gwine to git after the niggers some way or another, an' when they does, where is Jerry gwine to be? I'm gwine to look at dat newspaper they been talkin' 'bout, an' 'les'n my mind changes mightily, I'm gwine to keep my mouth shut an' stan' in wid the Angry-Saxon race—as they calls deyselves nowadays—an' keep on the right side of my bread an' meat. What nigger ever give me twenty cents in all my born days?"

"By the way, major," said the general, who lingered behind McBane as they were leaving, "is Miss Clara's marriage definitely settled upon?"

"Well, general, not exactly; but it's the understanding that they will marry when they are old enough."

"I was thinking," the general went on, "that if I were you I'd speak to Tom about cards and liquor. He gives more time to both than a young man can afford."

"Thank you, general, for the hint. I'll act upon it."

This political conference was fruitful in results. Acting upon the plans there laid out, McBane traveled extensively through the state, working up sentiment in favor of the new movement. He possessed a certain forceful eloquence; and white supremacy was so obviously the divine intention that he had merely to affirm the doctrine in order to secure adherents.

Carteret conducted the press campaign and held out to the Republicans of the North the glittering hope that, with the elimination of the negro vote and a proper deference to Southern feeling, a strong white Republican party might be built up in the New South.

61

# X

# Delamere Plays a Trump

CARTERET DID NOT FORGET WHAT GENERAL Belmont had said in regard to Tom. The opportunity to carry out this purpose was not long delayed. Old Mr. Delamere wished to sell some timber and sent Tom down to the Chronicle office to leave an advertisement. The major saw him at the desk, invited him into his sanctum and delivered him a mild lecture. The major was kind and talked in a fatherly way about the danger of extremes, the beauty of moderation and the value of discretion as a rule of conduct.

Delamere had turned red with anger while the major was speaking. He was impulsive and an effort was required to keep back the retort that sprang once or twice to his lips; but his conscience was not clear and he could not afford hard words with Clara's guardian and his grandfather's friend. Clara was rich and the most beautiful girl in town; they were engaged; he loved her as well as he could love anything of which he seemed sure; and he did not mean that any one else should have her.

"Thank you, major," he said, with well-simulated frankness. "I realize that I may have been a little careless, but my heart is all right, sir and I am glad that my conduct has been brought to your attention. I will be more careful of my company hereafter; for I love Clara and mean to try to be worthy of her."

Upon leaving the office, which was on the second floor, Tom met Ellis coming up the stairs. It had several times of late occurred to Tom that Ellis had a sneaking fondness for Clara. Tom had rather enjoyed the idea of a hopeless rival. But this interview with the major had so disquieted him that upon meeting Ellis upon the stairs he was struck by a sudden suspicion. He knew that Major Carteret seldom went to the Clarendon Club and that he must have got his information from some one else. Ellis was a member of the club and a frequent visitor. Who more likely than he to try to poison Clara's mind?

"That's the damned sneak who's been giving me away," he muttered. "I'll get even with him yet for this."

Ellis was an excellent judge of character and had formed a very decided opinion of Tom Delamere. To Ellis, unbiased by ancestral traditions, biased perhaps by jealousy, Tom Delamere was a type of the degenerate aristocrat. If, as he had often heard, it took three or four generations to make a gentleman and as many more to complete the curve and return to the base from which it started, Tom Delamere belonged somewhere on the downward slant, with large possibilities of further decline. Old Mr. Delamere, who might be taken as the apex of an ideal aristocratic development, had been distinguished, during his active life, as Ellis had learned, for courage and strength of will, courtliness of bearing, deference to his superiors, of whom there had been few, courtesy to his equals, kindness and consideration for those less highly favored and above all, a scrupulous sense of honor; his grandson Tom was merely the shadow without the substance, the empty husk without the grain. Of grace he had plenty. In manners he could be perfect, when he so chose. Courage and strength he had none. Ellis had seen this fellow, who boasted of his descent from a line of cavaliers, turn pale with fright and spring from a buggy to which was harnessed a fractious horse, which a negro stable-boy drove fearlessly. A valiant carpet-knight, skilled in all parlor exercises, great at whist or euchre, a dream of a dancer, unexcelled in cakewalk or "coon" impersonations, for which he was in large social demand, Ellis had seen him kick an inoffensive negro out of his path and treat a poor-white man with scant courtesy. He suspected Delamere of cheating at cards and knew that others entertained the same suspicion. For while regular in his own habits—his poverty would not have permitted him any considerable extravagance—Ellis' position

63

as a newspaper man kept him in touch with what was going on about town. He was a member, proposed by Carteret, of the Clarendon Club, where cards were indulged in within reasonable limits and a certain set were known to bet dollars in terms of dimes.

Delamere was careless, too, about money matters. He had a habit of borrowing, right and left, small sums which might be conveniently forgotten by the borrower and for which the lender would dislike to ask. Ellis had a strain of thrift, derived from a Scotch ancestry and a tenacious memory for financial details. Indeed, he had never had so much money that he could lose track of it. He never saw Delamere without being distinctly conscious that Delamere owed him four dollars, which he had lent at a time when he could ill afford to spare it. It was a prerogative of aristocracy, Ellis reflected, to live upon others and the last privilege which aristocracy in decay would willingly relinquish. Neither did the aristocratic memory seem able to retain the sordid details of a small pecuniary transaction.

No doubt the knowledge that Delamere was the favored lover of Miss Pemberton lent a touch of bitterness to Ellis' reflections upon his rival. Ellis had no grievance against the "aristocracy" of Wellington. The "best people" had received him cordially, though his father had not been of their caste; but Ellis hated a hypocrite and despised a coward and he felt sure that Delamere was both. Otherwise he would have struggled against his love for Clara Pemberton. His passion for her had grown with his appreciation of Delamere's unworthiness. As a friend of the family, he knew the nature and terms of the engagement and that if the marriage took place at all, it would not be for at least a year. This was a long time— many things might happen in a year, especially to a man like Tom Delamere. If for any reason Delamere lost his chance, Ellis meant to be next in the field. He had not made love to Clara, but he had missed no opportunity of meeting her and making himself quietly and unobtrusively agreeable.

On the day after this encounter with Delamere on the stairs

of the Chronicle office, Ellis, while walking down Vine Street, met old Mrs. Ochiltree. She was seated in her own buggy, which was of ancient build and pattern, driven by her colored coachman and man of all work.

"Mr. Ellis," she called in a shrill voice, having directed her coachman to draw up at the curb as she saw the young man approaching, "come here. I want to speak to you."

Ellis came up to the buggy and stood uncovered beside it.

"People are saying," said Mrs. Ochiltree, "that Tom Delamere is drinking hard and has to be carried home intoxicated, two or three times a week, by old Mr. Delamere's man Sandy. Is there any truth in the story?"

"My dear Mrs. Ochiltree, I am not Tom Delamere's keeper. Sandy could tell you better than I."

"You are dodging my question, Mr. Ellis. Sandy wouldn't tell me the truth and I know that you wouldn't lie—you don't look like a liar. They say Tom is gambling scandalously. What do you know about that?"

"You must excuse me, Mrs. Ochiltree. A great deal of what we hear is mere idle gossip and the truth is often grossly exaggerated. I'm a member of the same club with Delamere and gentlemen who belong to the same club are not in the habit of talking about one another. As long as a man retains his club membership, he's presumed to be a gentleman. I wouldn't say anything against Delamere if I could."

"You don't need to," replied the old lady, shaking her finger at him with a cunning smile. "You are a very open young man, Mr. Ellis and I can read you like a book. You are much smarter than you look, but you can't fool me. Good-morning."

Mrs. Ochiltree drove immediately to her niece's, where she found Mrs. Carteret and Clara at home. Clara was very fond of the baby and was holding him in her arms. He was a fine baby and bade fair to realize the bright hopes built upon him.

"You hold a baby very naturally, Clara," chuckled the old lady. "I suppose you are in training. But you ought to talk to Tom. I have just learned from Mr. Ellis that Tom is carried home drunk two or three times a week and that he is gambling in the most reckless manner imaginable."

Clara's eyes flashed indignantly. Ere she could speak, Mrs. Carteret exclaimed:—

"Why, Aunt Polly! did Mr. Ellis say that?"

"I got it from Dinah," she replied, "who heard it from her husband, who learned it from a waiter at the club. And"—

"Pshaw!" said Mrs. Carteret, "mere servants' gossip."

"No, it isn't, Olivia. I met Mr. Ellis on the street and asked him point blank and he didn't deny it. He's a member of the club and ought to know."

"Well, Aunt Polly, it can't be true. Tom is here every other night and how could he carry on so without showing the signs of it? and where would he get the money? You know he has only a moderate allowance."

"He may win it at cards—it's better to be born lucky than rich," returned Mrs. Ochiltree. "Then he has expectations and can get credit. There's no doubt that Tom is going on shamefully."

Clara's indignation had not yet found vent in speech; Olivia had said all that was necessary, but she had been thinking rapidly. Even if all this had been true, why should Mr. Ellis have said it? Or, if he had not stated it directly, he had left the inference to be drawn. It seemed a most unfair and ungentlemanly thing. What motive could Ellis have for such an act?

She was not long in reaching a conclusion which was not flattering to Ellis. Mr. Ellis came often to the house and she had enjoyed his society in a friendly way. That he had found her pleasant company had been very evident. She had never taken his attentions seriously, however, or regarded his visits as made especially to her, nor had the rest of the family treated them from that point of view. Her engagement to Tom Delamere, though not yet formally ratified, was so well understood by the world of Wellington that Mr. Ellis would scarcely have presumed to think of her as anything more than a friend.

This revelation of her aunt's, however, put a different face

66

upon his conduct. Certain looks and sighs and enigmatical remarks of Ellis, to which she had paid but casual attention and attached no particular significance, now recurred to her memory with a new meaning. He had now evidently tried, in a roundabout way, to besmirch Tom's character and undermine him in her regard. While loving Tom, she had liked Ellis well enough, as a friend; but he had abused the privileges of friendship and she would teach him a needed lesson.

Nevertheless, Mrs. Ochiltree's story had given Clara food for thought. She was uneasily conscious, after all, that there might be a grain of truth in what had been said, enough, at least, to justify her in warning Tom to be careful, lest his enemies should distort some amiable weakness into a serious crime.

She put this view of the case to Tom at their next meeting, assuring him, at the same time, of her unbounded faith and confidence. She did not mention Ellis' name, lest Tom, in righteous indignation, might do something rash, which he might thereafter regret. If any subtler or more obscure motive kept her silent as to Ellis, she was not aware of it, for Clara's views of life were still in the objective stage and she had not yet fathomed the deepest recesses of her own consciousness.

Delamere had the cunning of weakness. He knew, too, better than any one else could know, how much truth there was in the rumors concerning him and whether or not they could be verified too easily for him to make an indignant denial. After a little rapid reflection, he decided upon a different course.

"Clara," he said with a sigh, taking the hand which she generously yielded to soften any suggestion of reproach which he may have read into her solicitude, "you are my guardian angel. I do not know, of course, who has told you this pack of lies—for I can see that you have heard more than you have told me—but I think I could guess the man they came from. I am not perfect, Clara, though I have done nothing of which a gentleman should be ashamed. There is one sure way to stop the tongue of calumny. My home life is not ideal—grandfather is an old, weak man and the house needs the refining and softening influence of a lady's presence. I do not love club life, its ideals are not elevating. With you by my side, dearest, I should be preserved from every influence except the purest and the best. don't you think, dearest, that the major might be induced to shorten our weary term of waiting?"

"Oh, Tom," she demurred blushingly. "I shall be young enough at eighteen; and you are barely twent-yone."

But Tom proved an eloquent pleader and love a still more persuasive advocate. Clara spoke to the major the same evening, who looked grave at the suggestion and said he would think about it. They were both very young; but where both parties were of good family, in good health and good circumstances, an early marriage might not be undesirable. Tom was perhaps a little unsettled, but blood would tell in the long run and marriage always exercised a steadying influence.

The only return, therefore, which Ellis received for his well-meant effort to ward off Mrs. Ochiltree's embarrassing inquiries was that he did not see Clara upon his next visit, which was made one afternoon while he was on night duty at the office. In conversation with Mrs. Carteret he learned that Clara's marriage had been definitely agreed upon and the date fixed—it was to take place in about six months. Meeting Miss Pemberton on the street the following day, he received the slightest of nods. When he called again at the house, after a week of misery, she treated him with a sarcastic coolness which chilled his heart.

"How have I offended you, Miss Clara?" he demanded desperately, when they were left alone for a moment.

"Offended me?" she replied, lifting her eyebrows with an air of puzzled surprise. "Why, Mr. Ellis! What could have put such a notion into your head? Oh dear, I think I hear Dodie—I know you'll excuse me, Mr. Ellis, won't you? Sister Olivia will be back in a moment; and we're expecting Aunt Polly this afternoon—if you'll stay awhile she'll be glad to talk to you! You can tell her all the interesting news about your friends!"

# XI

# The Baby and the Bird

WHEN ELLIS, AFTER THIS REBUFF, HAD TAKEN HIS leave, Clara, much elated at the righteous punishment she had inflicted upon the slanderer, ran upstairs to the nursery and, snatching Dodie from Mammy Jane's arms, began dancing gayly with him round the room.

"Look a-here, honey," said Mammy Jane, "you better be careful wid dat chile, an' don't drop him on the floor'. My, my! but you two does make a pretty pictur'! You'll be wantin' ole Jane to come an' nurse yo' chillun some of these days," she chuckled unctuously.

Mammy Jane had been very much disturbed by the recent dangers through which little Dodie had passed; and his escape from strangulation, in the first place and then from the knife had impressed her as little less than miraculous. She was not certain whether this result had been brought about by her manipulation of the buried charm, or by the prayers which had been offered for the child, but was inclined to believe that both had cooperated to avert the threatened calamity. The favorable outcome of this particular incident had not, however, altered the general situation. Prayers and charms, after all, were merely temporary things, which must be constantly renewed and might be forgotten or overlooked; while the mole, on the contrary, neither faded nor went away. If its malign influence might for a time seem to disappear, it was merely lying dormant, like the germs of some deadly disease, awaiting its opportunity to strike at an unguarded spot.

Clara and the baby were laughing in great glee, when a mockingbird, perched on the topmost bough of a small tree

69

opposite the nursery window, burst suddenly into song, with many a trill and quaver. Clara, with the child in her arms, sprang to the open window.

"Sister Olivia," she cried, turning her face toward Mrs. Carteret, who at that moment entered the room, "come and look at Dodie."

The baby was listening intently to the music, meanwhile gurgling with delight and reaching his chubby hands toward the source of this pleasing sound. It seemed as though the mockingbird were aware of his appreciative audience, for he ran through the songs of a dozen different birds, selecting, with the discrimination of a connoisseur and entire confidence in his own powers, those which were most difficult and most alluring.

Mrs. Carteret approached the window, followed by Mammy Jane, who wandered over to join the admiring party. So absorbed were the three women in the baby and the bird that neither one of them observed a neat top buggy, drawn by a sleek sorrel pony, passing slowly along the street before the house. In the buggy was seated a lady and beside her a little boy, dressed in a child's sailor suit and a straw hat. The lady, with a wistful expression, was looking toward the party grouped in the open window.

Mrs Carteret, chancing to lower her eyes for an instant, caught the other woman's look directed toward her and her child. With a glance of cold aversion she turned away from the window.

Old Mammy Jane had observed this movement and had divined the reason for it. She stood beside Clara, watching the retreating buggy.

"Uhhuh!" she said to herself, "it's huh sister Janet! She married a doctor, an' all dat, an' she lives in a big house, an' she's been roun' the world an the Lawd knows where else; but Miss 'Livy don't like the sight of her, an' never will, as long as the sun rises an' sets. They certainly does favor one another—anybody might 'low they was twins, if they did n' know better. Well, well! Forty years ago who'd 'a' ever expected to see a

70

nigger gal ridin' in her own buggy? My, my! but I don't know—I don't know! It don't look right, an' it ain't gwine to las'!—you can't make me b'lieve!"

Meantime Janet, stung by Mrs. Carteret's look— the nearest approach she had ever made to a recognition of her sister's existence—had turned away with hardening face. She had struck her pony sharply with the whip, much to the gentle creature's surprise, when the little boy, who was still looking back, caught his mother's sleeve and exclaimed excitedly:—

"Look, look, mama! The baby—the baby!"

Janet turned instantly and with a mother's instinct gave an involuntary cry of alarm.

At the moment when Mrs. Carteret had turned away from the window and while Mammy Jane was watching Janet, Clara had taken a step forward and was leaning against the window-sill. The baby, convulsed with delight, had given a spasmodic spring and slipped from Clara's arms. Instinctively the young woman gripped the long skirt as it slipped through her hands and held it tenaciously, though too frightened for an instant to do more. Mammy Jane, ashen with sudden dread, uttered an inarticulate scream, but retained self-possession enough to reach down and draw up the child, which hung dangerously suspended, head downward, over the brick pavement below.

"Oh, Clara, Clara, how could you!" exclaimed Mrs. Carteret reproachfully; "you might have killed my child!"

She had snatched the child from Jane's arms and was holding him closely to her own breast. Struck by a sudden thought, she drew near the window and looked out. Twice within a few weeks her child had been in serious danger and upon each occasion a member of the Miller family had been involved, for she had heard of Dr. Miller's presumption in trying to force himself where he must have known he would be unwelcome.

Janet was just turning her head away as the buggy moved slowly off. Olivia felt a violent wave of antipathy sweep over her toward this baseborn sister who had thus thrust herself beneath her eyes. If she had not cast her brazen glance toward

71

the window, she herself would not have turned away and lost sight of her child. To this shameless intrusion, linked with Clara's carelessness, had been due the catastrophe, so narrowly averted, which might have darkened her own life forever. She took to her bed for several days and for a long time was cold toward Clara and did not permit her to touch the child.

Mammy Jane entertained a theory of her own about the accident, by which the blame was placed, in another way, exactly where Mrs. Carteret had laid it. Julia's daughter, Janet, had been looking intently toward the window just before little Dodie had sprung from Clara's arms. Might she not have cast the evil eye upon the baby and sought thereby to draw him out of the window? One would not ordinarily expect so young a woman to possess such a power, but she might have acquired it, for this very purpose, from some more experienced person. By the same reasoning, the mockingbird might have been a familiar of the witch and the two might have conspired to lure the infant to destruction. Whether this were so or not, the transaction at least wore a peculiar look. There was no use telling Miss 'Livy about it, for she didn't believe, or pretended not to believe, in witchcraft and conjuration. But one could not be too careful. The child was certainly born to be exposed to great dangers—the mole behind the left ear was an unfailing sign—and no precaution should be omitted to counteract its baleful influence.

While adjusting the baby's crib, a few days later, Mrs. Carteret found fastened under one of the slats a small bag of cotton cloth, about half an inch long and tied with a black thread, upon opening which she found a few small roots or fibres and a pinch of dried and crumpled herbs. It was a good-luck charm which Mammy Jane had placed there to ward off the threatened evil from the grandchild of her dear old mistress. Mrs. Carteret's first impulse was to throw the bag into the fire, but on second thoughts she let it remain. To remove it would give unnecessary pain to the old nurse. Of course these old negro superstitions were absurd—but if the charm did no good, it at least would do no harm.

# XII

# Another Southern Product

ONE MORNING SHORTLY AFTER THE OPENING OF the hospital, while Dr. Miller was making his early rounds, a new patient walked in with a smile on his face and a broken arm hanging limply by his side. Miller recognized in him a black giant by the name of Josh Green, who for many years had worked on the docks for Miller's father—and simultaneously identified him as the dust-begrimed negro who had stolen a ride to Wellington on the trucks of a passenger car.

"Well, Josh," asked the doctor, as he examined the fracture, "how did you get this? Been fighting again?"

"No, suh, I don't s'pose you could hardly call it a fight. One of dem dagoes off of a South American boat gimme some of his jaw, an' I give him a back answer, an' here I is wid a broken arm. He got hold of a stick befo' I could hit him."

"What became of the other man?" demanded Miller suspiciously.

"Lemme see," said Josh reflectively, "if I can 'member what did become of him! Oh, yes, I 'member now! They took him to the Marine Hospital in the ambulance, 'cause his leg was broke, an' I reckon somethin' must 'a' accidently hit him in the jaw, for he was scatterin' teeth all the way 'long the street. I didn't wan' to kill the man, for he might have somebody dependin' on him, an' I knows how that'd be to dem. But no man can call me a damn' low-down nigger and keep on enjoyin' good health right along."

"It was considerate of you to spare his life," said Miller dryly, "but you'll hit the wrong man some day. These are bad times for bad negroes. You'll get into a quarrel with a white man and at the end of it there'll be a lynching, or a funeral."

"I expect to die a violent death in a quarrel wid a white man," replied Josh, in a matter-of-fact tone, "an' furthermo', he's gwine to die at the same time, of a little befo'. I been takin' my own time 'bout killin' him; I ain't been crowdin' the man, but I'll be ready after a while, an' then he can look out!"

"And I suppose you 're merely keeping in practice on these other fellows who come your way. When I get your arm dressed, you'd better leave town till that fellow's boat sails; it may save you the expense of a trial and three months in the chain-gang. But this talk about killing a man is all nonsense. What has any man in this town done to you, that you should thirst for his blood?"

"No, suh, it ain't nonsense—it's straight, solem' fac'. I'm gwine to kill dat man as sho' as I 'm sitting in dis chair; an' they ain't nobody can say I ain't got a right to kill him. Does you 'member the Ku-Klux?"

"Yes, but I was a child at the time and recollect very little about them. It is a page of history which most people are glad to forget."

"Yes, suh; I was a chile, too, but I was right in it, an' so I 'members mo' about it 'n you does. My mammy an' daddy lived 'bout ten miles from here, up the river. One night a crowd of white men come to you' house an' took my daddy out an' shot him to death, an' scared my mammy so she ain't been herself from dat day to dis. I weren't mo' 'n ten years ole at the time, an' when my mammy saw the white men comin', she tol' me to run. I hid in the bushes an' seen the whole thing, an' it was branded on my memory, suh, like a red-hot iron brands the skin. The white folks had masks on, but one of 'em fell off— he was the boss, he was the head man, an' tol' the res' what to do—an' I seen his face. It was a easy face to 'member; an' I swo' then, 'way down deep in my heart, little as I was, dat some day of 'another I'd kill dat man. I ain't never had no doubt about it; it's jus' what I'm livin' for, an' I know I ain't gwine to die till I've done it. Some lives for one thing an' some for another, but dat's my job. I ain't been in no haste, for I'm not ole yet, an' dat

74

man is in good health. I'd like to see a little of the world befo' I takes chances on leavin' it sudden; an', mo'over, somebody's got to take care of the ole 'oman. But her time'll come some of these days, an then his time'll be come—an' prob'ly mine. But I ain't carin' 'bout myself: when I git thru wid him, it won' make no difference 'bout me."

Josh was in dead earnest. Miller recalled the expression he had seen on his patient's face, during the journey to Wellington. He had often seen Josh's mother, old Aunt Milly— "Silly Milly," the children called her—wandering aimlessly about the street, muttering to herself incoherently. He had vaguely understood that she was the victim of human cruelty. This was his first knowledge of the real facts of the case.

He realized, too, for a moment, the continuity of life, how inseparably the present is woven with the past, how certainly the future will be but the outcome of the present. He knew the timeworn explanation that the Ku-Klux movement, in the main, was merely an ebullition of boyish spirits, begun to amuse young white men by playing upon the fears and superstitions of ignorant negroes. Here, however, was its tragic side—the old wound still bleeding, the fruit of one tragedy, the seed of another. He could not approve of Josh's application of the Mosaic law of revenge and yet the incident was not without significance. Here was a negro who could remember an injury, who could shape his life to a definite purpose, if not a high or holy one. When his race reached the point where they would resent a wrong, there was hope that they might soon attain the stage where they would try and, if need be, die, to defend a right. This man, too, had a purpose in life and was willing to die that he might accomplish it. Miller was willing to give up his life to a cause. Would he be equally willing, he asked himself, to die for it? Miller had no prophetic instinct to tell him how soon he would have the opportunity to answer his own question. But he could not encourage Josh to carry out this dark and revengeful purpose. Every worthy consideration required him to dissuade his patient from such a desperate course.

75

"You had better put away these murderous fancies, Josh," he said seriously. "The Bible says that we should 'forgive our enemies, bless them that curse us and do good to them that despitefully use us.' "

"Yes, suh, I've learnt all dat in Sunday-school, an' I've heard the preachers say it time an' time again. But it 'pears to me dat dis forgetfulness an' forgiveness is mighty one-sided. The white folks don't forgive nothin' the niggers does. They got up the Ku-Klux, they said, on 'count of the carpet-baggers. They been talkin' 'bout the carpet-baggers ever since, an' they 'pears to forgot all 'bout the Ku-Klux. But I ain't forgot. The niggers is been train' to forgiveness; an' for fear they might forget how to forgive, the white folks gives 'em somethin' new every now an' then, to practice on. A white man can do what he wants to a nigger, but the minute the nigger gits back at him, up goes the nigger, an' don't come down tell somebody cuts him down. If a nigger gits a' office, of the race 'pears to be prosperin' too much, the white folks up an' kills a few, so dat the res' can keep on forgivin' an' being thankful dat dey're lef' alive. don't talk to me 'bout these white folks—I knows 'em, I does! If a nigger wants to git down on his marrowbones, an' eat dirt, an' call 'em 'marster,' he's a good nigger, There's room for him. But I ain't no white folks' nigger, I ain'. I don't call no man 'marster.' I don't wan' nothin' but what I work for, but I wants all of dat. I never molest no white man, 'less 'n he molest me first'. But when the ole 'oman dies, doctor, an' I gits a good chance at dat white man—there ain't no use talkin', suh!— There's gwine to be a mix-up, an' a funeral, of two funerals—of may be mo', if-anybody is careless enough to git in the way."

"Josh," said the doctor, "you 're feverish and don't know what you're talking about."

When Josh got better he would talk to him and dissuade him from this dangerous design. He had not asked the name of Josh's enemy, but the look of murderous hate which the dust-begrimed tramp of the railway journey had cast at Captain George McBane rendered any such question superfluous.

# XIII

# The Cakewalk

OLD MR. DELAMERE'S SERVANT, SANDY CAMPBELL, was in deep trouble.

A party of Northern visitors had been staying for several days at the St. James Hotel. The gentlemen of the party were concerned in a projected cotton mill, while the ladies were much interested in the study of social conditions and especially in the negro problem. As soon as their desire for information became known, they were taken courteously under the wing of prominent citizens and their wives, who gave them, at elaborate luncheons, the Southern white man's views of the negro, sighing sentimentally over the disappearance of the good old negro of before the war and gravely deploring the degeneracy of his descendants. They enlarged upon the amount of money the Southern whites had spent for the education of the negro and shook their heads over the inadequate results accruing from this unexampled generosity. It was sad, they said, to witness this spectacle of a dying race, unable to withstand the competition of a superior type. The severe reprisals taken by white people for certain crimes committed by negroes were of course not the acts of the best people, who deplored them; but still a certain charity should be extended towards those who in the intense and righteous anger of the moment should take the law into their own hands and deal out rough but still substantial justice; for no negro was ever lynched without incontestable proof of his guilt. In order to be perfectly fair and give their visitors an opportunity to see both sides of the question, they accompanied the Northern visitors to a colored church where they might hear a colored preacher, who had won a jocular popularity throughout the whole country by an oft-repeated sermon intended to demonstrate that the earth was flat like a pancake. This celebrated divine could always draw a white audience, except on the days when his no less distinguished white rival in the field of sensationalism preached his equally famous sermon to prove that hell was exactly one half mile, linear measure, from the city limits of Wellington. Whether accidentally or not, the Northern visitors had no opportunity to meet or talk alone with any colored person in the city except the servants at the hotel. When one of the party suggested a visit to the colored mission school, a Southern friend kindly volunteered to accompany them.

The visitors were naturally much impressed by what they learned from their courteous hosts and felt inclined to sympathize with the Southern people, for the negro is not counted as a Southerner, except to fix the basis of congressional representation. There might of course be things to criticise here and there, certain customs for which they did not exactly see the necessity and which seemed in conflict with the highest ideals of liberty but surely these courteous, soft-spoken ladies and gentlemen, entirely familiar with local conditions, who descanted so earnestly and at times pathetically upon the grave problems confronting them, must know more about it than people in the distant North, without their means of information. The negroes who waited on them at the hotel seemed happy enough and the teachers whom they had met at the mission school had been well-dressed, well-mannered and apparently content with their position in life. Surely a people who made no complaints could not be very much oppressed.

In order to give the visitors, ere they left Wellington, a pleasing impression of Southern customs and particularly of the joyous, happy-go-lucky disposition of the Southern darky and his entire contentment with existing conditions, it was decided by the hotel management to treat them, on the last night of their visit, to a little diversion, in the shape of a genuine negro cakewalk.

78

On the afternoon of this same day Tom Delamere strolled into the hotel and soon gravitated to the bar, where he was a frequent visitor. Young men of leisure spent much of their time around the hotel and no small part of it in the bar. Delamere had been to the club, but had avoided the cardroom. Time hanging heavy on his hands, he had sought the hotel in the hope that some form of distraction might present itself.

"Have you heard the latest, Mr. Delamere?" asked the bartender, as he mixed a cocktail for his customer.

"No, Billy; what is it?"

"There's to be a big cakewalk upstairs to-night. The Northern gentlemen an' ladies who are down here to see about the new cotton factory want to study the nigger some more and the boss has got up a cakewalk for 'em, 'mongst the waiters and chambermaids, with a little outside talent."

"Is it to be public?" asked Delamere.

"Oh, no, not generally, but friends of the house won't be barred out. The clerk'll fix it for you. Ransom, the head waiter, will be floor manager."

Delamere was struck with a brilliant idea. The more he considered it, the brighter it seemed. Another cocktail imparted additional brilliancy to the conception. He had been trying, after a feeble fashion, to keep his promise to Clara and was really suffering from lack of excitement.

He left the bar-room, found the head waiter, held with him a short conversation and left in his intelligent and itching palm a piece of money.

The cakewalk was a great success. The most brilliant performer was a late arrival, who made his appearance just as the performance was about to commence. The newcomer was dressed strikingly, the conspicuous features of his attire being a long blue coat with brass buttons and a pair of plaid trousers. He was older, too, than the other participants, which made his agility the more remarkable. His partner was a new chambermaid, who had just come to town and whom the head waiter introduced to the newcomer upon his arrival. The cake was awarded to this couple by a unanimous vote. The man

79

presented it to his partner with a grandiloquent flourish and returned thanks in a speech which sent the Northern visitors into spasms of delight at the quaintness of the darky dialect and the darky wit. To cap the climax, the winner danced a buck dance with a skill and agility that brought a shower of complimentary silver.

Ellis was off duty for the evening and dropped into the hotel office at about nine o'clock. He was invited up to see the cakewalk, which he rather enjoyed, for there was some graceful dancing and posturing. But the grotesque contortions of one participant had struck him as somewhat overdone, even for the comical type of negro. He recognized the fellow, after a few minutes' scrutiny, as the body-servant of old Mr. Delamere. The man's present occupation, or choice of diversion, seemed out of keeping with his employment as attendant upon an invalid old gentleman and strangely inconsistent with the gravity and decorum which had been so noticeable when this agile cakewalker had served as butler at Major Carteret's table, upon the occasion of the christening dinner. There was a vague suggestion of unreality about this performance, too, which Ellis did not attempt to analyze, but which recurred vividly to his memory upon a subsequent occasion.

Ellis had never pretended to that intimate knowledge of negro thought and character by which some of his acquaintances claimed the ability to fathom every motive of a negro's conduct and predict in advance what any one of the darker race would do under a given set of circumstances.

The champion cakewalker disappeared immediately after the close of the performance. The following week Sandy was summoned before the disciplinary committee of his church and charged with unchristian conduct, in the following particulars, to wit: dancing and participating in a sinful diversion called a cakewalk, which was calculated to bring the church into disrepute and make it the mockery of sinners.

Sandy protested his innocence vehemently, but in vain. The proof was overwhelming. He was positively identified by Sister 'Manda Patterson, the hotel cook, who had watched the

80

whole performance from the hotel corridor for the sole, single, solitary and only purpose, she averred, of seeing how far human wickedness could be carried by a professing Christian. The whole thing had been shocking and offensive to her and only a stern sense of duty had sustained her in looking on, that she might be qualified to bear witness against the offender. She had recognized his face, his clothes, his voice, his walk—there could be no shadow of doubt that it was Brother Sandy. This testimony was confirmed by one of the deacons, whose son, a waiter at the hotel, had also seen Sandy at the cakewalk.

Sandy stoutly insisted that he was at home the whole evening; that he had not been near the hotel for three months; that he had never in his life taken part in a cakewalk and that he did not know how to dance. It was replied that wickedness, like everything else, must have a beginning; that dancing was an art that could be acquired in secret and came natural to some people. In the face of positive proof, Sandy's protestations were of no avail; he was found guilty and suspended from church fellowship.

Refusing to confess his faults, Sandy glided into habits of which the church would not have approved. The consolation however, did not compensate him for the loss of standing in the church, which to him was a social club as well as a religious temple. At times, in conversation with young Delamere, he would lament his hard fate.

Tom laughed until he cried at the comical idea which Sandy's plaint always brought up, of half-a-dozen negro preachers sitting in solemn judgment upon that cakewalk—it had certainly been a good cakewalk!—and sending poor Sandy to spiritual Coventry.

"Cheer up, Sandy, cheer up!" he would say when Sandy seemed most depressed. "Go into my room and get yourself a good drink of liquor!"

Hoping to revive his drooping spirits, Sandy too often accepted the proffered remedy.

81

# XIV

# Old Mrs. Ochiltree

WHEN MRS. CARTERET HAD FULLY RECOVERED from the shock attendant upon the accident at the window, where little Dodie had so narrowly escaped death or serious injury, she ordered her carriage one afternoon and directed the coachman to drive her to Mrs. Ochiltree's.

Mrs. Carteret had discharged her young nurse only the day before and had sent for Mammy Jane, who was now recovered from her rheumatism, to stay until she could find another girl. The nurse had been ordered not to take the child to negroes' houses. In driving past the old homestead of her husband's family, now occupied by Dr. Miller and his family, Mrs. Carteret had seen her own baby's carriage standing in the yard.

When the nurse returned home, she was immediately discharged. She offered some sort of explanation, to the effect that her sister worked for Mrs. Miller and that some family matter had rendered it necessary for her to see her sister. The explanation only aggravated the offense: if Mrs. Carteret could have overlooked the disobedience, she would by no means have retained in her employment a servant whose sister worked for the Miller woman.

Old Mrs. Ochiltree had within a few months begun to show signs of breaking up. She was over seventy years old and had been of late, by various afflictions, confined to the house much of the time. More than once within the year, Mrs. Carteret had asked her aunt to come and live with her; but Mrs. Ochiltree, who would have regarded such a step as an acknowledgment of weakness, preferred her lonely independence. She resided in a small, old-fashioned house, standing back in the middle of a garden on a quiet street. Two old servants made up her modest household.

This refusal to live with her niece had been lightly borne, for Mrs. Ochiltree was a woman of strong individuality, whose comments upon her acquaintance, present or absent, were marked by a frankness at times no less than startling. This characteristic caused her to be more or less avoided. Mrs. Ochiltree was aware of this sentiment on the part of her acquaintance and rather exulted in it. She hated fools. Only fools ran away from her and that because they were afraid she would expose their folly. If most people were fools, it was no fault of hers and she was not obliged to indulge them by pretending to believe that they knew anything. She had once owned considerable property, but was reticent about her affairs and told no one how much she was worth, though it was supposed that she had considerable ready money, besides her house and some other real estate. Mrs. Carteret was her nearest living relative, though her grand-nephew Tom Delamere had been a great favorite with her. If she did not spare him her tongue-lashings it was nevertheless expected in the family that she would leave him something handsome in her will.

When the carriage drove up with Mrs. Carteret, her aunt was seated on the little front piazza, with her wrinkled hands folded in her lap, dozing the afternoon away in fitful slumber.

"Tie the horse, William," said Mrs. Carteret, "and then wake Aunt Polly and tell her I want her to come and drive with me."

William returned in a few moments with a fat, comfortable looking black woman, who curtsied to Mrs. Carteret at the gate and then going up to her mistress seized her by the shoulder and shook her vigorously.

"Wake up there, Miss Polly," she screamed, as harshly as her mellow voice would permit. "Miss 'Livy wants you to go drivin' wid 'of!"

"Dinah," exclaimed the old lady, sitting suddenly upright with a defiant assumption of wakefulness, "why do you take so long to come when I call? Bring me my bonnet and shawl. Don't you see my niece waiting for me at the gate?"

Leaning on William's arm, the old lady went slowly down the walk and was handed to the rear seat with Mrs. Carteret.

"How's the baby to-day, Olivia and why didn't you bring him?"

"He has a cold to-day and is a little hoarse," replied Mrs. Carteret.

The drive led past a brick building of modern construction.

"Hugh Poindexter," Mrs. Ochiltree exclaimed explosively, after a considerable silence, "has been building a new house, in place of the old family mansion burned during the war."

"It isn't Mr. Poindexter's house, Aunt Polly. That is the new colored hospital built by the colored doctor."

"The new colored hospital, indeed and the colored doctor! Before the war the negroes were all healthy and when they got sick we took care of them ourselves! Hugh Poindexter has sold the graves of his ancestors to a negro—I should have starved first!"

"Turn to the right, William," ordered Mrs. Carteret, addressing the coachman, "and come back past the other side of the hospital."

A turn to the right into another road soon brought them to the building, which stood slightly back from the street, with no intervening fence or inclosure. A sorrel pony in a light buggy was fastened to a hitching-post near the entrance. As they drove past, a lady came out of the front door, holding a pretty child about six years old.

"Who is that woman, Olivia?" asked Mrs. Ochiltree.

"I have not the honor of her acquaintance," returned Mrs. Carteret sharply. "Drive faster, William."

"I want to know who that woman is," persisted Mrs. Ochiltree querulously. "William," she cried shrilly, poking the coachman in the back with the end of her cane, "who is that woman?"

"Dat's Miss Miller, ma'am," said the coachman, touching his hat; "Doctor Miller's wife."

"What was her mother's name?"

"Her mother's name was Julia Brown. She's been dead these twenty years or mo'. Why, you knew Julia, Miss Polly!—she used to belong to yo' own father befo' the war; an' after the

84

war she kept house for—"

"Look to your horses, William!" exclaimed Mrs. Carteret sharply.

"It's that hussy's child," said Mrs. Ochiltree, turning to her niece with great excitement. "When your father died, I turned the mother and the child out into the street. The mother died and went to—the place provided for such as she. If I hadn't been just in time, Olivia, they would have turned you out. I saved the property for you and your son! You can thank me for it all!"

"Hush, Aunt Polly, for goodness' sake! William will hear you. Tell me about it when you get home... There's Mr. Delamere's Sandy! I wonder how his master is? Sandy, oh, Sandy!"

Sandy approached the carriage, lifting his hat with a slight exaggeration of Chesterfieldian elegance.

"How is Mr. Delamere, Sandy?" asked Mrs. Carteret, acknowledging Sandy's salutation with a nod and a smile.

"He ain't as peart as he has been, ma'am," replied Sandy, "but he's doin' tol'able well. The doctor say he's good for years yet, if he'll jes' take good care of hisself an' keep from gittin' excited; for since dat second stroke, excitement is dangerous for him."

"I'm sure you take the best care of him," returned Mrs. Carteret kindly.

"You can't do anything for him, Sandy," interposed old Mrs. Ochiltree, shaking her head slowly to emphasize her dissent. "All the doctors in creation couldn't keep him alive another year. I shall outlive him by twenty years, though we are not far from the same age."

"Lawd, ma'am!" exclaimed Sandy, lifting his hands in affected amazement—his study of gentle manners had been superficial—"whoever would 'a' s'picion' dat you an' Mars John was nigh the same age? I'd 'a' 'lowed you was ten years younger 'n him, easy, if you was a day!"

"Give my compliments to the poor old gentleman," returned Mrs. Ochiltree, with a simper of senile vanity, though her back

85

was weakening under the strain of the effort to sit erect that she might maintain this illusion of comparative youthfulness. "Bring him to see me some day when he is able to walk."

"Yes 'm, I will," rejoined Sandy.

Sandy made another deep bow and held his hat in his hand until the carriage had moved away. He had not condescended to notice the coachman at all, who was one of the young negroes of the new generation; while Sandy regarded himself as belonging to the quality and seldom stooped to notice those beneath him. It would not have been becoming in him, either, while conversing with white ladies, to have noticed a colored servant. Moreover, the coachman was a Baptist, while Sandy was a Methodist, though under a cloud and considered a Methodist in poor standing as better than a Baptist of any degree or sanctity.

"Lawd, Lawd!" chuckled Sandy, after the carriage had departed, "I never saw nothin' like the way dat ole lady do keep up her temper! Wid one foot in the grave, an' the other hoverin' on the edge, she talks 'bout my ole marster like he was in his second chil'hood. But I'm jes' willin' to bet dat he'll outlas' her! She ain't half the woman she was dat night I waited on the table at the christenin' party, when she 'lowed she wasn't feared of no man livin'."

86

# XV

## Mrs. Carteret Seeks an Explanation

AS A STONE DROPPED INTO A POOL OF WATER SETS in motion a series of concentric circles which disturb the whole mass in varying degree, so Mrs. Ochiltree's enigmatical remark had started in her niece's mind a disturbing train of thought. Had her words, Mrs. Carteret asked herself, any serious meaning, or were they the mere empty babblings of a clouded intellect?

"William," she said to the coachman when they reached Mrs. Ochiltree's house, "you may tie the horse and help us out. I shall be here a little while."

William helped the ladies down, assisted Mrs. Ochiltree into the house and then went round to the kitchen. Dinah was an excellent hand at potato-pone and other culinary delicacies dear to the Southern heart and William was a welcome visitor in her domain.

"Now, Aunt Polly," said Mrs. Carteret resolutely, as soon as they were alone, "I want to know what you meant by what you said about my father and Julia and this—this child of hers?"

The old woman smiled cunningly, but her expression soon changed to one more grave.

"Why do you want to know?" she asked suspiciously. "You've got the land, the houses and the money. You've nothing to complain of. Enjoy yourself and be thankful!"

"I'm thankful to God," returned Olivia, "for all his good gifts—and He has blessed me abundantly—but why should I be thankful to you for the property my father left me?"

"Why should you be thankful to me? You'd better ask why shouldn't you be thankful to me. What have I not done for you?"

"Yes, Aunt Polly, I know you've done a great deal. But why should I thank you for my inheritance?"

"Why should you thank me? Well, because I drove that woman and her brat away."

"But she had no right to stay, Aunt Polly, after father died."

"Perhaps not so surely as you think—if she had not been a negro. Had she been white, there might have been a difference. When I told her to go, she said—"

"What did she say, Aunt Polly," demanded Olivia eagerly.

Mrs. Ochiltree's eyes assumed an introspective expression and her story, as it advanced, became as keenly dramatic as though memory had thrown aside the veil of intervening years and carried her back directly to the events which she now described.

"Your father," she said, "while living with that woman, left home one morning the picture of health. Five minutes later he tottered into the house groaning with pain, stricken unto death by the hand of a just God, as a punishment for his sins."

Olivia gave a start of indignation, but restrained herself.

"I was at once informed of what had happened, for I had means of knowing all that took place in the household. Old Jane—she was younger then—had come with you to my house; but her daughter remained and through her I learned all that went on.

"I hastened immediately to the house, entered without knocking and approached Mr. Merkell's bedroom, which was on the lower floor and opened into the hall. The door was ajar and as I stood there for a moment I heard your father's voice.

" 'Listen, Julia,' he said, 'I shall not live until the doctor comes. But I wish you to know, dear Julia!'— he called her 'dear Julia!'—'before I die, that I have kept my promise. You did me one great service, Julia—you saved me from Polly Ochiltree!' Yes, Olivia, that is what he said! 'You have served me faithfully and well and I owe you a great deal, which I have tried to pay.'

" 'Oh, Mr. Merkell, dear Mr. Merkell,' cried the hypocritical hussy, falling to her knees by his bedside and shedding her crocodile tears, 'you owe me nothing. You have done more for me than I could ever repay. You will not die and leave me—no, no, it cannot be!'

" 'Yes, I am going to die—I am dying now, Julia. But listen —compose yourself and listen, for this is a more important matter. Take the keys from under my pillow, open the desk in the next room, look in the second drawer on the right and you will find an envelope containing three papers: one of them is yours, one is the paper I promised to make and the third is a letter which I wrote last night. As soon as the breath has left my body, deliver the envelope to the address indorsed upon it. Do not delay one moment, or you may live to regret it. Say nothing until you have delivered the package and then be guided by the advice which you receive—it will come from a friend of mine who will not see you wronged.'

"I slipped away from the door without making my presence known and entered, by a door from the hall, the room adjoining the one where Mr. Merkell lay. A moment later there was a loud scream. Returning quickly to the hall, I entered Mr. Merkell's room as though just arrived.

" 'How is Mr. Merkell?' I demanded.

" 'He is dead,' sobbed the woman, without lifting her head —she had fallen on her knees by the bedside. She had good cause to weep, for my time had come.

" 'Get up,' I said. 'You have no right here. You pollute Mr. Merkell's dead body by your touch. Leave the house immediately—your day is over!'

" 'I will not!' she cried, rising to her feet and facing me with brazen-faced impudence. 'I have a right to stay—he has given me the right!'

" 'Ha, ha!' I laughed. 'Mr. Merkell is dead and I am mistress here henceforth. Go and go at once—do you hear?'

" 'I hear, but I shall not heed. I can prove my rights! I shall not leave!'

" 'Very well,' I replied, 'we shall see. The law will decide.'

"I left the room, but did not leave the house. I concealed

myself where I could see what took place in the room adjoining the death-chamber.

"She entered the room a moment later, with her child on one arm and the keys in the other hand. Placing the child on the floor, she put the key in the lock and seemed surprised to find the desk already unfastened. She opened the desk, picked up a roll of money and a ladies' watch, which first caught her e ye and was reaching toward the drawer upon the right, when I interrupted her:—

" 'Well, thief, are you trying to strip the house before you leave it?'

"She gave an involuntary cry, clasped one hand to her bosom and with the other caught up her child and stood like a wild beast at bay.

" 'I am not a thief,' she panted. 'The things are mine!'

" 'You lie,' I replied. 'You have no right to them—no more right than you have to remain in this house!'

" 'I have a right,' she persisted, 'and I can prove it!'

"She turned toward the desk, seized the drawer and drew it open. Never shall I forget her look—never shall I forget that moment; it was the happiest of my life. The drawer was empty!

"Pale as death she turned and faced me.

" 'The papers!' she shrieked, 'the papers! You have stolen them!'

" 'Papers?' I laughed, 'what papers? Do you take me for a thief, like yourself?'

" 'There were papers here,' she cried, 'only a minute since. They are mine—give them back to me!'

" 'Listen, woman,' I said sternly, 'you are lying—or dreaming. My brother-in-law's papers are doubtless in his safe at his office, where they ought to be. As for the rest—you are a thief.'

" 'I am not,' she screamed; 'I am his wife. He married me and the papers that were in the desk will prove it.'

" 'Listen,' I exclaimed, when she finished—'listen carefully and take heed to what I say. You are a liar. You have no proofs —there never were any proofs of what you say, because it

90

never happened—It is absurd upon the face of it. Not one person in Wellington would believe it. Why should he marry you? He did not need to! You are merely lying—you are not even self-deceived. If he had really married you, you would have made it known long ago. That you did not is proof that your story is false.'

"She was hit so hard that she trembled and sank into a chair. But I had no mercy—she had saved your father from me —'dear Julia,' indeed!

" 'Stand up,' I ordered. 'Do not dare to sit down in my presence. I have you on the hip, my lady and will teach you your place.'

"She struggled to her feet and stood supporting herself with one hand on the chair. I could have killed her, Olivia! She had been my father's slave; if it had been before the war, I would have had her whipped to death.

" 'You are a thief,' I said, 'and of that there are proofs. I have caught you in the act. The watch in your bosom is my own, the money belongs to Mr. Merkell's estate, which belongs to my niece, his daughter Olivia. I saw you steal them. My word is worth yours a hundred times over, for I am a lady and you are —what? And now hear me- if ever you breathe to a living soul one word of this preposterous story, I will charge you with the theft and have you sent to the penitentiary. Your child will be taken from you and you shall never see it again. You have ten minutes to take your brat and your rags out of here forever. Before you go, put down your plunder on the desk!' She laid down the money and the watch and a few minutes later left the house with the child in her arms... Now Olivia, you know why you should be grateful to me."

Olivia had listened to her aunt's story with intense interest. One question had been hovering on her lips.

"What became of the papers, Aunt Polly?"

"Ha, ha!" chuckled Mrs. Ochiltree with a cunning look, "did I not tell you that she found no papers?"

# XVI

## Ellis Takes a Trick

LATE ONE AFTERNOON A HANDSOME TRAP, DRAWN by two spirited bays, drove up to Carteret's gate. Three places were taken by Mrs. Carteret, Clara and the major, leaving the fourth seat vacant.

"I've asked Ellis to drive out with us," said the major, as he took the lines from the colored man who had the trap in charge. "We'll go by the office and pick him up."

At the Chronicle office Ellis took the front seat beside the major. After leaving the city pavements, they bowled along merrily over an excellent toll-road, built of oyster shells from the neighboring sound, stopping at intervals to pay toll to the gate-keepers, most of whom were white women with tallow complexions and snuff-stained lips— the traditional "poor-white."

Occasionally our party passed a group of persons—mostly negroes approximating the pure type, for those of lighter color grew noticeably scarcer as the town was left behind. Now and then one of these would salute the party respectfully, while others glanced at them indifferently or turned away. There would have seemed, to a stranger, a lack of spontaneous friendliness between the people of these two races, as though each felt that it had no part or lot in the other's life. At one point the carriage drew near a party of colored folks who were laughing and jesting among themselves with great glee. Paying no attention to the white people, they continued to laugh and shout boisterously as the carriage swept by.

Major Carteret's countenance wore an angry look.

"The negroes around this town are becoming absolutely

insufferable," he said. "They are sadly in need of a lesson in manners."

Half an hour later they neared another group, who were also making merry. As the carriage approached, they became mute and silent as the grave until the major's party had passed.

"The negroes are a sullen race," remarked the major thoughtfully. "They will learn their lesson in a rude school and perhaps much sooner than they dream. By the way," he added, turning to the ladies, "what was the arrangement with Tom? Was he to come out this evening?"

"He came out early in the afternoon," replied Clara, "to go a-fishing. He is to join us at the hotel."

After an hour's drive they reached the hotel. Mrs. Carteret and Clara found seats on the veranda. Having turned the trap over to a hostler, the major joined a group of gentlemen, among whom was General Belmont and was soon deep in the discussion of the standing problem of how best to keep the negroes down.

Ellis remained by the ladies. Clara seemed restless and ill at ease. Half an hour elapsed and Delamere had not appeared.

"I wonder where Tom is," said Mrs. Carteret.

"I guess he hasn't come in yet from fishing," said Clara.

For Ellis the party was already one too large. He had accepted this invitation eagerly, hoping to make friends with Clara during the evening. The next best thing, he reasoned, to having a woman love you, is to have her dislike you violently—the main point is that you should be kept in mind and made the subject of strong emotions. He thought of the story of Hall Caine's, where the woman, after years of persecution at the hands of an unwelcome suitor, is on the point of yielding, out of sheer irresistible admiration for the man's strength and persistency, when the lover, unaware of his victory and despairing of success, seizes her in his arms and, springing into the sea, finds a watery grave for both. The analogy of this case with his own was, of course, not strong. He did not anticipate any tragedy in their relations; but he was glad to be thought of upon almost any terms. He would not

93

have done a mean thing to make her think of him; but if she did so because of a misconception, which he was given no opportunity to clear up, while at the same time his conscience absolved him from evil and gave him the compensating glow of martyrdom, it was at least better than nothing.

He would, of course, have preferred to be upon a different footing. It had been a pleasure to have her speak to him during the drive—they had exchanged a few trivial remarks in the general conversation. It was a greater pleasure to have her ask a favor of him—a pleasure which, in this instance, was partly offset when he interpreted her request to mean that he was to look for Tom Delamere. He accepted the situation gracefully, however and left the ladies alone.

Knowing Delamere's habits, he first went directly to the bar room—the atmosphere would be congenial, even if he were not drinking. Delamere was not there. Stepping next into the office, he asked the clerk if young Mr. Delamere had been at the hotel.

"Yes, sir," returned the man at the desk, "he was here at luncheon and then went out fishing in a boat with several other gentlemen. I think they came back about three o'clock. I'll find out for you."

He rang the bell, to which a colored boy responded.

"Front," said the clerk, "see if young Mr. Delamere's upstairs. Look in 255 or 256 and let me know at once."

The bell-boy returned in a moment.

"Yes, suh," he reported, with a suppressed grin, "he's in 256, suh."

"I wish you'd go up and tell him," said Ellis, "that—What are you grinning about?" he asked suddenly, noticing the waiter's expression.

"Nothin', suh, nothin' at all, suh," responded the negro. "What shall I tell Mr. Delamere, suh?"

"Tell him," resumed Ellis, watching the boy suspiciously— "no, I'll tell him myself."

He ascended the broad stair to the second floor. There was an upper balcony and a parlor, with a piano for the musically inclined. To reach these one had to pass along the hall upon which the room mentioned by the bell-boy opened. Ellis was quite familiar with the hotel. He could imagine circumstances under which he would not care to speak to Delamere; he would merely pass through the hall and glance into the room casually, as any one else might do and see what the darky downstairs might have meant by his impudence.

It took a moment to reach the room. The door was ajar. Two young men, were playing cards at a small table, next to an array of empty bottles and glasses. Sprawling on a lounge, with flushed face and disheveled hair, his collar unfastened, his vest buttoned awry, lay Tom Delamere in a drunken sleep, the fingers of his right hand clasp around the neck of a bottle which lay across his bosom. Ellis turned away in disgust and went back to the ladies.

"There seems to be no one here yet," he reported. "We came a little early for the evening crowd. The clerk says Tom Delamere was here to luncheon, but he hasn't seen him for several hours."

"He's not a very gallant cavalier," said Mrs. Carteret. "He ought to have been waiting for us."

Clara was clearly disappointed and made no effort to conceal her displeasure, leaving Ellis in doubt as to whether or not he were its object. Perhaps she suspected him of not having made a very thorough search. Her next remark might have borne such a construction.

"Sister Olivia," she said , "let's go up to the parlor. I can play the piano anyway, if there's no one to talk to."

"I find it very comfortable here, Clara," replied her sister placidly. "Mr. Ellis will go with you. You'll probably find someone in the parlor, or they'll come when you begin to play. I'm sure of that"

Clara's expression was not cordial, but she rose as if to go. If she went through the hall, the chances were at least even that she would see Delamere. Ellis did not care a rap for Delamere—if he chose to make a public exhibition of himself, it was his own affair; but to see him would surely spoil Miss Pemberton's evening and, in her frame

95

of mind, might lead to the suspicion that Ellis had prearranged the exposure. Even if she should not harbor this unjust thought, she would not love the witness of her discomfiture. We had rather not meet the persons who have seen, even though they never mention, the skeletons in our closets. Delamere had disposed of himself for the evening. Ellis would have a fairer field with Delamere out of sight and unaccounted for, than with Delamere in evidence in his present condition.

"Wouldn't you rather take a stroll on the beach?" he asked, in the hope of creating a diversion.

"No, I'm going to the parlor. You needn't come, Mr. Ellis, if you'd rather go down to the beach. I can quite as well go alone."

"I'd rather go with you," he said meekly.

They were moving toward the door opening into the hall, from which the broad staircase ascended. Ellis, whose thoughts did not always respond quickly to a sudden emergency, was puzzling his brain as to how he should save her from any risk of seeing Delamere. Through the side door leading from the hall into the of fice, he saw the bell-boy to whom he had spoken seated on the bench provided for the servants.

"Won't you wait for me just a moment, Miss Clara, "while I step into the office? I'll be with you in an instant."

Clara hesitated.

"Oh, certainly," she replied nonchalantly.

Ellis went direct to the bell-boy. "Sit right where you are," he said, "and don't move a hair. What is the lady in the hall doing?"

"She's got her back turned this way, suh. I 'spec' she's lookin' at the picture on the opposite wall, suh."

"All right," whispered Ellis, pressing a coin into the servant's hand. "I'm going up to the parlor with the lady. You go up ahead of us and keep in front of us along the hall. don't dare to look back. I shall keep on talking to the lady, so that you can tell by my voice where we are. When you get to room 256, go in, shut the door behind you: like you were called—

ask the gentlemen what they want—tell any kind of a lie you like—but keep the door shut until you're sure we've got by. Do you hear?"

"Yes, suh," replied the negro intelligently.

The plan worked without a hitch. Ellis talked steadily, about the hotel, the furnishings, all sorts of irrelevant subjects, to which Miss Pemberton paid little attention. She was angry with Delamere and took no pains to conceal her feelings. The bell-boy entered room 256 just before they reached the door. Ellis had heard loud talking as they approached and as they were passing there was a crash of broken glass, as though some object had been thrown at the door.

"What is the matter there?" exclaimed Clara, quickening her footsteps and instinctively drawing closer to Ellis.

"Someone dropped a glass, I presume," replied Ellis calmly.

Miss Pemberton glanced at him suspiciously. She was in a decidedly perverse mood. Seating herself at the piano, she played brilliantly for a quarter of an hour. Quite a number of couples strolled up to the parlor, but Delamere was not among them.

"Oh dear!" exclaimed Miss Pemberton, as she let her fingers fall upon the keys with a discordant crash, after the last note, "I don't see why we came out here tonight. Let's go back downstairs."

Ellis felt despondent. He had done his utmost to serve and to please Miss Pemberton, but was not likely, he foresaw, to derive much benefit from his opportunity. Delmare was evidently as much or more in her thoughts by reason of his absence than if he had been present. If the door should have been opened and she should see him from the hall upon their return, Ellis could not help it. He took the side next to the door, however, meaning to hurry past the room so that she might not recognize Delamere.

Fortunately the door was closed and all quiet within the room. On the stairway they met the bell-boy, rubbing his head with one hand and holding a bottle of seltzer upon a tray in the other. The boy was well enough trained to give no sign of recognition, though Ellis guessed the destination of the bottle.

Ellis hardly knew whether to feel pleased or disappointed at the success of his manouvres. He had spared Miss Pemberton some mortification, but he had saved Tom Delamere from merited exposure. Clara ought to know the truth, for her own sake.

On the beach, a few rods away, fires were burning, around which several merry groups had gathered. The smoke went mostly to one side, but a slight whiff came now and then to where Mrs. Carteret sat awaiting them.

"They're roasting oysters," said Mrs. Carteret. "I wish you'd bring me some, Mr. Ellis."

Ellis strolled down to the beach. A large iron plate, with a turned-up rim like a great baking-pan, supported by legs which held it off the ground, was set over a fire built upon the sand. This primitive oven was heaped with small oysters in the shell, taken from the neighboring sound and hauled up to the hotel by a negro whose pony cart stood near by. A wet coffee-sack of burlaps was spread over the oysters, which, when steamed sufficiently, were opened by a colored man and served gratis to all who cared for them.

Ellis secured a couple of plates of oysters, which he brought to Mrs. Carteret and Clara; they were small, but finely flavored.

Meanwhile Delamere, who possessed a remarkable faculty of recuperation from the effects of drink, had waked from his sleep and remembering his engagement, had exerted himself to overcome the ravages of the afternoon's debauch. A dash of cold water braced him up somewhat. A bottle of seltzer and a big cup of strong coffee still further strengthened his nerves.

When Ellis returned to the veranda, after having taken away the plates, Delamere had joined the ladies and was explaining the cause of his absence.

He had been overcome by the heat, he said, while out fishing and had been lying down ever since. Perhaps he ought to have sent for a doctor, but the fellows had looked after him. He hadn't sent word to his friends because he hadn't wished to spoil their evening.

"That was very considerate of you, Tom," said Mrs. Carteret dryly, "but you ought to have let us know. We have been worrying about you very much. Clara has found the evening dreadfully dull."

"Indeed, no, sister Olivia," said the young lady cheerfully, "I've been having a lovely time. Mr. Ellis and I have been up in the parlor; I played the piano; and we've been eating oysters and having a most delightful time. Won't you take me down there to the beach, Mr. Ellis? I want to see the fires. Come on."

"Can't I go?" asked Tom jealously.

"No, indeed, you mustn't stir a foot! You must not overtax yourself so soon; it might do you serious injury. Stay here with sister Olivia."

She took Ellis' arm with exaggerated cordiality. Delamere glared after them angrily. Ellis did not stop to question her motives, but took the goods the gods provided. With no very great apparent effort, Miss Pemberton became quite friendly and they strolled along the beach, in sight of the hotel, for nearly half an hour. As they were coming up she asked him abruptly—

"Mr. Ellis, did you know Tom was in the hotel?"

Ellis was looking across the sound, at the lights of a distant steamer which was making her way toward the harbor.

"I wonder," he said musingly, as though he had not heard her question, "if that is the Ocean Belle?"

"And was he really sick?" she demanded.

"She's later than usual this trip," continued Ellis, pursuing his thought. "She was due about five o'clock."

Miss Pemberton, under cover of the darkness, smiled a fine smile, which foreboded ill for some one. When they joined the party on the piazza, the major had come up and was saying that it was time to go. He had been engaged in conversation, for most of the evening, with General Belmont and several other gentlemen.

"Here comes the general now. Let me see. There are five of us. The general has offered me a seat in his buggy and Tom can go with you-all."

The general came and spoke to the ladies. Tom murmured his thanks; it would enable him to make up a part of the delightful evening he had missed.

When Mrs. Carteret had taken the rear seat, Clara promptly took the place beside her. Ellis and Delamere sat in front. When Delamere, who had offered to drive, took the reins, Ellis saw that his hands were shaking.

"Give me the lines," he whispered. "Your nerves are unsteady and the road is not well lighted."

Delamere prudently yielded the reins. He did not like Ellis' tone, which seemed sneering rather than expressive of sympathy with one who had been suffering. He wondered if the beggar knew anything about his illness. Clara had been acting strangely. It would have been just like Ellis to have slandered him. The upstart had no business with Clara, anyway. He would cheerfully have strangled Ellis, if he could have done so with safety to himself and no chance of discovery.

The drive homeward through the night was almost a silent journey. Mrs. Carteret was anxious about her baby. Clara did not speak, except now and then to Ellis with reference to some object in or near the road. Occasionally they passed a vehicle in the darkness, sometimes barely avoiding a collision. Far to the north the sky was lit up with the glow of a forest fire. The breeze from the Sound was deliciously cool. Soon the last toll-gate was passed and the lights of the town appeared.

Ellis threw the lines to William, who was waiting and hastenedto help the ladies out.

"Good-night, Mr. Ellis," said Clara sweetly, as she gave Ellis her hand. "Thank you for a very pleasant evening. Come up and see us soon."

She ran into the house without a word to Tom.

# XVII

## Captain McBane's Social Aspirations

IT WAS ONLY ELEVEN O'CLOCK AND DELAMERE, not being at all sleepy and feeling somewhat out of sorts as the combined results of his afternoon's debauch and the snubbing he had received at Clara's hands, directed the major's coachman, who had taken charge of the trap upon its arrival, to drive him to the St. James Hotel before returning the horses to the stable. First, however, the coachman left Ellis at his boarding-house, which was near by. The two young men parted with as scant courtesy as was possible without an open rupture.

Delamere hoped to find at the hotel some form of distraction to fill in an hour or two before going home. Ill fortune favored him by placing in his way the burly form of Captain George McBane, who was sitting in an armchair alone, smoking a midnight cigar, under the hotel balcony. Upon Delamere's making known his desire for amusement, the captain proposed a small game of poker in his own room.

McBane had been waiting for some such convenient opportunity. We have already seen that the captain was desirous of social recognition, which he had not yet obtained beyond the superficial acquaintance acquired by association with men about town. He had determined to assault society in its citadel by seeking membership in the Clarendon Club, of which most gentlemen of the best families of the city were members.

Membership in the Clarendon was the sine qua non of very high social standing and was strictly conditional, being based upon two or three things—birth, wealth and breeding. Breeding was the prime essential, but, with rare exceptions, must be backed by either birth or money.

Having decided, therefore, to seek admission into this social circle, the captain, who had either not quite appreciated the standard of the Clarendon's membership, or had failed to see that he fell beneath it, looked about for an intermediary through whom to approach the object of his desire. Possessing mental characteristics almost entirely opposite, Delamere and the captain had certain tastes in common and had smoked, drunk and played cards together more than once.

Still more to his purpose, McBane had detected Delamere trying to cheat him at cards. He had said nothing about this discovery, but had merely noted it as something which at some future time might prove useful.

The appearance of Delamere at a late hour, unaccompanied and wearing upon his countenance an expression in which the captain read aright the craving for mental and physical excitement, gave him the opportunity for which he had been looking. McBane was not the man to lose an opportunity, nor did Delamere require a second invitation. Neither was it necessary, during the game, for the captain to press upon his guest the contents of the decanter which stood upon the table within convenient reach.

The captain permitted Delamere to win from him several small amounts, after which he gradually increased the stakes and turned the tables.

Delamere, with every instinct of a gamester, was no more a match for McBane in self-control than in skill. When the young man had lost all his money, the captain expressed his entire willingness to accept notes of hand, for which he happened to have convenient blanks in his apartment.

When Delamere, flushed with excitement and wine, rose from the gaming table at two o'clock, he was vaguely conscious that he owed McBane a considerable sum, but not how much.

"Just one thousand dollars even," McBane remarked.

The announcement of this total had as sobering an effect up on Delamere as though he had been suddenly deluged with a shower of cold water. For a moment he caught his breath. He had not a dollar in the world with which to pay this sum. His only source of income was an allowance from his grandfather, the monthly installment of which, drawn that very day, he had just lost to McBane, before starting in upon the notes of hand.

"I'll give you your revenge another time," said McBane, as they rose. "Luck is against you to-night and I'm unwilling to take advantage of a clever young fellow like you. Meantime," he added, tossing the notes of hand carelessly on a bureau, "don't worry about these bits of paper. Such small matters shouldn't cut any figure between friends; but if you are around the hotel tomorrow, I should like to speak to you upon another subject."

"Very well, captain," returned Tom ungraciously.

Delamere had been completely beaten with his own weapons. He had tried desperately to cheat McBane. He knew perfectly well that McBane had discovered his efforts and had cheated him in turn, for the captain's play had clearly been gauged to meet his own. The biter had been bit and could not complain of the outcome.

The following afternoon McBane met Delamere at the hotel and bluntly requested the latter to propose him for membership in the Clarendon Club.

Delamere was annoyed at this request. His aristocratic gorge rose at the presumption of this son of an overseer and ex-driver of convicts. McBane was good enough to win money from, or even to lose money to, but not good enough to be recognized as a social equal. He would instinctively have blackballed McBane had he been proposed by some one else; with what grace could he put himself forward as the sponsor for this impossible social aspirant? Moreover, it was clearly a vulgar, cold-blooded attempt on McBane's part to use his power over him for a personal advantage.

"Well, now, Captain McBane," returned Delamere diplomatically, "I've never put any one up yet and it's not regarded as good form for so young a member as myself to propose candidates. I'd much rather you'd ask some older man."

"Oh, well," replied McBane, "just as you say, only I thought you had cut your eye teeth."

Delamere was not pleased with McBane's tone. There was a sneering savagery about it, too, that left Delamere uneasy. He was, in a measure, in McBane's power. He could not pay the thousand dollars, unless it fell from heaven, or he could win it from some one else. He would not dare go to his grandfather for help. Mr. Delamere did not even know that his grandson gambled. He might not have objected, perhaps, to a gentleman's game, with moderate stakes, but he would certainly, Tom knew very well, have looked upon a thousand dollars as a preposterous sum to be lost at cards by a man who had nothing with which to pay it. It was part of Mr. Delamere's creed that a gentleman should not make debts that he was not reasonably able to pay.

There was still another difficulty. If he had lost the money to a gentleman and it had been his first serious departure from Mr. Delamere's perfectly well understood standard of honor, Tom might have risked a confession and thrown himself on his grandfather's mercy.

He thought of old Mrs. Ochiltree. If she were a liberal soul, she could give him a thousand dollars now, when he needed it, instead of making him wait until she died, which might not be for ten years or more, for a legacy which was steadily growing less and might be entirely exhausted if she lived long enough—some old people were very tenacious of life! She was a careless old woman, too, he reflected and very foolishly kept her money in the house. Latterly she had been growing weak and childish. Some day she might be robbed and then his prospective inheritance from that source would vanish into thin air!

With regard to this debt to McBane, if he could not pay it, he could at least gain a long respite by proposing the captain at the club. True, he would undoubtedly be blackballed, but before this inevitable event his name must remain posted for several weeks, during which interval McBane would be conciliatory. On the other hand, to propose McBane would arouse suspicion of his own motives; it might reach his grandfather's ears and lead to a demand for an explanation, which it would be difficult to make. Clearly, the better plan would be to temporize with McBane, with the hope that something might intervene to remove this cursed obligation.

"Suppose, captain," he said affably, "we leave the matter open for a few days. This is a thing that can't be rushed. I'll feel the pulse of my friends and yours and when we get the lay of the land, the affair can be accomplished much more easily."

"Well, that's better," returned McBane, somewhat mortified.

McBane ordered and paid for more drinks and they parted on amicable terms

"We'll let these notes stand for the time being, Tom," said McBane, with significant emphasis, when they separated.

Delamere winced at the familiarity. McBane had never before been so personal. He had addressed the young aristocrat first as "Mr. Delamere," then, as their acquaintance advanced, as "Delamere." He had now reached the abbreviated christian name stage of familiarity. There was no lower depth to which Tom could sink, unless McBane should invent a nickname by which to address him.

He did not like McBane's manner—it was characterized by a veiled insolence which was exceedingly offensive. He would go over to the club and try his luck with some honest player— perhaps something might turn up to relieve him from his embarrassment.

He put his hand in his pocket mechanically—and found it empty! In the present state of his credit, he could hardly play without money.

A thought struck him. He hastened home, where he found Sandy dusting his suit of clothes. Mr. Delamere had departed for Belleview about two o'clock, leaving Sandy to follow him in the morning.

"Hello, Sandy," exclaimed Tom, with an assumed jocularity which he was very far from feeling, "what are you doing with those gorgeous garments?"

'I'm a-dustin' off 'em, Mister Tom, dat's what I'm adoin'.

There's somethin' wrong 'bout these clothes of mine—I don't never seem to be able to keep 'em clean no mo'. If I b'lieved in dem ole-timey sayin's, I'd 'low there was a witch come here every night an' took 'em out an' wore 'em, of took me out an' rid me in 'em."

"Sandy," asked Tom irrelevantly, "have you any money in the house?"

"Yes, suh, I got the money Mars John give me to git dem things to take out to Belleview in the mornin'."

"I mean money of your own."

"I got a quarter to buy tobacco wid," returned Sandy.

"Is that all? Haven't you some saved up?"

"Well, yes, Mister Tom," returned Sandy, with evident reluctance, "There's a few dollars put away in my bureau drawer for a rainy day—not much, suh."

"I'm a little short this afternoon, Sandy and need some money right away. Let me take what you have for a day or two, Sandy andI'll return it with good interest."

"Now, Mister Tom," said Sandy seriously, "I don't mind lettin' you take my money, but I hopes you ain't gwine to use it for gamblin'. It ain't right, Mister Tom, it ain't right! An' I only does it for the sake of the family honor."

"That's right, Sandy," replied Tom approvingly; "but the family honor is as safe in my hands as in grandfather's own and I'm going to use the money for an excellent purpose, in fact to relieve a case of genuine distress; and I'll hand it back to you in a day or two—perhaps tomorrow. Fetch me the money, Sandy—that's a good darky!"

"All right, Mister Tom, you shall have the money; but I wants to tell you, suh, dat in all the years I has worked for yo' gran'daddy, he has never called me a 'darky' to my face, suh. Co'se I knows there's white folks an' black folks—but there's manners, suh, there's manners, an' gentlemen oughta be the ones to use 'em, suh, if they ain't to be forgot entirely!"

"There, there, Sandy," returned Tom in a conciliatory tone, "I beg your pardon! I've been associating with some Northern white folks at the hotel and picked up the word from them. You're a high-toned colored gentleman, Sandy—the finest one on the footstool."

Still muttering to himself, Sandy retired to his own room, which was in the house, so that he might be always near his master. He soon returned with a time-stained leather pocket-book and a coarse-knit cotton sock, from which two receptacles he painfully extracted a number of bills and coins.

"You count dat, Mister Tom, so I'll know how much I'm lettin' you have."

"This isn't worth anything," said Tom, pushing aside one roll of bills. "It's Confederate money."

"So it is, suh. It ain't worth nothin' now; but it has been money, an' who can tell but what it might be money agin? The rest of dem bills is greenbacks—dey'll pass all right, I reckon."

The good money amounted to about fifty dollars, which Delamere thrust eagerly into his pocket.

"You won't say anything to grandfather about this, will you, Sandy," he said, as he turned away.

"No, suh, co'se I won't! Does I ever tell him 'bout yo' gwines-on? If I did," he added to himself, as the young man disappeared down the street, "I wouldn't have time to do nothin' else hardly. I don't know whether I'll ever see dat money or no, do' I 'magine the ole gentleman wouldn't lemme lose it if he knew. But I ain't gwine to tell him, whether I git my money back or no, for he is jes' so wrap up in dat boy there. B'lieve it'd jes' break his heart to fin' out how he's been gwine on. Doctor Price has told me not to let the ole gentleman git excited, or else there's no tellin' what might happen. He's been good to me, he has, an' I'm gwine to take care of him—dat's what I is, as long as I has the chance."

Delamere went directly to the club and soon lounged into the card-room, where several of the members were engaged in play. He sauntered here and there, too much absorbed in his own thoughts to notice that the greetings he received were less cordial than those usually exchanged between the members of a small and select so appropriately called "Gus," Davidson came into the room, Tom stepped toward him.

"Will you take a hand in a game, Gus?"

"Don't care if I do," said the other. "Let's sit over here. "

Davidson led the way to a table near the fireplace. Davidson took the seat opposite the fireplace, leaving Delamere with his back to it.

Delamere staked half of Sandy's money and lost. He staked the rest and determined to win, because he could not afford to lose. He had just reached out his hand to gather in the stakes, when he was charged with cheating at cards, of which two members, who had quietly entered the room and posted themselves behind the screen, had secured specific proof.

A meeting of the membership committee was hastily summoned, it being an hour at which most of them might be found at the club. To avoid a scandal and to save the feelings of a prominent family, Delamere was given an opportunity to resign quietly from the club, on condition that he paid all his gambling debts within three days and took an oath never to play cards again for money. This latter condition was made at the suggestion of an elderly member, who apparently believed that a man who would cheat at cards would stick at perjury.

Delamere acquiesced very promptly. The taking of the oath was easy. The payment of some fifteen hundred dollars of debt was a different matter. He went away from the club thoughtfully and it may be said, in full justice to a past which was far from immaculate, that in his present thoughts he touched a depth of scoundrelism far beyond anything of which he had as yet deemed himself capable. When a man of good position, of whom much is expected, takes to evil courses, his progress is apt to resemble that of a well-bred woman who had started on the downward path—the pace is all the swifter because of the distance which must be traversed to reach the bottom. Delamere had made rapid headway; having hitherto played with sin, his servant had now become his master and held him in an iron grip.

# XVIII

## Sandy Sees Clearly

HAVING FINISHED CLEANING HIS CLOTHES, Sandy went swiftly out to the house's kitchen for supper, after which he found himself with nothing to do. Mr. Delamere's absence relieved him from attendance at the house during the evening. He might have smoked his pipe tranquilly in the kitchen until bedtime, had not the cook intimated, rather pointedly, that she expected other company. To a man of Sandy's tact a word was sufficient, and he resigned himself to seeking companionship elsewhere.

Under normal circumstances, Sandy would have attended prayer-meeting on this particular evening of the week; but still cherishing what he considered the just resentment of a man falsely accused, he stifled the inclination which by long habit led him toward the church, and set out for the house of a friend with whom it occurred to him that he might spend the evening pleasantly. Unfortunately, his friend proved to be not at home, so Sandy turned his footsteps toward the lower part of the town, where the streets were well lighted, and on pleasant evenings quite animated. On the way he met Josh Green, whom he had known for many years, though their paths did not often cross. In his loneliness Sandy accepted an invitation to go with Josh and have a drink—a single drink.

When Sandy was going home about eleven o'clock, such was the potent effect of the single drink and those which had followed it, he was scared almost into soberness by a remarkable apparition. As it seemed to Sandy, he saw himself hurrying along in front of himself toward the house. Possibly the muddled condition of Sandy's intellect had so affected his judgment as to vitiate any conclusion he might draw, but Sandy was quite sober enough to perceive that the figure ahead of him wore his best clothes and looked exactly like him, but seemed to be in something more of a hurry, a discrepancy which Sandy at once corrected by quickening his own pace so as to maintain as nearly as possible an equal distance between himself and his double. The situation was certainly an incomprehensible one, and savored the supernatural.

"If dat's me gwine 'long in front," mused Sandy, "then who is dis behin' here? There ain't but one of me, an' my hand wouldn't leave my body 'til I was dead. If dat's me in front, then I must be my own hand an' whichever one of us is the ha'nt, the other must be dead an' don't know it. I don't know what to make of no such gwines on, I don't. Maybe it ain't me after all, but it certainly do look like me."

When the apparition disappeared in the house by the side door, Sandy stood in the yard for several minutes, under the shade of an elm-tree, before he could make up his mind to enter the house. He took courage, however, upon the reflection that after all, it was only the bad liquor he had drunk. Bad liquor often made people see double.

He entered the house. It was dark, except for a light in Tom Delamere's room. Sandy tapped softly at the door.

"Who's there?" came Delamere's voice, in a somewhat startled tone, after a momentary silence.

"It's me, suh; Sandy."

They both spoke softly. It was the rule of the house when Mr. Delamere had retired, and though he was not at home, habit held its own sway.

"Just a moment, Sandy."

Sandy waited patiently in the hall until the door was opened. If the room showed any signs of haste or disorder, Sandy was too full of his own thoughts to notice them.

"What do you want, Sandy?" asked Tom.

"Mister Tom," asked Sandy solemnly, "if I was in yo' place,

110

an' you was in my place, an' we was both in the same place, where would I be?"

Tom looked at Sandy keenly, with a touch of apprehension. Did Sandy mean anything in particular by this enigmatical inquiry, and if so, what? But Sandy's face clearly indicated a state of mind in which consecutive thought was improbable; and after a brief glance Delamere breathed more freely.

"I give it up, Sandy," he responded lightly. "That's too deep for me."

" 'Scuse me, Mister Tom, but is you heard or seen anybody or anything come in the house for the las' ten minutes?"

"Why, no, Sandy, I haven't heard any one. I came from the club an hour ago. I had forgotten my key, and Sally got up and let me in, and then went back to bed. I've been sitting here reading ever since. I should have heard any one who came in."

"Mister Tom," inquired Sandy anxiously, "would you 'low dat I'd been drinkin' too much?"

"No, Sandy, I should say you were sober enough, though of course you may have had a few drinks. Perhaps you'd like another? I've got something good here."

"No, suh, Mister Tom, no, suh! No mo' liquor for me suh, never! When liquor can make a man see his own ha'nt, it's 'bout time for dat man to quit drinkin', it sho' is! Goodnight, Mister Tom."

As Sandy turned to go, Delamere was stuck by a sudden and daring thought. The creature of impulse, he acted upon it immediately.

"By the way, Sandy," he exclaimed carelessly, "I can pay you back that money you were good enough to lend me this afternoon. I think I'll sleep better if I have the debt off my mind, and I shouldn't wonder if you would. You don't mind having it in gold, do you?"

"No, indeed, suh," replied Sandy. "I ain't seen no gold for so long dat the sight of it'd be good for my eyes."

Tom counted out ten five-dollar gold pieces upon the table at his elbow.

111

"And here's another, Sandy," he said, adding an eleventh, "as interest for the use of it."

"Thank y', Mister Tom. I didn't spec' no intres', but I don't never 'fuse gold when I can git it."

"And here," added Delamere, reaching carelessly into a bureau drawer, "is a little old silk purse that I've had since I was a boy. I'll put the gold in it, Sandy; it will hold it very nicely."

"Thank y', Mister Tom. You're a gentleman, suh, an' worthy of the family name. Good-night, suh, an' I hope yo' dreams'll be pleasanter 'n' mine. If it weren't for dis gold kinder takin' my mind off of dat ha'nt, I don't s'pose I'd be able to do much sleepin' to-night. Good-night, suh."

"Good-night, Sandy."

Whether or not Delamere slept soundly, or was troubled by dreams, pleasant or unpleasant, it is nevertheless true that he locked his door, and sat up an hour later, looking through the drawers of his bureau, and burning several articles in the little iron stove which constituted part of the bedroom furniture.

It is also true that he rose very early, before the household was stirring. The cook slept in a room off the kitchen, which was in an outhouse in the back yard. She was just stretching herself, preparatory to getting up, when Tom came to her window and said that he was going off fishing, to be gone all day and that he would not wait for breakfast.

# XIX

# A Midnight Walk

ELLIS LEFT THE OFFICE OF THE MORNING
Chronicle about eleven o'clock the same evening and set out to
walk home.

At the Clarendon Club, where he had gone, a couple of
hours before, to verify a certain news item for the morning
paper, he had heard a story about Tom Delamere which, he
imagined, would spike that gentleman's guns for all time, so
far as Miss Pemberton was concerned. So grave an affair as
cheating at cards could never be kept secret—it was certain to
reach her ears; and Ellis was morally certain that Clara would
never marry a man who had been dishonored. With the
best intentions in the world, it was no more than human nature
that he should feel a certain elation in the thought that his rival
had been practically disposed of, and the field left clear;
especially since this good situation had been brought about
merely by the unmasking of a hypocrite, who had held him at
an unfair disadvantage in the race for Clara's favor.

The night was quiet, except for the faint sound of distant
music now and then, or the mellow laughter of some group of
revelers. Ellis met but few pedestrians, but as he neared old Mr.
Delamere's, he saw two men walking in the same direction as
his own, on the opposite side of the street. He had observed
that they kept at about an equal distance apart, and that the
second, from the stealthy manner in which he was making his
way, was anxious to keep the first in sight, without disclosing
his own presence. This aroused Ellis' curiosity, which was
satisfied in some degree when the man in advance stopped
beneath a lamp-post and stood for a moment looking across the

street, with his face plainly visible in the yellow circle of light. A dark face, and Ellis recognized it instantly as that of old Mr. Delamere's body servant, whose personal appearance had been very vividly impressed upon Ellis at the christening dinner at Major Carteret's. He had seen Sandy once since, too, at the hotel cakewalk. The negro had a small bundle in his hand, the nature of which Ellis could not make out.

When Sandy had stopped beneath the lamp-post, the man who was following him had dodged behind a tree trunk. When Sandy moved on, Ellis, who had stopped in turn, saw the man in hiding come out and follow Sandy. When this second man came in range of the light, Ellis wondered that there should be two men so much alike. The first of the two had undoubtedly been Sandy. Ellis had recognized the peculiar, old-fashioned coat that Sandy had worn upon the two occasions when he had noticed him. Barring this difference, and the somewhat unsteady gait of the second man, the two were as much alike as twin brothers.

When they had entered Mr. Delamere's house, one after the other—in the stillness of the night Ellis could perceive that each of them tried to make as little noise as possible—Ellis supposed that they were probably relatives, both employed as servants, or that some younger negro, taking Sandy for a model was trying to pattern himself after his superior. Why all this mystery, of course he could not imagine, unless the younger man had been out without permission and was trying to avoid the accusing eye of Sandy. Ellis was vaguely conscious that he had seen the other negro somewhere, but he could not for the moment place him—there were so many negroes, nearly three negroes to one white man in the city of Wellington!

The subject, however, while curious, was not important as compared with the thoughts of his sweetheart which drove it from his mind. Clara had been kind to him the night before—whatever her motive, she had been kind, and could not consistently return to her attitude of coldness. With Delamere hopelessly discredited, Ellis hoped to have at least fair play—with fair play, he would take his chances of the outcome.

114

# XX

# A Shocking Crime

ON FRIDAY MORNING, WHEN OLD MRS. OCHILTREE'S cook Dinah went to wake her mistress, she was confronted with a sight that well-nigh blanched her ebony cheek and caused her eyes almost to start from her head with horror.

As soon as she could command her trembling limbs sufficiently to make them carry her, she rushed out of the house and down the street, bareheaded, covering in an incredibly short time the few blocks that separated Mrs. Ochiltree's residence from that of her niece.

She hastened around the house, and finding the back door open and the servants stirring, ran into the house and up the stairs with the familiarity of an old servant, not stopping until she reached the door of Mrs. Carteret's chamber, at which she knocked in great agitation.

Entering in response to Mrs. Carteret's invitation, she found the lady, dressed in a simple wrapper, superintending the morning toilet of little Dodie, who was a wakeful child and insisted upon rising with the birds, for whose music he still showed a great fondness, in spite of his narrow escape while listening to the mockingbird.

"What is it, Dinah?" asked Mrs. Carteret, alarmed at the frightened face of her aunt's old servitor.

"Oh my Lawd, Miss 'Livy, my Lawd, my Lawd! My legs is tremblin' so dat I can't hardly hold my hands steady 'nuff to say what I got to say! Oh Lawd have mussy on us poor sinners! Whatever is gwine to happen in dis world of sin an' sorrow!"

"What in the world is the matter, Dinah?" demanded Mrs.

Carteret, whose own excitement had increased with the length of this preamble. "Has anything happened to Aunt Polly?"

"Somebody done broke in the house las' night, Miss 'Livy, an' kill' Miss Polly, an' lef' her layin' dead on the floor', in her own blood, wid her cedar ches' broke' open, an' everything scattered roun' the floor'! O my Lawd, my Lawd, my Lawd, my Lawd!"

Mrs. Carteret was shocked beyond expression. She ran immediately to the scene of the tragedy. Before the thought of this violent death all her aunt's faults faded into insignificance, and only her good qualities were remembered.

More than one motive, however, lent wings to Mrs. Carteret's feet. Her aunt's incomplete disclosures on the day of the drive past the hospital had been weighing up on Mrs. Carteret's mind and she had intended to make another effort this very day, to get an answer to her question about the papers which the woman had claimed were in existence. Suppose her aunt had really found such papers— papers which would seem to prove the preposterous claim made by her father's mulatto mistress? Suppose that, with the fatuity which generally leads human beings to keep compromising documents, her aunt had presumed these papers? If they should be found there in the house, there might be a scandal, if nothing worse, and this was to be avoided at all hazards.

Guided by some fortunate instinct, Dinah had as yet informed no one but Mrs. Carteret of her discovery. If they could reach the house before the murder became known to any third person, she might be the first to secure access to the remaining contents of the cedar chest, which would be likely to be held as evidence in case the officers of the law forestalled her own arrival.

They found the house wrapped in the silence of death. Mrs. Carteret entered the chamber of the dead woman. Upon the floor, where it had fallen, lay the body in a pool of blood, the strongly marked countenance scarcely more grim in the

116

rigidity of death than it had been in life. A gaping wound in the head accounted easily for the death. The cedar chest stood open, its strong fastenings having been broken by a steel bar which still lay beside it. Near it were scattered pieces of old lace, antiquated jewelry, tarnished silverware—the various mute souvenirs of the joys and sorrows of a long and active life.

Kneeling by the open chest, Mrs. Carteret glanced hurriedly through its contents. There were no papers there except a few old deeds and letters. She had risen with a sigh of relief, when she perceived the end of a paper projecting from beneath the edge of a rug which had been carelessly rumpled, probably by the burglar in his hasty search for plunder. This paper, or sealed envelope as it proved to be, which evidently contained some inclosure, she seized, and at the sound of approaching footsteps thrust hastily into her own bosom.

The sight of two agitated women rushing through the quiet streets at so early an hour in the morning had attracted attention and aroused curiosity, and the story of the murder, having once become known, spread with the customary rapidity of bad news. Very soon a policeman, and a little later a sheriff's officer, arrived at the house and took charge of the remains to await the arrival of the coroner.

By nine o'clock a coroner's jury had been summoned, who, after brief deliberation, returned a verdict of willful murder at the hands of some person or persons unknown, while engaged in the commission of a burglary.

No sooner was the verdict announced than the community, or at least the white third of it, resolved itself spontaneously into acommittee of the whole to discover the perpetrator of this dastardly crime, which, at this stage of the affair, seemed merely one of robbery and murder.

Suspicion was at once directed toward the negroes, as it always is when an unexplained crime is committed in a Southern community. The suspicion was not entirely an illogical one. Having been, for generations, trained up to thriftlessness, theft,and immorality, against which only

117

thirty years of very limited opportunity can be offset, during which brief period they have been denied in large measure the healthful social stimulus and sympathy which holds most men in the path of rectitude, colored people might reasonably be expected to commit at least a share of crime proportionate to their numbers. The population of the town was at least two thirds colored. The chances were, therefore, in the absence of evidence, at least two to one that a man of color had committed the crime. The Southern tendency to charge the negroes with all the crime and immorality of that region, unjust and exaggerated as the claim may be, was therefore not without a logical basis to the extent above indicated.

It must not be imagined that any logic was needed, or any reasoning consciously worked out. The mere suggestion that the crime had been committed by a negro was equivalent to proof against any negro that might be suspected and could not prove his innocence. A committee of white men was hastily formed. Acting independently of the police force, which was practically ignored as likely to favor the negroes, this committee set to work to discover the murderer.

The spontaneous activity of the whites was accompanied by a visible shrinkage of the colored population. This could not be taken as any indication of guilt, but was merely a recognition of the palpable fact that the American habit of lynching had so whetted the thirst for black blood that a negro suspected of crime had to face at least the possibility of a short shrift and a long rope, not to mention more gruesome horrors, without the intervention of judge or jury. Since to have a black face at such a time was to challenge suspicion, and since there was neither the martyr's glory nor the saint's renown in being killed for some one else's crime, and very little hope of successful resistance in case of an attempt at lynching, it was obviously the part of prudence for those thus marked to seek immunity in a temporary disappearance from public view.

# XXI

# The Necessity of an Example

ABOUT TEN O'CLOCK ON THE MORNING OF THE discovery of the murder, Captain McBane and General Belmont, as though moved by a common impulse, found themselves at the office of the Morning Chronicle. Carteret was expecting them, though there had been no appointment made. These three resourceful and energetic minds, representing no organized body, and clothed with no legal authority, had so completely arrogated to themselves the leadership of white public sentiment as to come together instinctively when an event happened which concerned the public, and, as this murder presumably did, involved the matter of race.

"Well, gentlemen," demanded McBane impatiently, "what are we going to do with the scoundrel when we catch him?"

"They've got the murderer," announced a reporter, entering the room.

"Who is he?" they demanded in a breath.

"A nigger by the name of Sandy Campbell, a servant of old Mr. Delamere."

"How did they catch him?"

"Our Jerry saw him last night, going toward Mrs. Ochiltree's house, and a white man saw him coming away, half an hour later."

"Has he confessed?"

"No, but he might as well. When the posse went to arrest him, they found him cleaning the clothes he had worn last night, and discovered in his room a part of the plunder. He denies it strenuously, but it seems a clear case."

"There can be no doubt," said Ellis, who had come into the

119

room behind the reporter. "I saw the negro last night, at twelve o'clock, going into Mr. Delamere's yard, with a bundle in his hand."

"He is the last negro I should have suspected," said Carteret. "Mr. Delamere had implicit confidence in him."

"All niggers are alike," remarked McBane sententiously. "The only way to keep them from stealing is not to give them the chance. A nigger will steal a cent off a dead man's eye. He has assaulted and murdered a white woman—an example should be made of him."

Carteret recalled very distinctly the presence of this negro at his own residence on the occasion of little Theodore's christening dinner. He remembered having questioned the prudence of letting a servant know that Mrs. Ochiltree kept money in the house. Mr. Delamere had insisted strenuously upon the honesty of this particular negro. The whole race, in the major's opinion, was morally undeveloped, and only held within bounds by the restraining influence of the white people. Under Mr. Delamere's thumb this Sandy had been a model servant—faithful, docile, respectful, and self-respecting; but Mr. Delamere had grown old, and had probably lost in a measure his moral influence over his servant. Left to his own degraded ancestral instincts, Sandy had begun to deteriorate, and a rapid decline had culminated in this robbery and murder—and who knew what other horror? The criminal was a negro, the victim a white woman— it was only reasonable to expect the worst.

"He'll swing for it," observed the general.

Ellis went into another room, where his duty called him.

"He should burn for it," averred McBane. "I say, burn the nigger."

"This," said Carteret, "is something more than an ordinary crime, to be dealt with by the ordinary processes of law. It is a murderous and fatal assault upon a woman of our race—upon our race in the person of its womanhood, its crown and flower. If such crimes are not punished with swift and terrible directness, the whole white womanhood of the South is in

120

danger."

"Burn the nigger," repeated McBane automatically.

"Neither is this a mere sporadic crime," Carteret went on. "It is symptomatic; it is the logical and inevitable result of the conditions which have prevailed in this town for the past year. It is the last straw."

"Burn the nigger," reiterated McBane. "We seem to have the right nigger, but whether we have or not, burn a nigger. It is an assault upon the white race, in the person of old Mrs. Ochiltree, committed by the black race, in the person of some nigger. It would justify the white people in burning any nigger. The example would be all the more powerful if we got the wrong one. It would serve notice on the niggers that we shall hold the whole race responsible for the misdeeds of each individual."

"In ancient Rome," said the general, "when a master was killed by a slave, all his slaves were put to the sword."

"We couldn't afford that before the war," said McBane, "but the niggers don't belong to anybody now, and there's nothing to prevent our doing as we please with them. A dead nigger is no loss to any white man. I say, burn the nigger."

"I do not believe," said Carteret, who had gone to the window and was looking out—"I do not believe that we need trouble ourselves personally about his punishment. I should judge, from the commotion in the street, that the public will take the matter into its own hands. I, for one, would prefer that any violence, however justifiable, should take place without my active intervention."

"It won't take place without mine, if I know it," exclaimed McBane, starting for the door.

"Hold on a minute, captain," exclaimed Carteret. "There's more at stake in this matter than the life of a black scoundrel. Wellington is in the hands of negroes and scallywags. What better time to rescue it?"

"It's a trifle premature," replied the general. "I should have preferred to have this take place, if it was to happen, say three months hence, on the eve of the election—but discussion always provokes thirst with me; I wonder if I could get Jerry to

121

bring us some drinks?"

Carteret summoned the porter. Jerry's usual manner had taken on an element of self-importance, resulting in what one might describe as a sort of condescending obsequiousness. Though still a porter, he was also a hero, and wore his aureole.

"Jerry," said the general kindly, "the white people are very much pleased with the assistance you have given them in apprehending this scoundrel Campbell. You have rendered a great public service, Jerry, and we wish you to know that it is appreciated."

"Thank y', General, thank y', suh! I always tries to do my duty, suh, an' stan' by dem dat stan's by me. Dat lowdown nigger oughta be lynched, suh, don't you think, of else burnt? There ain't nothin' too bad to happen to him."

"No doubt he will be punished as he deserves, Jerry," returned the general, "and we will see that you are suitably rewarded. Go across the street and get me three Calhoun cocktails. I seem to have nothing less than a two-dollar bill, but you may keep the change, Jerry—all the change."

Jerry was very happy. He had distinguished himself in the public view, for to Jerry, as to the white people themselves, the white people were the public. He had won the goodwill of the best people, and had already begun to reap a tangible reward. It is true that several strange white men looked at him with lowering brows as he crossed the street, which was curiously empty of colored people; but he nevertheless went firmly forward, panoplied in the consciousness of his own rectitude, and serenely confident of the protection of the major and the major's friends.

"Jerry is about the only negro I have seen since nine o'clock," observed the general when the porter had gone. "If this were election day, where would the negro vote be?"

"In hiding, where most of the negro population is today," answered McBane. "It's a pity, if old Mrs. Ochiltree had to go this way, that it couldn't have been deferred a month or six weeks."

Carteret frowned at this remark, which, coming from

McBane, seemed lacking in human feeling, as well as in respect to his wife's dead relative.

"But," resumed the general, "if this negro is lynched, as he well deserves to be, it will not be without its effect. We still have in reserve for the election a weapon which this affair will only render more effective. What became of the piece in the negro paper?"

"I have it here," answered Carteret. "I was just about to use it as the text for an editorial."

"Save it awhile longer," responded the general. "This crime itself will give you text enough for a four-volume work."

When this conference ended, Carteret immediately put into press an extra edition of the Morning Chronicle, which was soon upon the streets, giving details of the crime, which was characterized as an atrocious assault upon a defenseless old lady, whose age and sex would have protected her from harm at the hands of any one but a brute in the lowest human form. This event, the Chronicle suggested, had only confirmed the opinion which had been of late growing upon the white people, that drastic efforts were necessary to protect the white women of the South against brutal, lascivious, and murderous assaults at the hands of negro men. It was only another significant example of the results which might have been foreseen from the application of a false and pernicious political theory, by which ignorance, clothed in a little brief authority, was sought to be exalted over knowledge, vice over virtue, an inferior and degraded race above the heaven-crowned Anglo-Saxon. If an outraged people, justly infuriated, and impatient of the slow processes of the courts, should assert their inherent sovereignty, which the law after all were merely intended to embody, and should choose, in obedience to the higher law, to set aside, temporarily, the ordinary judicial procedure, it would serve as a warning and an example to the vicious elements of the community, of the swift and terrible punishment which would fall, like the judgment of God, upon any one who laid sacrilegious hands upon white womanhood.

123

# XXII

# How Not to Prevent a Lynching

DR. MILLER, WHO HAD SAT UP LATE THE NIGHT before with a difficult case at the hospital, was roused, about eleven o'clock, from a deep and dreamless sleep. Struggling back into consciousness, he was informed by his wife, who stood by his bedside, that Mr. Watson, the colored lawyer, wished to see him upon a matter of great importance.

"Nothing but a matter of life and death would make me get up just now," he said with a portentous yawn.

"This is a matter of life and death," replied Janet. "Old Mrs. Polly Ochiltree was robbed and murdered last night, and Sandy Campbell has been arrested for the crime—and they are going to lynch him!"

"Tell Watson to come right up," exclaimed Miller, springing out of bed. "We can talk while I'm dressing."

Watson explained the situation. Campbell had been arrested on the charge of murder. He had been seen, during the night, in the neighborhood of the scene of the crime, by two different persons, a negro and a white man, and had been identified later while entering Mr. Delamere's house, where he lived and where damning proofs of his guilt had been discovered; the most important item of which was an old-fashioned knit silk purse, recognized as Mrs. Ochiltree's, and several gold pieces of early coinage, of which the murdered woman was known to have a number. Watson brought with him one of the first copies procurable of the extra edition of the Chronicle, which contained these facts and further information.

They were still talking when Mrs. Miller, knocking at the door, announced that big Josh Green wished to see the doctor

124

about Sandy Campbell. Miller took his collar and necktie in his hand and went downstairs, where Josh was waiting.

"Doctor," said Green, "the white folks is talkin' 'bout lynchin' Sandy Campbell for killin' ole Miss Ochiltree. He never done it, an' they oughtn' to be 'lowed to lynch him."

"They ought not to lynch him, even if he committed the crime," returned Miller, "but still less if he didn't. What do you know about it?"

"I know he was wid me, suh, las' night, at the time when they say ole Miss Ochiltree was killed. We was down to Sam Taylor's place, having a little game of cards an' a little liquor. Then we lef there an' went up as far as the corner of Main an' Vine Streets, where we parted, an' Sandy went 'long towards home. Mo'over, they say he had on check' britches an' a blue coat. When Sandy was wid me he had on gray clothes, an' when we separated he weren't in no shape to be changin' his clothes, let 'lone robbin' or killin' anybody."

"Your testimony ought to prove an alibi for him," declared Miller.

"There ain't gwine to be no chance to prove nothin', 'less'n we can do it mighty quick! They say they 're gwine to lynch him to-night—some on 'em is talkin' 'bout burnin' him. My idea is to hunt up the niggers an' git 'em to stan' together an' guard the jail."

"Why shouldn't we go to the principal white people of the town and tell them Josh's story, and appeal to them to stop this thing until Campbell can have a hearing?"

"It wouldn't do any good," said Watson despondently; "their blood is up. It seems that some colored man attacked Mrs. Ochiltree—and he was a murderous villain, whoever he may be. To quote Josh would destroy the effect of his story—we know he never harmed any one but himself"—

"An' a few careless people what got in my way," corrected Josh.

"He has been in court several times for fighting—and that's against him. To have been at Sam Taylor's place is against Sandy, too, rather than in his favor. No, Josh, the white people

125

would believe that you were trying to shield Sandy, and you would probably be arrested as an accomplice. "

"But look a-here, Mr. Watson—Dr. Miller, is we-all jes' got to set down here, widout openin' you' mouths, an' let des white folks hang or burn a man what we know ain't guilty? Dat ain't no law, nor justice, nor nothin'! If you-all won't help, I'll do somethin' myself! There's two niggers to one white man in dis town, an' I'm sho' I can fin' fifty of 'em what'll fight, if they can fin' anybody to lead 'em."

"Now hold on, Josh," argued Miller; "what is to be gained by fighting? Suppose you got your crowd together and surrounded the jail—what then?"

"There'd be a clash," declared Watson, "and instead of one dead negro there'd be fifty. The white people are claiming now that Campbell didn't stop with robbery and murder. A special edition of the Morning Chronicle, just out, suggests a further purpose, and has all the old shopworn talk about race purity and supremacy and imperative necessity, which always comes to the front whenever it is sought to justify some outrage on the colored folks. The blood of the whites is up, I tell you!"

"The whole thing is profoundly discouraging," said Miller sadly.

"The white folks don't want too good an opinion of the niggers—" said Josh sullenly. "If they had a good opinion of 'em, they wouldn't have no excuse for 'busin' an' hangin' an' burnin' 'em. But if they can't keep from doin' it, let 'em git the right man! Dis way of pickin' up the first' nigger they comes across, an' stringin' him up regardless, ought to be stop', an' stop' right now!"

"Yes, that's the worst of lynch law," said Watson; "but we are wasting valuable time. One of our race is about to be put to death without judge or jury, because he is a negro, for if he were white he would not be lynched. It is thus made a race issue. What can we do to protect him?"

"We can fight, if we have to," replied Josh resolutely.

"Well, now, let us see. Suppose the colored people armed themselves? Messages would at once be sent to every town and

126

county in the neighborhood. White men from all over the state, armed to the teeth, would at the slightest word pour into town on every railroad train, and extras would be run for their benefit."

"They're already coming in," said Watson.

"We might go to the sheriff," suggested Miller, "and demand that he telegraph the governor to call out the militia."

"I spoke to the sheriff an hour ago," replied Watson. "He has a white face and a whiter liver. He does not dare call out the militia to protect a negro charged with such a brutal crime;—and if he did, the militia are white men, and who can say that their efforts would not be directed to keeping the negroes out of the way, in order that the white devils might do their worst?"

"We might call on the general government," said Miller. "Surely the President would intervene."

"Such a demand would be of no avail," returned Watson. "The government can only intervene under certain conditions, of which it must be informed through designated channels. It never sees anything that is not officially called to its attention. The whole negro population of the South might be slaughtered before the necessary red tape could be spun out to inform the President that a state of anarchy prevailed. There's no hope there."

"Then what we gwine to do?" demanded Josh indignantly; "jes' set here an' let 'em hang Sandy, or burn him?"

"God knows!" exclaimed Miller. "The outlook is dark, but we should at least try to do something. There must be some white men in the town who would stand for law and order— there's no possible chance for Sandy to escape hanging by due process of law, if he is guilty. We might at least try half a dozen gentlemen."

"We'd better leave Josh here," said Watson. "He's too truculent. If he went on the street he'd make trouble, and if he accompanied us he'd do more harm than good. Wait for us here, Josh, until we've seen what we can do. We'll be back in half an hour."

127

In half an hour they had both returned.

"It's no use," reported Watson gloomily. "I called at the mayor's office and found it locked. He is doubtless afraid on his own account, and would not dream of asserting his authority. I then looked up Judge Everton, who has always seemed to be fair. My reception was cold. He admitted that lynching was, as a rule, unjustifiable, but maintained that there were exceptions to all rules—that laws were made, after all, to express the will of the people in regard to the ordinary administration of justice, but that in an emergency the sovereign people might assert itself and take the law into its own hands— the creature was not greater than the creator. He laughed at my suggestion that Sandy was innocent. 'If he is innocent,' he said, 'then produce the real criminal. You negroes are standing in your own light when you try to protect such dastardly scoundrels as this Campbell, who is an enemy of society and not fit to live. I shall not move in the matter. If a negro wants the protection of the law, let him obey the law.' A wise judge—a second Daniel come to judgment! If this were the law, there would be no need of judges or juries."

"I called on Dr. Price," said Miller, "my good friend Dr. Price, who would rather lie than hurt my feelings. 'Miller,' he declared, 'this is no affair of mine, or yours. I have too much respect for myself and my profession to interfere in such a matter, and you will accomplish nothing, and only lessen your own influence, by having anything to say.' 'But the man may be innocent,' I replied; 'there is every reason to believe that he is.' He shook his head pityingly. 'You are self-deceived, Miller; your prejudice has warped your judgment. The proof is overwhelming that he robbed this old lady, laid violent hands upon her, and left her dead. If he did no more, he has violated the written and unwritten law of the Southern States. I could not save him if I would, Miller, and frankly, I would not if I could. If he is innocent, his people can console themselves with the reflection that Mrs. Ochiltree was also innocent, and balance one crime against the other, the white against the black. Of course I shall take no part in whatever may be done—but it

128

is not my affair, nor yours. Take my advice, Miller, and keep out of it.'

"That is the situation," added Miller, summing up. "Their friendship for us, a slender stream at the best, dries up entirely when it strikes their prejudices. There is seemingly not one white man in Wellington who will speak a word for law, order, decency, or humanity. Those who do not participate will stand idly by and see an untried man deliberately and brutally murdered. Race prejudice is the devil unchained."

"Well, then, suh," said Josh, "where does we stan' now? what is we gwine to do? I wouldn't mind fightin', for my time ain't come yet—I feels dat in my bones. What we gwine to do, dat's what I wanna know."

"What does old Mr. Delamere have to say about the matter?" asked Miller suddenly. "Why haven't we thought of him before? Has he been seen?"

"No," replied Watson gloomily, "and for a good reason— he is not in town. I came by the house just now, and learned that he went out to his country place yesterday afternoon, to remain a week. Sandy was to have followed him out there this morning—it's a pity he didn't go yesterday. The old gentleman has probably heard nothing about the matter."

"How about young Delamere?"

"He went away early this morning, down the river, to fish. He'll probably not hear of it before night, and he's only a boy anyway, and could very likely do nothing," said Watson.

Miller looked at his watch.

"Belleview is ten miles away," he said. "It is now eleven o'clock. I can drive out there in an hour and a half at the farthest. I'll go and see Mr. Delamere—he can do more than any living man, if he is able to do anything at all. There's never been a lynching here, and one good white man, if he choose, may stem the flood long enough to give justice a chance. Keep track of the white people while I'm gone, Watson; and you, Josh, learn what the colored folks are saying, and do nothing rash until I return. In the meantime, do all that you can to find out who did commit this most atrocious murder."

# XXIII

# Belleview

MILLER DID NOT REACH HIS DESTINATION without interruption, but in the course of time he arrived at the entrance gate of Belleview.

This old colonial plantation, rich in legendary lore and replete with historic distinction, had been in the Delamere family for nearly two hundred years. Enlarged and improved from generation to generation, it stood, like a baronial castle, upon a slight eminence from which could be surveyed the large demesne still belonging to the estate, which had shrunk greatly from its colonial dimensions. While still embracing several thousand acres, part forest and part cleared land, it had not of late years been profitable; in spite of which Mr. Delamere, with the conservatism of his age and caste, had never been able to make up his mind to part with any considerable portion of it. Here, in pleasant weather, surrounded by the scenes which he loved, old Mr. Delamere spent much of the time during his declining years.

Dr. Miller had once passed a day at Belleview, upon Mr. Delamere's invitation. In earlier years Mr. Delamere had been a practicing lawyer, and had numbered Miller's father among his clients. He had always been regarded as friendly to the colored people, and, until age and ill health had driven him from active life, had taken a lively interest in their advancement since the abolition of slavery. Upon the public opening of Miller's new hospital, he had made an effort to be present, and had made a little speech of approval and encouragement which had manifested his kindliness and given Miller much pleasure.

It was with the consciousness, therefore, that he was

approaching a friend, as well as Sandy's master, that Miller's mind was chiefly occupied as his tired horse, scenting the end of his efforts, bore him with a final burst of speed along the last few rods of the journey; for the urgency of Miller's errand, involving as it did the issues of life and death, did not permit him to enjoy the charm of mossy oak or forest reaches, or even to appreciate the noble front of Belleview House when it at last loomed up before him.

"Well, William," said Mr. Delamere, as he gave his hand to Miller from the armchair in which he was seated under the broad and stately portico. "I didn't expect to see you out here. You'll excuse my not rising—I'm none too firm on my legs. Did you see anything of my man Sandy back there on the road? He ought to have been here by nine o'clock, and it's now one. Sandy is punctuality itself, and I don't know how to account for his delay."

Clearly there need be no time wasted in preliminaries. Mr. Delamere had gone directly to the subject in hand.

"He will not be here to-day, sir," replied Miller. "I have come to you on his account."

In a few words Miller stated the situation.

"Preposterous!" exclaimed the old gentleman, with more vigor than Miller had supposed him to possess. "Sandy is absolutely incapable of such a crime as robbery, to say nothing of murder; and as for the rest, that is absurd upon the face of it! And so the poor old woman is dead! Well, well, well! she could not have lived much longer anyway; but Sandy did not kill her—it's simply impossible! Why, I raised that boy! He was born on my place. I'd as soon believe such a thing of my own grandson as of Sandy! No negro raised by a Delamere would ever commit such a crime. I really believe, William, that Sandy has the family honor of the Delameres quite as much at heart as I have. Just tell them I say Sandy is innocent, and it will be all right."

"I'm afraid, sir," rejoined Miller, who kept his voice up so that the old gentleman could understand without having it suggested that Miller knew he was hard of hearing, "that you

131

don't quite appreciate the situation. I believe Sandy innocent; you believe him innocent; but there are suspicious circumstances which do not explain themselves, and the white people of the city believe him guilty, and are going to lynch him before he has a chance to clear himself."

"Why doesn't he explain the suspicious circumstances?" asked Mr. Delamere. "Sandy is truthful and can be believed. I would take Sandy's word as quickly as another man's oath."

"He has no chance to explain," said Miller. "The case is prejudged. A crime has been committed. Sandy is charged with it. He is black, and therefore he is guilty. No colored lawyer would be allowed in the jail, if one should dare to go there. No white lawyer will intervene. He'll be lynched tonight, without judge, jury, or preacher, unless we can stave the thing off for a day or two."

"Have you seen my grandson?" asked the old gentleman. "Is he not looking after Sandy?"

"No, sir. It seems he went down the river this morning to fish, before the murder was discovered; no one knows just where he has gone, or at what hour he will return."

"Well, then," said Mr. Delamere, rising from his chair with surprising vigor, "I shall have to go myself. No faithful servant of mine shall be hanged for a crime he didn't commit, so long as I have a voice to speak or a dollar to spend. There'll be no trouble after I get there, William. The people are naturally wrought up at such a crime. A fine old woman—she had some detestable traits, and I was always afraid she wanted to marry me, but she was of an excellent family and had many good points—an old woman of one of the best families, struck down by the hand of a murderer! You must remember, William, that blood is thicker than water, and that the provocation is extreme, and that a few hotheads might easily lose sight of the great principles involved and seek immediate vengeance, without too much discrimination. But they are good people, William, and when I have spoken, and they have an opportunity for the sober second thought, they will do nothing rashly, but will wait for the operation of the law, which will, of course, clear Sandy. "

"I'm sure I hope so," returned Miller. "Shall I try to drive you back, sir, or will you order your own carriage?"

"My horses are fresher, William, and I'll have them brought around. You can take the reins, if you will— I'm rather old to drive—and my man will come behind with your buggy."

In a few minutes they set out along the sandy road. Having two fresh horses, they made better headway than Miller had made coming out, and reached Wellington easily by three o'clock.

"I think, William," said Mr. Delamere, as they drove into the town, "that I had first better talk with Sandy He may be able to explain away the things that seem to connect him with this atrocious affair; and that will put me in a better position to talk to other people about it."

Miller drove directly to the county jail. Thirty or forty white men, who seemed to be casually gathered near the door, closed up when the carriage approached. The sheriff, who had seen them from the inside, came to the outer door and spoke to the visitor through a grated wicket.

"I wish to see my servant, Sandy Campbell, who is said to be in your custody." said Mr. Delamere, when he had made his way to the entrance with the aid of his cane.

The sheriff hesitated. Meantime there was some parleying in low tones among the crowd outside. No one interfered, however, and in a moment the door opened sufficiently to give entrance to the old gentleman, after which it closed quickly and clangorously behind him.

Feeling no desire to linger in the locality, Miller, having seen his companion enter the jail, drove the carriage round to Mr. Delamere's house, and leaving it in charge of a servant with instructions to return for his master in a quarter of an hour hastened to his own home to meet Watson and Josh and report the result of his efforts.

# XXIV

## Two Southern Gentlemen

THE IRON BOLT RATTLED IN THE LOCK, THE DOOR of a cell swung open, and when Mr. Delamere had entered was quickly closed again.

"Well, Sandy!"

"Oh, Mars John! Is you fell from heaven to help me out of here? I prayed the Lawd to send you, an' He answered my prayer, an' here you is, Mars John—here you is! Oh, Mars John, git me out of dis place!"

"Tut, tut, Sandy!" answered his master; "of course I'll get you out. That's what I've come for. How in the world did such a mistake ever happen? You would no more commit such a crime than I would!"

"No, suh, 'deed I wouldn', an' you know I wouldn'! I wouldn't want to bring no disgrace on the family dat raise' me, nor to make no trouble for you, suh; but here I is suh, lock' up in jail, an' folks talkin' 'bout hangin' me for somethin' dat never entered my min', suh. I swea' to God I never thought of such a thing!"

"Of course you didn't, Sandy," returned Mr. Delamere soothingly; "and now the next thing, and the simplest thing, is to get you out of this. I'll speak to the officers, and at the preliminary hearing to-morrow I'll tell them all about you, and they will let you go. You won't mind spending one night in jail for your sins."

"No, suh, if I was sho' I'd be 'lowed to spen' it here. But they say dey're gwine to lynch me tonight—I can hear 'em talkin' from the winders of the cell, suh."

"Well, I say, Sandy, that they shall do no such thing! Lynch

134

a man brought up by a Delamere, for a crime of which he is innocent? Preposterous! I'll speak to the authorities and see that you are properly protected until this mystery is unraveled. If Tom had been here, he would have had you out before now, Sandy. My grandson is a genuine Delamere, is he not, Sandy?"

"Yes, suh, yes, suh," returned Sandy, with a lack of enthusiasm which he tried to conceal from his master. "An' I s'pose if he hadn't gone fishin' so soon dis mornin', he'd 'a' been lookin' after me, suh."

"It has been my love for him and your care of me, Sandy," said the old gentleman tremulously, "that have kept me alive so long; but now explain to me everything concerning this distressing matter, and I shall then be able to state your case to better advantage."

"Well, suh," returned Sandy, "I might as well tell the whole tale an' not hol' nothin' back. I was kind of lonesome las' night, an' since I been turned outta the church on account of dat cakewalk I didn't go to, so help me God! I didn't feel like gwine to prayer-meetin', so I went roun' to see Solomon Williams, an' he weren't home, an' then I walk' down street an' met Josh Green, an' he ax' me inter Sam Taylor's place, an' I got roun' there wid Josh till 'bout 'leven o'clock, when I started back home. I went straight to the house, suh, an' went to bed an' to sleep widout sayin' a word to a single soul excep' Mister Tom, who was sitting up readin' a book when I come in. I wish I may drop dead in my tracks, suh, if dat ain't the God's truth, suh, every word of it!"

"I believe every word of it, Sandy; now tell me about the clothes that you are said to have been found cleaning, and the suspicious articles that were found in your room?"

"Dat's what beats me, Mars John," replied Sandy, shaking his head mournfully. "when I lef' home las' night after supper, my clothes was all put away in the closet in my room, folded up on the shelf to keep the moths out. They was my good clothes—the blue coat dat you wore to the weddin' Forty years ago, an' dem there plaid pants I gun Mister Cohen for' dollars for three years ago; an' when I looked in my closet dis mornin', suh, befo' I got ready to start for Belleview, there was my clothes layin' on the floor', all muddy an' crumple' up, des like somebody had wore 'em in a fight! Somebody else had worn my clothes—of else there 'd been some witchcraf', of some sort of devilment gwine on dat I can't make out, suh, to save my soul!"

"There was no witchcraft, Sandy, but that there was some devilry might well be. Now, what other negro, who might have been mistaken for you, could have taken your clothes? Surely no one about the house?"

"No, suh, no, suh. It couldn't 'a' been Jeff, for he was at Belleview wid you; an' it couldn't 'a' been Billy, for he was too little to wear my clothes; an' it couldn't 'a' been Sally, for she's a 'oman. It's a mystery to me, suh!"

"Have you no enemies? Is there any one in Wellington whom you imagine would like to do you an injury?"

"Not a livin' soul dat I knows of, suh. I've been turned out of the church, but I don't know who my enemy is there, of if it was all a mistake, like dis  jailin' is; but the Devil is in dis somewhere,.Mars John—an' I got my reasons for sayin' so."

"What do you mean, Sandy?"

Sandy related his experience of the preceding evening: how he had seen the apparition preceding him to the house, and how he had questioned Tom upon the subject.

"There's some mystery here, Sandy," said Mr. Delamere reflectively. "Have you told me all, now, upon your honor? I am trying to save your life, Sandy, and I must be able to trust your word implicitly. You must tell me every circumstance; a very little and seemingly unimportant bit of evidence may sometimes determine the issue of a great lawsuit. There is one thing especially, Sandy: where did you get the gold which was found in your trunk?"

Sandy's face lit up with hopefulness.

"Why, Mars John, I can 'splain dat part easy. Dat was money I had lent out, an' I got back from—But no, suh, I promise' not to tell."

"Circumstances absolve you from your promise, Sandy.

136

Your life is of more value to you than any other thing. If you will explain where you got the gold, and the silk purse that contained it, which is said to be Mrs. Ochiltree's, you will be back home before night."

Old Mr. Delamere watched Sandy with all the awakened instincts of the trial lawyer. He could see clearly enough that, in beginning to account for the possession of the gold, Sandy had started off with his explanation in all sincerity. At the mention of the silk purse, however, his face had blanched to an ashen gray, and the words had frozen upon his lips.

A less discerning observer might have taken these things as signs of guilt, but not so Mr. Delamere.

"Well, Sandy," said his master encouragingly, "go on. You got the gold from"—

Sandy remained silent. He had had a great shock, and had taken a great resolution.

"Mars John," he asked dreamily, "you don't b'lieve dat I done dis thing?"

"Certainly not, Sandy, else why should I be here?"

"An' nothin' wouldn't make you b'lieve it, suh?"

"No, Sandy—I could not believe it of you. I've known you too long and too well."

"An' you wouldn't b'lieve it, not even if I wouldn't say one word mo' about it?"

"No, Sandy, I believe you no more capable of this crime than I would be—or my grandson, Tom. You'll not be so foolish, so absurdly foolish, Sandy, as to keep silent and risk your life merely to shield some one else, when by speaking you might clear up this mystery and be restored at once to liberty. Just tell me where you got the gold," added the old gentleman persuasively. "Come, now, Sandy, that's a good fellow!"

"Mars John," asked Sandy softly, "when my daddy, 'way back yonder befo' the war, was about to be sol' away from his wife an' chillun, you bought him an' dem, an' kept us all on yo' place together, didn't you, suh?"

"Yes, Sandy, and he was a faithful servant, and proved worthy of all I did for him."

"And when he had worked for you ten years, suh, you set him free?"

"Yes, Sandy, he had earned his freedom."

"An' when the war broke out, an' my folks was scattered, an' I didn't have nothin' to do nor nowhere to go, you kept me on yo' place, and took me to wait on you, suh, didn't you?"

"Yes, Sandy, and you have been a good servant and a good friend; but tell me now about this gold, and I'll go and get you out of this, right away, for I need you, Sandy, and you'll not be of any use to me shut up here!"

"Jes' hol' on a minute befo' you go, John; for if dem people outside should git hold of me befo' you does git me out of here, I may never see you no mo', suh, in dis worl'. When Mars Billy McLean shot me by mistake, while we was out huntin' dat day, who was it boun' up my wounds an' kept me from bleedin' to death, an' me two miles on his own shoulders to a doctor?"

"Yes, Sandy, and when black Sally ran away with your young mistress and Tom, when Tom was a baby, who stopped the runaway, and saved their lives at the risk of his own?"

"Dat weren't nothin' suh; anybody could 'a' done dat, what was strong enough an' swif' enough. You is been good to me, suh, all these years, an' I've tried to do my duty by you, suh, an' by Mister Tom, who was yo' own grandson, an' de las' one of de family."

"Yes, you have, Sandy, and when I am gone, which will not be very long, Tom will take care of you, and see that you never want. But we are wasting valuable time, Sandy, in these old reminiscences. Let us get back to the present. Tell me about the gold, now, so that I may at once look after your safety. It may not even be necessary for you to remain here all night."

"Jes' one word mo', Mars John, befo' you go! I know you're gwine to do de bes' you can for me, an' I'm sorry I can't help you no mo' wid it; but if there should be any accident, or if you can't git me out of here, don't bother yo' mind 'bout it no mo', suh, an' don't git yo'self excited, for you know de doctor says, suh, dat you can't stand excitement; but jes' leave me in de hands of the Lawd, suh—He'll look after me, here or hereafter.

138

I know I've fell from grace mo' than once, but I've done made my peace wid Him in dis here jailhouse, suh, an' I ain't 'feared to die—if I have to. I ain't got no wife nor chillun to mourn for me, an' I'll die knownin' dat I've done my duty to dem dat hired me, an' trusted me, an' had claims on me. For I was raise' by a Delamere, suh, an' all de ole Delameres was gentlemen, an' their principles spread to de niggers 'round 'em, suh; an' if I has to die for somethin' I did n' do—I can die, suh, like a gentleman!

But as for dat gol', suh, I ain't gwine to say one word mo' 'bout it to nobody in dis worl'!"

Nothing could shake Sandy's determination. Mr. Delamere argued, expostulated, but all in vain. Sandy would not speak.

Mr. Delamere felt less confident of the outcome than when he had entered the jail, but was resolved that no effort should be spared to secure protection for Sandy until there had been full opportunity for the truth to become known.

"Take good care of your prisoner, sheriff," he said sternly, as he was conducted to the door. "He will not be long in your custody, and I shall see that you are held strictly accountable for his safety."

"I'll do what I can, sir," replied the sheriff in an even tone and seemingly not greatly impressed by this warning. "If the prisoner is taken from me, it will be because the force that comes for him is too strong for resistance."

"There should be no force too strong for an honest man in your position to resist—whether successfully or not is beyond the question. The officer who is intimidated by threats, or by his own fears, is recreant to his duty, and no better than the mob which threatens him. But you will have no such test, Mr. Wemyss! I shall see to it myself that there is no violence!"

# XXV

# The Honor of a Family

MR. DELAMERE'S COACHMAN, WHO, IN accordance with instructions left by Miller, had brought the carriage around to the jail and was waiting anxiously at the nearest corner, drove up with some trepidation as he saw his master emerge from the prison. The old gentleman entered the carriage and gave the order to be driven to the office of the Morning Chronicle. According to Jerry, the porter, whom he encountered at the door, Carteret was in his office, and Mr. Delamere, with the aid of his servant, climbed the stairs painfully and found the editor at his desk.

"Carteret," exclaimed Mr. Delamere, "what is all this talk about lynching my man for murder and robbery and criminal assault! It's perfectly absurd! The man was raised by me; he had lived in my house forty years. He has been honest, faithful, and trustworthy. He would no more be capable of this crime than you would, or my grandson Tom. Sandy has too much respect for the family to do anything that would reflect disgrace upon it."

"My dear Mr. Delamere," asked Carteret, with an indulgent smile, "how could a negro possibly reflect discredit upon a white family? I should really like to know."

"How, sir? A white family raised him. Like all the negroes, he has been clay in the hands of the white people. They are what we have made them, or permitted them to become."

"We are not God, Mr. Delamere! We do not claim to have created these—masterpieces."

"No; but we thought to overrule God's laws, and we enslaved these people for our greed, and sought to escape the manstealer's curse by laying to our souls the flattering unction that we were making of barbarous negroes civilized and Christian men. If we did not, if instead of making them Christians we have made some of them brutes, we have only ourselves to blame, and if these prey upon society, it is our just punishment! But my negroes, Carteret, were well raised and well behaved. This man is innocent of this offense, I solemnly affirm, and I want your aid to secure his safety until a fair trial can be had."

"On your bare word, sir?" asked Carteret, not at all moved by this outburst.

Old Mr. Delamere trembled with anger, and his withered cheek flushed darkly, but he restrained his feelings, and answered with an attempt at calmness:—

"Time was, sir, when the word of a Delamere was held as good as his bond, and those who questioned it were forced to maintain their skepticism upon the field of honor. Time was, sir, when the law was enforced in this state in a manner to command the respect of the world! Our lawyers, our judges, our courts, were a credit to humanity and civilization. I fear I have outlasted my epoch—I have lived to hear of white men, the most favored of races, the heirs of civilization, the conservators of liberty, howling like red Indians around a human being slowly roasting at the stake."

"My dear sir," said Carteret soothingly, "you should undeceive yourself. This man is no longer your property. The negroes are no longer under our control, and with their emancipation ceased our responsibility. Their insolence and disregard for law have reached a point where they must be sternly rebuked."

"The law," retorted Mr. Delamere, "furnishes a sufficient penalty for any crime, however heinous, and our code is by no means lenient. To my old-fashioned notions, death would seem an adequate punishment for any crime, and torture has been abolished in civilized countries for a hundred years. It would be better to let a crime go entirely unpunished, than to use it as a pretext for turning the whole white population into a mob of

141

primitive savages, dancing in hellish glee around the mangled body of a man who has never been tried for a crime. All this, however, is apart from my errand, which is to secure your assistance in heading off this mob until Sandy can have a fair hearing and an opportunity to prove his innocence."

"How can I do that, Mr. Delamere?"

"You are editor of the Morning Chronicle. The Chronicle is the leading newspaper of the city. This morning's issue practically suggested the mob; the same means will stop it. I will pay the expense of an extra edition, calling off the mob, on the ground that newly discovered evidence has shown the prisoner's innocence."

"But where is the evidence?" asked Carteret.

Again Mr. Delamere flushed and trembled. "My evidence, sir! I say the negro was morally incapable of the crime. A man of forty-five does not change his nature over-night. He is no more capable of a disgraceful deed than my grandson would be!"

Carteret smiled sadly.

"I am sorry, Mr. Delamere," he said, "that you should permit yourself to be so exercised about a worthless scoundrel who has forfeited his right to live. The proof against him is overwhelming. As to his capability of crime, we will apply your own test. You have been kept in the dark too long, Mr. Delamere—indeed, we all have—about others as well as this negro. Listen, sir: last night, at the Clarendon Club, Tom Delamere was caught cheating outrageously at cards. He had been suspected for some time; a trap was laid for him, and he fell into it. Out of regard for you and for my family, he has been permitted to resign quietly, with the understanding that he first pay off his debts, which are considerable."

Mr. Delamere's face, which had taken on some color in the excitement of the interview, had gradually paled to a chalky white while Carteret was speaking. His head sunk forward; already an old man, he seemed to have aged ten years in but little more than as many seconds.

"Can this be true?" he demanded in a hoarse whisper. "Is

142

it—entirely authentic?"

"True as gospel; true as it is that Mrs. Ochiltree has been murdered, and that this negro killed her. Ellis was at the club a few minutes after the affair happened, and learned the facts from one of the participants. Tom made no attempt at denial. We have kept the matter out of the others papers, and I would have spared your feelings—I surely would not wish to wound them—but the temptation proved too strong for me, and it seemed the only way to convince you: it was your own test. If a gentleman of a distinguished name and an honorable ancestry, with all the restraining forces of social position surrounding him, to hold him in check, can stoop to dishonor, what is the improbability of an illiterate negro's being at least capable of crime?"

"Enough, sir," said the old gentleman. "You have proved enough. My grandson may be a scoundrel—I can see, in the light of this revelation, how he might be; and he seems not to have denied it. I maintain, nevertheless, that my man Sandy is innocent of the charge against him. He has denied it, and it has not been proved. Carteret, I owe that negro my life; he, and his father before him, have served me and mine faithfully and well. I cannot see him killed like a dog, without judge or jury—no, not even if he were guilty, which I do not believe!"

Carteret felt a twinge of remorse for the pain he had inflicted upon this fine old man, this ideal gentleman of the ideal past—the past which he himself so much admired and regretted. He would like to spare his old friend any further agitation; he was in a state of health where too great excitement might prove fatal. But how could he? The negro was guilty, and sure to die sooner or later. He had not meant to interfere, and his intervention might be fruitless.

"Mr. Delamere," he said gently, "there is but one way to gain time. You say the negro is innocent. Appearances are against him. The only way to clear him is to produce the real criminal, or prove an alibi. If you, or some other white man of equal standing, could swear that the negro was in your presence last night at any hour when this crime could have

143

taken place, it might be barely possible to prevent the lynching for the present; and when he is tried, which will probably be not later than next week, he will have every opportunity to defend himself, with you to see that he gets no less than justice. I think it can be managed, though there is still a doubt. I will do my best, for your sake, Mr. Delamere—solely for your sake, be it understood, and not for that of the negro, in whom you are entirely deceived."

"I shall not examine your motives, Carteret," replied the other, "if you can bring about what I desire."

"Whatever is done," added Carteret, "must be done quickly. It is now four o'clock; no one can answer for what may happen after seven. If he can prove an alibi, there may yet be time to save him. White men might lynch a negro on suspicion; they would not kill a man who was proven, by the word of white men, to be entirely innocent."

"I do not know," returned Mr. Delamere, shaking his head sadly. "After what you have told me, it is no longer safe to assume what white men will or will not do;—what I have learned here has shaken my faith in humanity. I am going away, but shall return in a short time. Shall I find you here?"

"I will await your return," said Carteret.

He watched Mr. Delamere pityingly as the old man moved away on the arm of the coachman waiting in the hall. He did not believe that Mr. Delamere could prove an alibi for his servant, and without some positive proof the negro would surely die—as he well deserved to die.

# XXVI

## The Discomfort of Ellis

MR. ELLIS WAS VAGUELY UNCOMFORTABLE. IN THE first excitement following the discovery of the crime, he had given his bit of evidence, and had shared the universal indignation against the murderer. When public feeling took definite shape in the intention to lynch the prisoner, Ellis felt a sudden sense of responsibility growing upon himself. When he learned, an hour later, that it was proposed to burn the negro, his part in the affair assumed a still graver aspect; for his had been the final word to fix the prisoner's guilt.

Ellis did not believe in lynch law. He had argued against it, more than once, in private conversation, and had written several editorials against the practice, while in charge of the Morning Chronicle during Major Carteret's absence. A young man, however, and merely representing another, he had not set up as a reformer, taking rather the view that this summary method of punishing crime, with all its possibilities of error, to say nothing of the resulting disrespect of the law and contempt for the time-honored methods of establishing guilt, was a mere temporary symptom of the unrest caused by the unsettled relations of the two races at the South. There had never before been any special need for any vigorous opposition to lynch law, so far as the community was concerned, for there had not been a lynching in Wellington since Ellis had come there, eight years before, from a smaller town, to seek a place for himself in the world of action. Twenty years before, indeed, there had been wild doings, during the brief Ku-Klux outbreak, but that was before Ellis' time—or at least when he was but a child. He had come of a Quaker family—the modified Quakers of the

South—and while sharing in a general way the Southern prejudice against the negro, his prejudices had been tempered by the peaceful tenets of his father's sect. His father had been a Whig, and a non-slaveholder; and while he had gone with the South in the civil war so far as a man of peace could go, he had not done so for love.

As the day wore on, Ellis' personal responsibility bore more heavily upon him. Suppose he had been wrong? He had seen the accused negro, he had recognized him by his clothes, his whiskers, his spectacles, and his walk; but he had also seen another man, who resembled Sandy so closely that but for the difference in their clothes, he was forced to acknowledge, he could not have told them apart. Had he not seen the first man, he would have sworn with even greater confidence that the second was Sandy. There had been, he recalled, about one of the men—he had not been then nor was he now able to tell which—something vaguely familiar, and yet seemingly discordant to whichever of the two it was, or, as it seemed to him now, to any man of that race. His mind reverted to the place where he had last seen Sandy, and then a sudden wave of illumination swept over him, and filled him with horror. The cakewalk—the dancing—the speech— they were not Sandy's at all, nor any negro's! It was a white man who had stood in the light of the street lamp, so that the casual passer-by might see and recognize in him old Mr. Delamere's servant. The scheme was a dastardly one, and worthy of a heart that was something worse than weak and vicious.

Ellis resolved that the negro should not, if he could prevent it, die for another's crime; but what proof had he himself to offer in support of his theory? Then again if he denounced Tom Delamere as the murderer, it would involve, in all probability, the destruction of his own hopes with regard to Clara. Of course she could not marry Delamere after the disclosure—the disgraceful episode at the club would have been enough to make that reasonably certain; it had put a nail in Delamere's coffin but this crime had driven it in to the head and clinched it. On the other hand, would Miss Pemberton ever speak again

146

to the man who had been the instrument of bringing disgrace upon the family? Spies, detectives, police officers, may be useful citizens, but they are rarely pleasant company for other people. We fee the executioner, but we do not touch his bloody hand. We might feel a certain tragic admiration for Brutus condemning his sons to death, but we would scarcely invite Brutus to dinner after the event. It would harrow our feelings too much.

Perhaps, thought Ellis, there might be a way out of the dilemma. It might be possible to save this innocent negro without, for the time being, involving Delamere. He believed that murder will out, but it need not be through his initiative. He determined to go to the jail and interview the prisoner, who might give such an account of himself as would establish his innocence beyond a doubt. If so, Ellis would exert himself to stem the tide of popular fury. If, as a last resort, he could save Sandy only by denouncing Delamere, he would do his duty, let it cost him what it might.

The gravity of his errand was not lessened by what he saw and heard on the way to the jail. The anger of the people was at a white heat. A white woman had been assaulted and murdered by a brutal negro. Neither advanced age, nor high social standing, had been able to protect her from the ferocity of a black savage. Her sex, which should have been her shield and buckler, had made her an easy mark for the villainy of a black brute. To take the time to try him would be a criminal waste of public money. To hang him would be too slight a punishment for so dastardly a crime. An example must be made.

Already the preparations were under way for the impending execution. A T-rail from the railroad yard had been procured, and men were burying it in the square before the jail. Others were bringing chains, and a load of pine wood was piled in convenient proximity. Some enterprising individual had begun the erection of seats from which, for a pecuniary consideration, the spectacle might be the more easily and comfortably viewed.

147

Ellis was stopped once or twice by persons of his acquaintance. From one he learned that the railroads would run excursions from the neighboring towns in order to bring spectators to the scene; from another that the burning was to take place early in the evening, so that the children might not be kept up beyond their usual bedtime. In one group that he passed he heard several young men discussing the question of which portions of the negro's body they would prefer for souvenirs. Ellis shuddered and hastened forward. Whatever was to be done must be done quickly, or it would be too late. He saw that already it would require a strong case in favor of the accused to overcome the popular verdict.

Going up the steps of the jail, he met Mr. Delamere, who was just coming out, after a fruitless interview with Sandy.

"Mr. Ellis," said the old gentleman, who seemed greatly agitated, "this is monstrous!"

"It is indeed, sir!" returned the younger man. "I mean to stop it if I can. The negro did not kill Mrs. Ochiltree. "

Mr. Delamere looked at Ellis keenly, and, as Ellis recalled afterwards, there was death in his eyes. Unable to draw a syllable from Sandy, he had found his servant's silence more eloquent than words. Ellis felt a presentiment that this affair, however it might terminate, would be fatal to this fine old man, whom the city could ill spare, in spite of his age and infirmities

"Mr. Ellis," asked Mr. Delamere, in a voice which trembled with ill-suppressed emotion, "do you know who killed her?"

Ellis felt a surging pity for his old friend; but every step that he had taken toward the jail had confirmed and strengthened his own resolution that this contemplated crime, which he dimly felt to be far more atrocious than that of which Sandy was accused, in that it involved a whole community rather than one vicious man, should be stopped at any cost. Deplorable enough had the negro been guilty, it became, in view of his certain innocence, an unspeakable horror, which for all time would cover the city with infamy.

"Mr. Delamere," he replied, looking the elder man squarely in the eyes, "I think I do—and I am very sorry. "

"And who was it, Mr. Ellis?"

He put the question hopelessly, as though the answer were a foregone conclusion.

"I do not wish to say at present," replied Ellis, with a remorseful pang, "unless it becomes absolutely necessary, to save the negro's life. Accusations are dangerous—as this case proves—unless the proof be certain.'

For a moment it seemed as though Mr. Delamere would collapse upon the spot. Rallying almost instantly, however, he took the arm which Ellis involuntarily offered, and said with an effort:—

"Mr. Ellis, you are a gentleman whom it is an honor to know. If you have time, I wish you would go with me to my house—I can hardly trust myself alone—and thence to the Chronicle office. This thing shall be stopped, and you will help me stop it."

It required but a few minutes to cover the half mile that lay between the prison and Mr. Delamere's residence.

# XXVII

## The Vagaries of the Higher Law

MR. DELAMERE WENT IMMEDIATELY TO HIS grandson's room, closing and locking the door behind him. He had requested Ellis to wait in the carriage.

The bed had been made, and the room was in order. There was a bureau in the room through which Mr. Delamere searched. Finding one of the drawers locked, he tried it with a key of his own, and being unable to unlock it, took a poker from beside the stove and broke it ruthlessly open.

The contents confirmed what he had heard concerning his grandson's character. Thrown together in disorderly confusion were bottles of wine and whiskey; soiled packs of cards; a dice-box with dice; a box of poker chips, several revolvers, and a number of photographs and paper-covered books.

He searched the room more carefully, and found, in the wood-box by the small heating stove which stood in the room, a torn and crumpled bit of paper. Stooping to pick this up, his eye caught a gleam of something yellow beneath the bureau.

He smoothed out the paper. It was the lower half of a label, or part of the cover of a small box, torn diagonally from corner to corner. From the business card at the bottom, which gave the name of a firm of manufacturers of theatrical supplies in a Northern city, and from the letters remaining upon the upper and narrower half, the bit of paper had plainly formed part of the wrapper of a package of burnt cork.

Folding this damning piece of evidence, Delamere knelt and with the aid of his cane drew out from under the bureau the yellow object which had attracted his attention. It was a five-dollar gold piece dated from the beginning of the century.

To make assurance doubly sure, Mr. Delamere summoned the cook from the kitchen in the back yard. Sally said that Mr. Tom had got up early, knocked at her window and had told her that she need not bother about breakfast for him, as he had had a cold bite from the pantry; that he was going hunting and fishing, and would be gone all day. According to Sally, he had come in about ten o'clock the night before. He had forgotten his night key, Sandy was out, and she had admitted him with her own key. He had said that he was very tired and was going immediately to bed.

Mr. Delamere seemed perplexed; the crime had been committed later in the evening than ten o'clock. The cook cleared up the mystery.

"He must 'a' been dead tired, suh, for I went back to his room fifteen or twenty minutes after he come in to fin' out what he wanted for breakfas'; an' I knock' two or three times, real hard, an' Mister Tom did n' wake up no mo' than de dead. He surely-had a good sleep, or he'd never 'a' got up so early."

"Thank you, Sally," said Mr. Delamere, when the woman had finished, "that will do."

"Will you be home to supper, suh?" asked the cook.

"Yes."

In a few minutes Delamere was driving rapidly with Ellis toward the office of the Morning Chronicle. Ellis could see that Mr. Delamere had discovered something of tragic import. Neither spoke. Ellis gave all his attention to the horses, and Mr. Delamere remained wrapped in his own sombre reflections.

At the office, they were informed by Jerry that Major Carteret was engaged with General Belmont and Captain McBane. Mr. Delamere knocked at the door of the inner office, which was opened by Carteret in person.

"Oh, it is you, Mr. Delamere."

"Carteret," exclaimed Mr. Delamere, "I must speak to you immediately, and alone."

"Excuse me a moment, gentlemen," said Carteret, turning to those within the room. "I'll be back in a moment—don't go away."

151

Ellis had left the room, closing the door behind him. Mr. Delamere and Carteret were quite alone.

"Carteret," declared the old gentleman, "this murder must not take place."

" 'Murder' is a hard word," replied the editor, frowning slightly.

"It is the right word," rejoined Mr. Delamere, decidedly. "It would be a foul and most unnatural murder, for Sandy did not kill Mrs. Ochiltree."

Carteret with difficulty restrained a smile of pity. His old friend was very much excited, as the tremor in his voice gave proof. The criminal was his trusted servant, who had proved unworthy of confidence. No one could question Mr. Delamere's motives; but he was old, his Judgment was no longer to be relied upon. It was a great pity that he should so excite and overstrain himself about a worthless negro, who had forfeited his life for a dastardly crime. Mr. Delamere had had two paralytic strokes, and a third might prove fatal. He must be dealt with gently.

"Mr. Delamere," he said, with patient tolerance, "I think you are deceived. There is but one sure way to stop this execution. If your servant is innocent, you must produce the real criminal. If the negro, with such overwhelming proofs against him, is not guilty, who is?"

"I will tell you who is," replied Mr. Delamere. "The murderer is"—the words came with a note of anguish, as though torn from his very heart—"the murderer is Tom Delamere, my own grandson!"

"Impossible, sir!" exclaimed Carteret, starting back involuntarily. "That could not be! The man was seen leaving the house, and he was black!"

"All cats are gray in the dark, Carteret; and moreover, nothing is easier than for a white man to black his face. God alone knows how many crimes have been done in this guise! Tom Delamere, to get the money to pay his gambling debts, committed this foul murder, and then tried to fasten it upon as honest and faithful a soul as ever trod the earth."

152

Carteret, though at first overwhelmed by this announcement, perceived with quick intuition that it might easily be true. It was but a step from fraud to crime, and in Delamere's need of money there lay a palpable notice for robbery—the murder may have been an afterthought. Delamere knew as much about the cedar chest as the negro could have known, and more.

But a white man must not be condemned without proof positive.

"What foundation is there, sir," he asked, "for this astounding charge?"

Mr. Delamere related all that had taken place since he had left Belleview a couple of hours before, and as he proceeded, step by step, every word carried conviction to Carteret. Tom Delamere's skill as a mimic and a negro impersonator was well known; he had himself laughed at more than one of his performances. There had been a powerful motive, and Mr. Delamere's discoveries had made clear the means. Tom's unusual departure, before breakfast, on a fishing expedition was a suspicious circumstance. There was a certain devilish ingenuity about the affair which he would hardly have expected of Tom Delamere, but for which the reason was clear enough. One might have thought that Tom would have been satisfied with merely blacking his face, and leaving to chance the identification of the negro who might be apprehended. He would hardly have implicated, out of pure malignity, his grandfather's old servant, who had been his own care-taker for many years. Here, however, Carteret could see where Tom's own desperate position operated to furnish a probable motive for the crime. The surest way to head off suspicion from himself was to direct it strongly toward some particular person, and this he had been able to do conclusively by his access to Sandy's clothes, his skill in making up to resemble him, and by the episode of the silk purse. By placing himself beyond reach during the next day, he would not be called upon to corroborate or deny any statements which Sandy might make, and in the very probable case that the crime should be summarily avenged, any such statements on Sandy's part would be regarded as mere desperate subterfuges of the murderer to save his own life. It was a bad affair.

"The case seems clear," said Carteret reluctantly but conclusively. "And now, what shall we do about it?"

"I want you to print a handbill," said Mr. Delamere "and circulate it through the town, stating that Sandy Campbell is innocent and Tom Delamere guilty of this crime. If this is not done, I will go myself and declare it to all who will listen, and I will publicly disown the villain who is no more grandson of mine. There is no deeper sink of iniquity into which he could fall."

Carteret's thoughts were chasing one another tumultuously. There could be no doubt that the negro was innocent, from the present aspect of affairs, and he must not be lynched; but in what sort of position would the white people be placed, if Mr. Delamere carried out his Spartan purpose of making the true facts known? The white people of the city had raised the issue of their own superior morality, and had themselves made this crime a race question. The success of the impending "revolution," for which he and his confreres had labored so long, depended in large measure upon the maintenance of their race prestige, which would be injured in the eyes of the world by such a fiasco. While they might yet win by sheer force, their cause would suffer in the court of morals, where they might stand convicted as pirates, instead of being applauded as patriots. Even the negroes would have the laugh on them—the people whom they hoped to make approve and justify their own despoilment. To be laughed at by the negroes was a calamity only less terrible than failure or death.

Such an outcome of an event which had already been heralded to the four corners of the earth would throw a cloud of suspicion upon the stories of outrage which had gone up from the South for so many years, and had done so much to win the sympathy of the North for the white South and to alienate it from the colored people. The reputation of the race was threatened. They must not lynch the negro, and yet, for the

154

credit of the town, its aristocracy, and the race, the truth of this ghastly story must not see the light—at least not yet.

"Mr. Delamere," he exclaimed, "I am shocked and humiliated. The negro must be saved, of course, but— consider the family honor."

"Tom is no longer a member of my family. I disown him. He has covered the family name—my name, sir— with infamy. We have no longer a family honor. I wish never to hear his name spoken again!"

For several minutes Carteret argued with his old friend. Then he went into the other room and consulted with General Belmont.

As a result of these conferences, and of certain urgent messages sent out, within half an hour thirty or forty of the leading citizens of Wellington were gathered in the Morning Chronicle office. Several other curious persons, observing that there was something in the wind, and supposing correctly that it referred to the projected event of the evening, crowded in with those who had been invited.

Carteret was in another room, still arguing with Mr. Delamere. "It's a mere formality, sir," he was saying suavely, "accompanied by a mental reservation. We know the facts; but this must be done to justify us, in the eyes of the mob, in calling them off before they accomplish their purpose."

"Carteret," said the old man, in a voice eloquent of the struggle through which he had passed, "I would not perjure myself to prolong my own miserable existence another day, but God will forgive a sin committed to save another's life. Upon your head be it, Carteret, and not on mine!"

"Gentlemen," said Carteret, entering with Mr. Delamere the room where the men were gathered, and raising his hand for silence, "the people of Wellington were on the point of wreaking vengeance upon a negro who was supposed to have been guilty of a terrible crime. The white men of this city, impelled by the highest and holiest sentiments, were about to take steps to defend their hearthstones and maintain the purity and ascendancy of their race. Your purpose sprung from hearts

155

wounded in their tenderest susceptibilities."

" 'Rah, 'rah!" shouted a tipsy sailor, who had edged in with the crowd.

"But this same sense of justice," continued Carteret oratorically, "which would lead you to visit swift and terrible punishment upon the guilty, would not permit you to slay an innocent man. Even a negro, as long as he behaves himself and keeps in his place, is entitled to the protection of the law. We may be stern and unbending in the punishment of crime, as befits our masterful race, but we hold the scales of justice with even and impartial hand."

" 'Rah, impartial hand!" cried the tipsy sailor, who was immediately ejected with slight ceremony.

"We have discovered, beyond a doubt, that the negro Sandy Campbell, now in custody, did not commit this robbery and murder, but that it was perpetrated by some unknown man, who has fled from the city. Our venerable and distinguished fellow townsman, Mr. Delamere, in whose employment this Campbell has been for many years, will vouch for his character, and states, furthermore, that Campbell was with him all last night, covering any hour at which this crime could have been committed."

"If Mr. Delamere will swear to that," said some one in the crowd, "the negro should not be lynched."

There were murmurs of dissent. The preparations had all been made. There would be great disappointment if the lynching did not occur.

"Let Mr. Delamere swear, if he wants to save the nigger," came again from the crowd.

"Certainly," assented Carteret. "Mr. Delamere can have no possible objection to taking the oath. Is there a notary public present, or a justice of the peace?"

A man stepped forward. "I am a justice of the peace," he announced.

"Very well, Mr. Smith," said Carteret, recognizing the speaker. "With your permission, I will formulate the oath, and Mr. Delamere may repeat it after me, if he will. I solemnly swear—"

"I solemnly swear—"

Mr. Delamere's voice might have come from the tomb, so hollow and unnatural did it sound.

"So help me God,"—

"So help me God,"—

"That the negro Sandy Campbell, now in jail on the charge of murder, robbery, and assault, was in my presence last night between the hours of eight and two o'clock."

Mr. Delamere repeated this statement in a firm voice; but to Ellis, who was in the secret, his words fell upon the ear like dods dropping upon the coffin in an open grave.

"I wish to add," said General Belmont, stepping forward, "that it is not our intention to interfere, by anything which may be done at this meeting, with the orderly process of the law, or to advise the prisoner's immediate release. The prisoner will remain in custody, Mr. Delamere, Major Carteret, and I guaranteeing that he will be proved entirely innocent at the preliminary hearing tomorrow morning."

Several of those present looked relieved; others were plainly disappointed; but when the meeting ended, the news went out that the lynching had been given up. Carteret immediately wrote and had struck off a handbill giving a brief statement of the proceedings, and sent out a dozen boys to distribute copies among the people in the streets. That no precaution might be omitted, a call was issued to the Wellington Grays, the crack independent military company of the city, who in an incredibly short time were on guard at the jail.

Thus a slight change in the point of view had demonstrated the entire ability of the leading citizens to maintain the dignified and orderly processes of the law whenever they saw fit to do so.

The night passed without disorder, beyond the somewhat rough handling of two or three careless negroes that came in the way of small parties of the disappointed who had sought alcoholic consolation.

At ten o'clock the next morning, a preliminary hearing of the charge against Campbell was had before a magistrate. Mr. Delamere, perceptibly older and more wizened than he had seemed the day before, and leaning heavily on the arm of a servant, repeated his statement of the evening before. Only one or two witnesses were called, among whom was Mr. Ellis, who swore positively that in his opinion the prisoner was not the man whom he had seen and at first supposed to be Campbell. The most sensational piece of testimony was that of Dr. Price, who had examined the body, and who swore that the wound in the head was not necessarily fatal, and might have been due to a fall—that she had more than likely died of shock attendant upon the robbery, she being of advanced age and feeble health. There was no evidence, he said, of any personal violence.

Sandy was not even bound over to the grand jury, but was discharged upon the ground that there was not sufficient evidence upon which to hold him. Upon his release he received the congratulations of many present, some of whom would cheerfully have done him to death a few hours before. With the childish fickleness of a mob, they now experienced a satisfaction almost as great as, though less exciting than, that attendant upon taking life. We speak of the mysteries of inanimate nature. The workings of the human heart are the profoundest mystery of the universe. One moment they make us despair of our kind, and the next we see in them the reflection of the divine image. Sandy, having thus escaped from the Mr. Hyde of the mob, now received the benediction of its Dr. Jekyll. Being no cynical philosopher, and realizing how nearly the jaws of death had closed upon him, he was profoundly grateful for his escape, and felt not the slightest desire to investigate or criticise any man's motives.

With the testimony of Dr. Price, the worst feature of the affair came to an end. The murder eliminated or rendered doubtful, the crime became a mere vulgar robbery, the extent of which no one could estimate, since no living soul knew how much money Mrs. Ochiltree had had in the cedar chest. The absurdity of the remaining charge became more fully apparent

158

in the light of the reaction from the excitement of the day before.

Nothing further was ever done about the case; but though the crime went unpunished, it carried evil in its train. As we have seen, the charge against Campbell had been made against the whole colored race. All over the United States the Associated Press had flashed the report of another dastardly outrage by a burly black brute—all black brutes it seems are burly—and of the impending lynching with its prospective horrors. This news, being highly sensational in its character, had been displayed in large black type on the front pages of the daily papers. The dispatch that followed, to the effect that the accused had been found innocent and the lynching frustrated, received slight attention, if any, in a fine-print paragraph on an inside page. The facts of the case never came out at all. The family honor of the Delameres was preserved, and the prestige of the white race in Wellington was not seriously impaired.

Upon leaving the preliminary hearing, old Mr. Delamere had requested General Belmont to call at his house during the day upon professional business. This the general did in the course of the afternoon.

"Belmont," said Mr. Delamere, "I wish to make my will. I should have drawn it with my own hand; but you know my motives, and can testify to my soundness of mind and memory."

He thereupon dictated a will, by the terms of which he left to his servant, Sandy Campbell, three thousand dollars, as a mark of the testator's appreciation of services rendered and sufferings endured by Sandy on behalf of his master. After some minor dispositions, the whole remainder of the estate was devised to Dr. William Miller, in trust for the uses of his hospital and training school for nurses, on condition that the institution be incorporated and placed under the management of competent trustees. Tom Delamere was not mentioned in the will.

"There, Belmont," he said, "that load is off my mind. Now,

if you will call in some witnesses—most of my people can write—I shall feel entirely at ease."

The will was signed by Mr. Delamere, and witnessed by Jeff and Billy, two servants in the house, neither of whom received any information as to its contents, beyond the statement that they were witnessing their master's will.

"I wish to leave that with you for safe keeping, Belmont," said Mr. Delamere, after the witnesses had retired. "Lock it up in your safe until I die, which will not be very long, since I have no further desire to live."

An hour later Mr. Delamere suffered a third paralytic stroke, from which he died two days afterwards, without having in the meantime recovered the power of speech.

The will was never produced. The servants stated, and General-Belmont admitted, that Mr. Delamere had made a will a few days before his death; but since it was not discoverable, it seemed probable that the testator had destroyed it. This was all the more likely, the general was inclined to think, because the will had been of a most unusual character. What the contents of the will were, he of course did not state, it having been made under the seal of professional secrecy.

This suppression was justified by the usual race argument: Miller's hospital was already well established, and, like most negro institutions, could no doubt rely upon Northern philanthropy for any further support it might need. Mr. Delamere's property belonged of right to the white race, and by the higher law should remain in the possession of white people. Loyalty to one's race was a more sacred principle than deference to a weak old man's whims.

Having reached this conclusion, General Belmont's first impulse was to destroy the will; on second thoughts he locked it carefully away in his safe. He would hold it awhile. It might some time be advisable to talk the matter over with young Delamere, who was of a fickle disposition and might wish to change his legal adviser.

# XXVIII

## In Season and Out

WELLINGTON SOON RESUMED ITS CALM, AND IN A few weeks the intended lynching was only a memory. The affair had been dropped as absolutely as though it had never occurred. No colored man ever learned the reason of this sudden change of front, and Sandy Campbell's loyalty to his old employer's memory kept him silent. Tom Delamere did not offer to retain Sandy in his service, though he presented him with most of the old gentleman's wardrobe. At this time he had not been informed of the contents of his grandfather's latest will. Major Carteret gave Sandy employment as a butler, thus making a sort of vicarious atonement, on the part of the white race, of which the major felt himself in a way the embodiment, for the risk to which Sandy had been subjected.

Sandy was restored to the bosom of the church and was no longer tempted to stray from the path of rectitude, but became even a more rigid Methodist than before his recent troubles.

Tom Delamere did not call upon Clara again in the character of a lover. Indeed, the social atmosphere of Wellington remained so frigid toward Delamere that he left town, and did not return for several months.

Ellis was aware that Delamere had been thrown over but a certain delicacy restrained him from following up immediately the advantage which the absence of his former rival gave him. As for Dr. Miller, he never learned of Mr. Delamere's good intentions toward his institution, but regretted the old gentleman's death as the loss of a sincere friend and well-wisher of his race in their unequal struggle.

Despite the untiring zeal of Carteret and his associates, the

161

campaign for the restriction of the suffrage, which was to form the basis of a permanent white supremacy, had seemed to languish for a while after the Ochiltree affair. The lull, however, was only temporary, and more apparent than real, for the forces adverse to the negro were merely gathering strength for a more vigorous assault. In the South, an obscure jealousy of the negro's progress, an obscure fear of the very equality so contemptuously denied, furnished a rich soil for successful agitation. Statistics of crime, ingeniously manipulated, were made to present a fearful showing against the negro. Vital statistics were made to prove that he had degenerated from an imaginary standard of physical excellence which had existed under the benign influence of slavery. Constant lynchings emphasized his impotence, and bred everywhere a growing contempt for his rights. The negro had become a target at which any one might try a shot. Schoolboys gravely debated the question as to whether or not the negro should exercise the franchise. The pessimist gave him up in despair; while the optimist, smilingly confident that everything would come out all right in the end, also turned aside and went his buoyant way to more pleasing themes.

For a time there were white men in the state who opposed any reactionary step unless it were of general application. They were conscientious men, who had learned the ten commandments and wished to do right; but this class was a small minority, and their objections were soon silenced by the all-powerful race argument. Selfishness is the most constant of human motives. Patriotism, humanity, or the love of God may lead to sporadic outbursts which sweep away the heaped-up wrongs of centuries; but they languish at times, while the love of self works on ceaselessly, unwearyingly, burrowing always at the very roots of life, and heaping up fresh wrongs for other centuries to sweep away. The state was at the mercy of venal and self-seeking politicians, bent upon regaining their ascendancy at any cost, stultifying their own minds by vague sophistries and high-sounding phrases, which deceived none but those who wished to be deceived, and these but imperfectly; and dulling the public conscience by a loud clamor in which the calm voice of truth was for the moment silenced. So the cause went on.

Carteret, as spokesman of the campaign, and sincerest of all its leaders, performed prodigies of labor. The Morning Chronicle proclaimed, in season and out, the doctrine of "White Supremacy." Leaving the paper in charge of Ellis, the major made a tour of the state, rousing the white people of the better class to an appreciation of the terrible danger which confronted them in the possibility that a few negroes might hold a few offices or dictate the terms upon which white men should fill them. Difficulties were explained away. The provisions of the Federal Constitution, it was maintained, must yield to the "higher law," and if the Constitution could neither be altered nor bent to this end, means must be found to circumvent it.

The device finally hit upon for disfranchising the colored people in this particular state was the notorious "grandfather clause. " After providing various restrictions of the suffrage, based upon education, character, and property, which it was deemed would in effect disfranchise the colored race, an exception was made in favor of all citizens whose fathers or grandfathers had been entitled to vote prior to 1867. Since none but white men could vote prior to 1867, this exception obviously took in the poor and ignorant whites, while the same class of negroes were excluded.

It was ingenious, but it was not fair. In due time a constitutional convention was called, in which the above scheme was adopted and submitted to a vote of the people for ratification. The campaign was fought on the color line. Many white Republicans, deluded with the hope that by the elimination of the negro vote their party might receive accessions from the Democratic ranks, went over to the white party. By fraud in one place, by terrorism in another, and everywhere by the resistless moral force of the united whites, the negroes were reduced to the apathy of despair, their few white allies demoralized, and the amendment adopted by a large majority. The negroes were taught that this is a white man's country, and that the sooner they made up their minds to this fact, the better for all concerned. The white people would be good to them so long as they behaved themselves and kept their place. As theoretical equals— practical equality being forever out of the question, either by nature or by law— there could have been nothing but strife between them, in which the weaker party would invariably have suffered most.

Some colored men accepted the situation thus outlined, if not as desirable, at least as inevitable. Most of them, however, had little faith in this condescending friendliness which was to take the place of constitutional rights. They knew they had been treated unfairly; that their enemies had prevailed against them; that their friends had stood passively by and seen them undone. Many of the most enterprising and progressive left the state, and those who remain still labor under a sense of wrong and outrage which renders them distinctly less valuable as citizens.

The great steal was made, but the thieves did not turn honest—the scheme still showed the mark of the burglar's tools. Sins, like chickens, come home to roost. The South paid a fearful price for the wrong of negro slavery; in some form or other it will doubtless reap the fruits of this later iniquity.

Drastic as were these "reforms," the results of which we have anticipated somewhat, since the new Constitution was not to take effect immediately, they moved all too slowly for the little coterie of Wellington conspirators, whose ambitions and needs urged them to prompt action. Under the new Constitution it would be two full years before the "nigger amendment" became effective, and meanwhile the Wellington district would remain hopelessly Republican. The committee decided, about two months before the fall election, that an active local campaign must be carried on, with a view to discourage the negroes from attending the polls on election day.

The question came up for discussion one forenoon in a

meeting at the office of the Morning Chronicle, at which all of the "Big Three" were present.

"Something must be done," declared McBane, "and that damn quick. Too many white people are saying that it will be better to wait until the amendment goes into effect. That would mean to leave the niggers in charge of this town for two years after the state has declared for white supremacy! I'm opposed to leaving it in their hands one hour—them's my sentiments!"

This proved to be the general opinion, and the discussion turned to the subject of ways and means.

"What became of that editorial in the nigger paper?" inquired the general in his blandest tones, cleverly directing a smoke ring toward the ceiling. "It lost some of its point back there, when we came near lynching that nigger; but now that that has blown over, why wouldn't it be a good thing to bring into play at the present juncture? Let's read it over again."

Carteret extracted the paper from the pigeon-hole where he had placed it some months before. The article was read aloud with emphasis and discussed phrase by phrase. Of its wording there could be little criticism—it was temperately and even cautiously phrased. As suggested by the general, the Ochiltree affair had proved that it was not devoid of truth. Its great offensiveness lay in its boldness: that a negro should publish in a newspaper what white people would scarcely acknowledge to themselves in secret was much as though a Russian moujik or a German peasant should rush into print to question the divine right of the Lord's Anointed. The article was racial lese-majeste in the most aggravated form. A peg was needed upon which to hang a coup d'etat, and this editorial offered the requisite opportunity. It was unanimously decided to republish the obnoxious article, with comment adapted to fire the inflammable Southern heart and rouse it against any further self-assertion of the negroes in politics or elsewhere.

"The time is ripe!" exclaimed McBane. "In a month we can have the niggers so scared that they won't dare stick their heads out of doors on 'lection day."

"I wonder," observed the general thoughtfully, after this

conclusion had been reached, "if we couldn't have Jerry fetch us some liquor?"

Jerry appeared in response to the usual summons. The general gave him the money, and ordered three Calhoun cocktails. When Jerry returned with the glasses on a tray, the general observed him with pointed curiosity.

"What in hell is the matter with you, Jerry? Your black face is splotched with brown and yellow patches and your hair shines as though you had fallen headforemost into a firkin of butter. What's the matter with you?"

Jerry seemed much embarrassed by this inquiry.

"Nothin', suh, nothin'," he stammered. "It's—it's jes' somethin' I been puttin' on my hair, suh, to improve de quality, suh."

"Jerry," returned the general, bending a solemn look upon the porter, "you have been playing with edged tools, and your days are numbered. You have been reading the Afro-American Banner."

He shook open the paper, which he had retained in his hand, and read from one of the advertisements:—

" 'Kinky, curly hair made straight in two applications. Dark skins lightened two shades; mulattoes turned perfectly white.'

"This stuff is rank poison, Jerry," continued the general with a mock solemnity which did not impose upon Jerry, who nevertheless listened with an air of great alarm. He suspected that the general was making fun of him; but he also knew that the general would like to think that Jerry believed him in earnest; and to please the white folks was Jerry's consistent aim in life. "I can see the signs of decay in your face, and your hair will all fall out in a week or two at the latest—mark my words!"

McBane had listened to this pleasantry with a sardonic sneer. It was a waste of valuable time. To Carteret it seemed in doubtful taste. These grotesque advertisements had their tragic side. They were proof that the negroes had read the handwriting on the wall. These pitiful attempts to change their physical characteristics were an acknowledgment, on their own

166

part, that the negro was doomed, and that the white man was to inherit the earth and hold all other races under his heel. For, as the months had passed, Carteret's thoughts, centering more and more upon the negro, had led him farther and farther, until now he was firmly convinced that there was no permanent place for the negro in the United States, if indeed anywhere in the world, except under the ground. More pathetic even than Jerry's efforts to escape from the universal doom of his race was his ignorance that even if he could, by some strange alchemy, bleach his skin and straighten his hair, there would still remain, underneath it all, only the unbleached darky—the ass in the lion's skin.

When the general had finished his facetious lecture, Jerry backed out of the room shamefacedly, though affecting a greater confusion than he really felt. Jerry had not reasoned so closely as Carteret, but he had realized that it was a distinct advantage to be white—an advantage which white people had utilized to secure all the best things in the world, and he had entertained the vague hope that by changing his complexion he might share this prerogative. While he suspected the general's sincerity, he nevertheless felt a little apprehensive lest the general's prediction about the effects of the face-bleach and other preparations might prove true—the general was a white gentleman and ought to know—and decided to abandon their use.

This purpose was strengthened by his next interview with the major. When Carteret summoned him, an hour later, after the other gentlemen had taken their leave, Jerry had washed his head thoroughly and there remained no trace of the pomade. An attempt to darken the lighter spots in his cuticle by the application of printer's ink had not proved equally successful—the retouching left the spots as much too dark as they had formerly been too light.

"Jerry," said Carteret sternly, "when I hired you to work for the Chronicle, you were black. The word 'negro' means 'black.' The best negro is a black negro, of the pure type, as it came from the hand of God. If you wish to get along well with the white people, the blacker you are the better—white people do not like negroes who want to be white. A man should be content to remain as God made him and where God placed him. So no more of this nonsense. Are you going to vote at the next election?"

"What would you 'vise me to do, suh?" asked Jerry cautiously.

"I do not advise you. You ought to have sense enough to see where your own interests lie. I put it to you whether you cannot trust yourself more safely in the hands of white gentlemen, who are your true friends, than in the hands of ignorant and purchasable negroes and unscrupulous white scoundrels?"

"There's no doubt about it, suh," assented Jerry, with a vehemence proportioned to his desire to get back into favor. "I ain't gwine to have nothin' to do wid de 'lection, suh! If I don't vote, I can keep my job, can't I, suh?"

The major eyed Jerry with an air of supreme disgust. What could be expected of a race so utterly devoid of tact? It seemed as though this negro thought a white gentleman might want to bribe him to remain away from the polls; and the negro's willingness to accept the imaginary bribe demonstrated the venal nature of the colored race—its entire lack of moral principle!

"You will retain your place, Jerry," he said severely, "so long as you perform your duties to my satisfaction and behave yourself properly."

With this grandiloquent subterfuge Carteret turned to his next article on white supremacy. Jerry did not delude himself with any fine-spun sophistry. He knew perfectly well that he held his job upon the condition that he stayed away from the polls at the approaching election. Jerry was a fool. But while no one may be entirely wise, there are degrees of folly, and Jerry was not all kinds of a fool.

# XXIX

# Mutterings of the Storm

EVENTS MOVED RAPIDLY DURING THE NEXT FEW days. The reproduction, in the Chronicle, of the article from the Afro-American Banner, with Carteret's inflammatory comment, took immediate effect. It touched the Southern white man in his most sensitive spot. To him such an article was an insult to white womanhood, and must be resented by some active steps—mere words would be no answer at all. To meet words with words upon such a subject would be to acknowledge the equality of the negro and his right to discuss or criticise the conduct of the white people.

The colored people became alarmed at the murmurings of the whites, which seemed to presage a coming storm. A number of them sought to arm themselves, but ascertained, upon inquiring at the stores, that no white merchant would sell a negro firearms. Since all the dealers in this sort of merchandise were white men, the negroes had to be satisfied with oiling up the old army muskets which some of them possessed, and the few revolvers with which a small rowdy element generally managed to keep themselves supplied. Upon an effort being made to purchase firearms from a Northern city, the express company, controlled by local men, refused to accept the consignment. The white people, on the other hand, procured both arms and ammunition in large quantities, and the Wellington Grays drilled with great assiduity at their armory.

All this went on without any public disturbance of the town's tranquillity. A stranger would have seen nothing to excite his curiosity. The white people did their talking among

169

themselves, and merely grew more distant in their manner toward the colored folks, who instinctively closed their ranks as the whites drew away. With each day that passed the feeling grew more tense. The editor of the Afro-American Banner, whose office had been quietly garrisoned for several nights by armed negroes, became frightened, and disappeared from the town between two suns.

The conspirators were jubilant at the complete success of their plans. It only remained for them to so direct this aroused public feeling that it might completely accomplish the desired end—to change the political complexion of the city government and assure the ascendancy of the whites until the amendment should go into effect. A revolution, and not a riot, was contemplated.

With this end in view, another meeting was called at Carteret's office.

"We are now ready," announced General Belmont, "for the final act of this drama. We must decide promptly, or events may run away from us."

"What do you suggest?" asked Carteret.

"Down in the American tropics," continued the general, "they have a way of doing things. I was in Nicaragua, ten years ago, when Paterno's revolution drove out Igorroto's government. It was as easy as falling off a log. Paterno had the arms and the best men. Igorroto was not looking for trouble, and the guns were at his breast before he knew it. We have the guns. The negroes are not expecting trouble, and are easy to manage compared with the fiery mixture that flourishes in the tropics."

"I should not advocate murder," returned Carteret. "We are animated by high and holy principles. We wish to right a wrong, to remedy an abuse, to save our state from anarchy and our race from humiliation. I don't object to frightening the negroes, but I am opposed to unnecessary bloodshed."

"I'm not quite so particular," struck in McBane. "They need to be taught a lesson, and a nigger more or less wouldn't be missed. There's too many of 'em now."

"Of course," continued Carteret, "if we should decide upon a certain mode of procedure, and the negroes should resist, a different reasoning might apply; but I will have no premeditated murder."

"In Central and South America," observed the general reflectively, "none are hurt except those who get in the way. "

"There'll be no niggers hurt," said McBane contemptuously, "unless they strain themselves running. One white man can chase a hundred of 'em. I've managed five hundred at a time. I'll pay for burying all the niggers that are killed."

The conference resulted in a well-defined plan, to be put into operation the following day, by which the city government was to be wrested from the Republicans and their negro allies.

"And now," said General Belmont, "while we are cleansing the Augean stables, we may as well remove the cause as the effect. There are several negroes too many in this town, which will be much the better without them. There's that yellow lawyer, Watson. He's altogether too mouthy, and has too much business. Every nigger that gets into trouble sends for Watson, and white lawyers, with families to support and social positions to keep up, are deprived of their legitimate source of income."

"There's that damn nigger real estate agent," blurted out McBane. "Billy Kitchen used to get most of the nigger business, but this darky has almost driven him to the poorhouse. A white business man is entitled to a living in his own profession and his own home. That nigger don't belong here nohow. He came from the North a year or two ago, and is hand in glove with Barber, the nigger editor, which is enough of itself to damn him. He'll have to go!"

"How about the collector of the port?"

"We'd better not touch him. It would bring the government down upon us, which we want to avoid. We don't need to worry about the nigger preachers either. They want to stay here, where the loaves and the fishes are. We can make 'em write letters to the newspapers justifying our course, as a condition of their remaining."

171

"What about Billings?" asked McBane. Billings was the white Republican mayor. "Is that skunk to be allowed to stay in town?"

"No," returned the general, "every white Republican office-holder ought to be made to go. This town is only big enough for Democrats, and negroes who can be taught to keep their place."

"What about the colored doctor," queried McBane, "with the hospital, and the diamond ring, and the carriage?"

"I shouldn't interfere with Miller," replied the general decisively. "He's a very good sort of a negro, doesn't meddle with politics, nor tread on any one else's toes. His father was a good citizen, which counts in his favor. He's spending money in the community too, and contributes to its prosperity."

"That sort of nigger, though, sets a bad example," retorted McBane. "They make it all the harder to keep the rest of 'em down."

" 'One swallow does not make a summer,' " quoted the general. "When we get things arranged, there'll be no trouble. A stream cannot rise higher than its fountain, and a smart nigger without a constituency will no longer be an object of fear. I say, let the doctor alone."

"He'll have to keep mighty quiet, though," muttered McBane discontentedly. "I don't like smart niggers. I've had to shoot several of them in the course of my life."

"Personally, I dislike the man," interposed Carteret, "and if I consulted my own inclinations, would say expel him with the rest; but my grievance is a personal one, and to gratify it in that way would be a loss to the community. I wish to be strictly impartial in this matter, and to take no step which cannot be entirely justified by a wise regard for the public welfare."

"What's the use of all this hypocrisy, gentlemen?" sneered McBane. "Every last one of us has an axe to grind! The major may as well put an edge on his. We'll never get a better chance to have things our way. If this nigger doctor annoys the major, we'll run him out with the rest. This is a white man's country, and a white man's city, and no nigger has any business here

172

when a white man wants him gone!"

Carteret frowned darkly at this brutal characterization of their motives. It robbed the enterprise of all its poetry, and put a solemn act of revolution upon the plane of a mere vulgar theft of power. Even the general winced.

"I would not consent," he said irritably, "to Miller's being disturbed."

McBane made no further objection.

There was a discreet knock at the door.

"Come in," said Carteret.

Jerry entered. "Mister Ellis wants to speak to you a minute, suh," he said.

Carteret excused himself and left the room.

"Jerry," said the general, "you lump of ebony, the sight of you reminds me! If your master doesn't want you for a minute, step across to Mr. Brown's and tell him to send me three cocktails."

"Yes, suh," responded Jerry, hesitating. The general had said nothing about paying.

"And tell him, Jerry, to charge them. I'm short on change to-day."

"Yes, suh; yes, suh," replied Jerry, as he backed out of the presence, adding, when he had reached the hall: "There ain't no change for Jerry dis time, sho': I'll jes' make dat for' cocktails, an' de General won't never know de difference. I ain't gwine 'cross de road for nothin', not if I knows it."

Half an hour later, the conspirators dispersed. They had fixed the hour of the proposed revolution, the course to be pursued, the results to be obtained; but in stating their equation they had overlooked one factor—God, or Fate, or whatever one may choose to call the Power that holds the destinies of man in the hollow of his hand.

173

# XXX

# The Missing Papers

MRS. CARTERET WAS VERY MUCH DISTURBED. IT was supposed that the shock of her aunt's death had affected her health, for since that event she had fallen into a nervous condition. Mrs. Ochiltree had left no will, and no property of any considerable value except her homestead, which descended to Mrs. Carteret as the natural heir. Whatever she may have had on hand in the way of ready money had undoubtedly been abstracted from the cedar chest by the midnight marauder. Her niece's grief was held to mark a deep seated affection for the grim old woman who had reared her.

An examination, not long after her aunt's death, of the papers found near the cedar chest on the morning after the murder had contributed to Mrs. Carteret's enlightenment, but had not promoted her peace of mind. When Mrs. Carteret reached home, after her hurried exploration of the cedar chest, she thrust into a bureau drawer the envelope she had found. So fully was her mind occupied, for several days, with the funeral, and with the excitement attending the arrest of Sandy Campbell, that she deferred the examination of the contents of the envelope until near the end of the week.

One morning, while alone in her chamber, she drew the envelope from the drawer, and was holding it in her hand, hesitating as to whether or not she should open it, when the baby in the next room began to cry. The child's cry seemed like a warning, and yielding to a vague uneasiness, she put the paper back.

"Phil," she said to her husband at luncheon, "Aunt Polly said some strange things to me one day before she died—I don't know whether she was quite in her right mind or not; but suppose that my father had left a will by which it was provided that half his property should go to that woman and her child?"

"Your Aunt Polly was in her dotage, and merely dreaming. Your father would never have been such a fool; but even if he had, no such will could have stood the test of the courts."

"So that legally, as well as morally," said Mrs. Carteret, "the will would have been of no effect?"

"Not the slightest. A jury would soon have broken down the legal claim. As for any moral obligation, there would have been nothing moral about the affair. The only possible consideration for such a gift was an immoral one. I don't wish to speak harshly of your father, my dear, but his conduct was gravely reprehensible. The woman herself had no right or claim whatever- she would have been whipped and expelled from the town, if justice—blind, bleeding justice, then prostrate at the feet of slaves and aliens—could have had her way!"

"But the child"—

"The child was in the same category. Who was she, to have inherited the estate of your ancestors, of which, a few years before, she would herself have formed a part? But the discussion is all in the air, Olivia. Your father never did and never would have left such a will."

This conversation relieved Mrs. Carteret's uneasiness. Going to her room shortly afterwards, she took the envelope from her bureau drawer and drew out a bulky paper. The haunting fear that it might be such a will as her aunt had suggested was now removed. It might be just as well, she thought, to throw the paper in the fire without looking at it. She wished to think as well as might be of her father, and she felt that her respect for his memory would not be strengthened by the knowledge that he had meant to leave his estate away from her; for her aunt's words had been open to the construction that she was to have been left destitute. Curiosity strongly prompted her to read the paper. Perhaps the will contained no such provision as she had feared.

She unfolded the document. It was written on legal paper,

in her father's own hand. It was a will, by which, in one item, her father devised to his daughter Janet, the child of the woman known as Julia Brown, the sum of ten thousand dollars, and a certain plantation or tract of land a short distance from the town of Wellington. The rest and residue of his estate, after deducting all legal charges and expenses, was bequeathed to his beloved daughter, Olivia Merkell.

Mrs. Carteret breathed a sigh of relief. Her father had not preferred another to her, but had left to his lawful daughter the bulk of his estate. She felt at the same time a growing indignation at the thought that that woman should so have wrought upon her father's weakness as to induce him to think of leaving so much valuable property to her bastard—property which by right should go, and now would go, to her own son, to whom by every rule of law and decency it ought to descend.

Mrs. Carteret came out from her chamber and threw the offending paper into the fire, and watched it slowly burn. When it had been consumed, the carbon residue of one sheet still retained its form, and she could read the words on the charred portion. A sentence, which had escaped her eye in her rapid reading, stood out in ghostly black upon the gray background:—

"All the rest and residue of my estate I devise and bequeath to my daughter Olivia Merkell, the child of my beloved first wife."

Mrs. Carteret had not before observed the word "first." Instinctively she stretched toward the fire the poker which she held in her hand, and at its touch the shadowy remnant fell to pieces, and nothing but ashes remained upon the hearth.

Not until the next morning did she think again of the envelope which had contained the paper she had burned. Opening the drawer where it lay, the oblong blue envelope confronted her. The sight of it was distasteful. The indorsed side lay uppermost, and the words seemed like a mute reproach:—

"The Last Will and Testament of Samuel Merkell."

Snatching up the envelope, she glanced into it mechanically

176

as she moved toward the next room, and perceived a thin folded paper which had heretofore escaped her notice. When opened, it proved to be a certificate of marriage, in due form, between Samuel Merkell and Julia Brown. It was dated from a county in South Carolina, about two years before her father's death.

For a moment Mrs. Carteret stood gazing blankly at this faded slip of paper. Her father had married this women!—at least he had gone through the form of marriage with her, for to him it had surely been no more than an empty formality. The marriage of white and colored persons was forbidden by law. Only recently she had read of a case where both the parties to such a crime, a colored man and a white woman, had been sentenced to long terms in the penitentiary. She even recalled the circumstances. The couple had been living together unlawfully—they were very low people, whose private lives were beneath the public notice—but influenced by a religious movement pervading the community, had sought, they said at the trial, to secure the blessing of God upon their union. The higher law, which imperiously demanded that the purity and prestige of the white race be preserved at any cost, had intervened at this point.

Mechanically she moved toward the fireplace, so dazed by this discovery as to be scarcely conscious of her own actions. She surely had not formed any definite intention of destroying this piece of paper when her fingers relaxed unconsciously and let go their hold upon it. The draught swept it toward the fireplace. A moment later the record of poor Julia's marriage was scattered to the four winds of heaven, as her poor body had long since mingled with the dust of earth.

The letter remained unread. In her agitation at the discovery of the marriage certificate, Olivia had almost forgotten the existence of the letter. It was addressed to "John Delamere, Esq., as Executor of my Last Will and Testament," while the lower left-hand corner bore the direction: "To be delivered only after my death, with seal unbroken."

The seal was broken already; Mr. Delamere was dead; the

letter could never be delivered. Mrs. Carteret unfolded it and read:—

*MY DEAR DELAMERE—I have taken the liberty of naming you as executor of my last will, because you are my friend, and the only man of my acquaintance whom I feel that I can trust to carry out my wishes, appreciate my motives, and preserve the silence I desire.*

*I have, first, a confession to make. Enclosed in this letter you will find a certificate of marriage between my child Janet's mother and myself. While I have never exactly repented of this marriage, I have never had the courage to acknowledge it openly. If I had not married Julia, I fear Polly Ochiltree would have married me by main force—as she would marry you or any other gentleman unfortunate enough to fall in the way of this twice-widowed man-hunter. When my wife died, three years ago, her sister Polly offered to keep house for me and the child. I would sooner have had the devil in the house, and yet I trembled with alarm—there seemed no way of escape—it was so clearly and obviously the proper thing.*

*But she herself gave me my opportunity. I was on the point of consenting, when she demanded, as a condition of her coming, that I discharge Julia, my late wife's maid. She was laboring under a misapprehension in regard to the girl, but I grasped at the straw, and did everything to foster her delusion. I declared solemnly that nothing under heaven would induce me to part with Julia. The controversy resulted in my permitting Polly to take the child, while I retained the maid.*

*Before Polly put this idea into my head, I had scarcely looked at Julia, but this outbreak turned my attention toward her. She was a handsome girl, and, as I soon found out, a good girl. My wife, who raised her, was a Christian woman, and had taught her modesty and virtue. She was free. The air was full of liberty, and equal rights, and all the abolition claptrap, and she made marriage a condition of her remaining longer in the house. In a moment of weakness I took her away to a place where we were not known, and married her. If she had left me, I should have fallen a victim to Polly Ochiltree—to which any fate was preferable.*

*And then, old friend, my weakness kept to the fore. I was ashamed*

178

of this marriage, and my new wife saw it. Moreover, she loved me—too well, indeed, to wish to make me unhappy. The ceremony had satisfied her conscience, had set her right, she said, with God; for the opinions of men she did not care, since I loved her—she only wanted to compensate me, as best she could, for the great honor I had done my handmaiden—for she had read her Bible, and I was the Abraham to her Hagar, compared with whom she considered herself at a great advantage. It was her own proposition that nothing be said of this marriage. If any shame should fall on her, it would fall lightly, for it would be undeserved. When the child came, she still kept silence. No one, she argued, could blame an innocent child for the accident of birth, and in the sight of God this child had every right to exist; while among her own people illegitimacy would involve but little stigma.

I need not say that I was easily persuaded to accept this sacrifice; but touched by her fidelity, I swore to provide handsomely for them both. This I have tried to do by the will of which I ask you to act as executor. Had I left the child more, it might serve as a ground for attacking the will; my acknowledgment of the tie of blood is sufficient to justify a reasonable bequest.

I have taken this course for the sake of my daughter Olivia, who is dear to me, and whom I would not wish to make ashamed; and in deference to public opinion, which it is not easy to defy. If, after my death, Julia should choose to make our secret known, I shall of course be beyond the reach of hard words; but loyalty to my memory will probably keep her silent. A strong man would long since have acknowledged her before the world and taken the consequences; but, alas! I am only myself, and the atmosphere I live in does not encourage moral heroism. I should like to be different, but it is God who hath made us, and not we ourselves!

Nevertheless, old friend, I will ask of you one favor. If in the future this child of Julia's and of mine should grow to womanhood; if she should prove to have her mother's gentleness and love of virtue; if, in the new era which is opening up for her mother's race, to which, unfortunately, she must belong, she should become, in time, an educated woman; and if the time should ever come when, by virtue of her education or the development of her people, it would be to her a source of shame or unhappiness that she was an illegitimate child—if

179

*you are still alive, old friend, and have the means of knowing or divining this thing, go to her and tell her, for me, that she is my lawful child, and ask her to forgive her father's weakness.*

*When this letter comes to you, I shall have passed to— the Beyond; but I am confident that you will accept this trust, for which I thank you now, in advance, most heartily.*

The letter was signed with her father's name, the same signature which had been attached to the will.

As the day wore on, Mrs. Carteret grew still less at ease. To herself, marriage was a serious thing—to a right thinking woman the most serious concern of life. A marriage certificate, rightfully procured, was scarcely less solemn, so far as it went, than the Bible itself. She had burned the pretended marriage certificate because it meant nothing. Nevertheless, she could not ignore the knowledge of another such marriage, of which every one in the town knew—a celebrated case, indeed, where a white man, of a family quite as prominent as her father's, had married a colored woman during the military occupation of the state just after the civil war. The legality of the marriage had never been questioned. It had been fully consummated by twenty years of subsequent cohabitation. No amount of social persecution had ever shaken the position of the husband. With an iron will he had stayed on in the town, a living protest against the established customs of the South and though his children were negroes, though he had never appeared in public with his wife, no one had ever questioned the validity of his marriage or the legitimacy of his offspring. Mrs. Carteret felt decidedly uncomfortable. She had destroyed the marriage certificate, but its ghost still haunted her.

Major Carteret, having just eaten a good dinner, was in a very agreeable humor when, that same evening, his wife brought up again the subject of their previous discussion.

"Phil," she asked, "Aunt Polly told me that once, long before my father died, when she went to remonstrate with him for keeping that woman in the house, he threatened to marry Julia if Aunt Polly ever said another word to him about the

180

matter. Suppose he had married her, and had then left a will—would the marriage have made any difference, so far as the will was concerned?"

Major Carteret laughed. "Your Aunt Polly," he said, "was a remarkable woman, with a wonderful imagination, which seems to have grown more vivid as her memory and judgment weakened. Why should your father marry his negro housemaid? Mr. Merkell was never rated as a fool—he had one of the clearest heads in Wellington. Your father was never capable of such a folly."

"Of course I am only supposing a case," returned Olivia. "Imagining such a case, just for the argument, would the marriage have been legal?"

"That would depend. If he had married her during the military occupation, or in South Carolina, the marriage would have been valid, though morally and socially outrageous."

"And if he had died afterwards, leaving a will?"

"The will would have controlled the disposition of his estate, in all probability."

"Suppose he had left no will?"

"You are getting the matter down pretty fine, my dear! The woman would have taken one third of the real estate for life, and could have lived in the homestead until she died. She would also have had half the other property—the money and goods and furniture, everything except the land—and the negro child would have shared with you the balance of the estate."

Mrs. Carteret lapsed into a troubled silence. Her father had married the woman. In her heart she had no doubt of the validity of the marriage. If the marriage had been valid, Julia's child had been legitimate. The will she had burned gave this sister of hers—she shuddered at the word—but a small part of the estate. Under the law, which intervened now that there was no will, the property should have been equally divided. If the woman had been white—but the woman had not been white, and the same rule of moral conduct did not, could not, in the very nature of things, apply, as between white people! For, if this were not so, slavery had been, not merely an economic mistake, but a great crime against humanity.

If she should make known the facts she had learned, it would mean what?—a division of her father's estate, a recognition of the legality of her father's relations with Julia. Such a stain upon her father's memory would be infinitely worse than if he had not married her. To have lived with her without marriage was a social misdemeanor, at which society in the old days had winked, or at most had frowned. To have married her was to have committed the unpardonable social sin. Such a scandal Mrs. Carteret could not have endured. Should she seek to make restitution, it would necessarily involve the disclosure of at least some of the facts. Had she not destroyed the will, she might have compromised with her conscience by producing it and acting upon its terms, which had been so stated as not to disclose the marriage. This was now rendered impossible by her own impulsive act; she could not mention the will at all, without admitting that she had destroyed it.

Mrs. Carteret found herself in what might be called, vulgarly, a moral "pocket." She could, of course, remain silent. Mrs. Carteret was a good woman, according to her lights, with a cultivated conscience, to which she had always looked as her mentor and infallible guide.

Hence Mrs. Carteret, after this painful discovery, remained for a long time ill at ease—so disturbed, indeed, that her mind reacted upon her nerves, which had never been strong; and her nervousness affected her strength, which had never been great, until Carteret, whose love for her had been deepened and strengthened by the advent of his son, became alarmed for her health, and spoke very seriously to Dr. Price concerning it.

# XXXI

# The Shadow of a Dream

MRS. CARTERET AWOKE, WITH A START, FROM A troubled dream. She had been sailing across a sunlit sea, in a beautiful boat, her child lying on a bright-colored cushion at her feet. Overhead the swelling sail served as an awning to keep off the sun's rays, which far ahead were reflected with dazzling brilliancy from the shores of a golden island. Her son, she dreamed, was a fairy prince, and yonder lay his kingdom, to which he was being borne, lying there at her feet, in this beautiful boat, across the sunlit sea.

Suddenly and without warning the sky was overcast. A squall struck the boat and tore away the sail. In the distance a huge billow—a great white wall of water—came sweeping toward their frail craft, threatening it with instant destruction. She clasped her child to her bosom, and a moment later found herself struggling in the sea, holding the child's head above the water. As she floated there, as though sustained by some unseen force, she saw in the distance a small boat approaching over the stormtossed waves. Straight toward her it came, and she had reached out her hand to grasp its side, when the rower looked back, and she saw that it was her sister. The recognition had been mutual. With a sharp movement of one oar the boat glided by, leaving her clutching at the empty air.

She felt her strength begin to fail. Despairingly she signaled with her disengaged hand; but the rower, after one mute, reproachful glance, rowed on. Mrs. Carteret's strength grew less and less. The child became heavy as lead. Herself floating in the water, as though it were her native element, she could no longer support the child. Lower and lower it sank—she was

183

powerless to save it or to accompany it— until, gasping wildly for breath, it threw up its little hands and sank, the cruel water gurgling over its head—when she awoke with a start and a chill, and lay there trembling for several minutes before she heard little Dodie in his crib, breathing heavily.

She rose softly, went to the crib, and changed the child's position to an easier one. He breathed more freely, and she went back to bed, but not to sleep.

She had tried to put aside the distressing questions raised by the discovery of her father's will and the papers accompanying it. Why should she be burdened with such a responsibility, at this late day, when the touch of time had well-nigh healed these old sores? Surely, God had put his curse not alone upon the slave, but upon the stealer of men! With other good people she had thanked Him that slavery was no more, and that those who once had borne its burden upon their consciences could stand erect and feel that they themselves were free. The weed had been cut down, but its roots remained, deeply imbedded in the soil, to spring up and trouble a new generation. Upon her weak shoulders was placed the burden of her father's weakness, her father's folly. It was left to her to acknowledge or not this shameful marriage and her sister's rights in their father's estate.

Balancing one consideration against another, she had almost decided that she might ignore this tie. To herself, Olivia Merkell—Olivia Carteret—the stigma of base birth would have meant social ostracism, social ruin, the averted face, the finger of pity or of scorn. All the traditional weight of public disapproval would have fallen upon her as the unhappy fruit of an unblessed union. To this other woman it could have had no such significance—it had been the lot of her race. To them, twenty-five years before, sexual sin had never been imputed as more than a fault. She had lost nothing by her supposed illegitimacy; she would gain nothing by the acknowledgment of her mother's marriage.

On the other hand, what would be the effect of this revelation upon Mrs. Carteret herself? To have it known that

184

her father had married a negress would only be less dreadful than to have it appear that he had committed some terrible crime. It was a crime now, by the laws of every Southern State, for white and colored persons to intermarry. She shuddered before the possibility that at some time in the future some person, none too well informed, might learn that her father had married a colored woman, and might assume that she, Olivia Carteret or her child, had sprung from this shocking alliance— a fate to which she would willingly have preferred death. No, this marriage must never be made known; the secret should remain buried forever in her own heart!

But there still remained the question of her father's property and her father's will. This woman was her father's child—of that there could be no doubt, it was written in her features no less than in her father's will. As his lawful child—of which, alas! there could also be no question—she was entitled by law to half his estate. Mrs. Carteret's problem had sunk from the realm of sentiment to that of material things, which, curiously enough, she found much more difficult. For, while the negro, by the traditions of her people, was barred from the world of sentiment, his rights of property were recognized. The question had become, with Mrs. Carteret, a question of meum and tuum. Had the girl Janet been poor, ignorant, or degraded, as might well have been her fate, Mrs. Carteret might have felt a vicarious remorse for her aunt's suppression of the papers; but fate had compensated Janet for the loss; she had been educated, she had married well, she had not suffered for lack of the money of which she had been defrauded, and did not need it now. She had a child, it is true, but this child's career would be so circumscribed by the accident of color that too much wealth would only be a source of unhappiness; to her own child, on the contrary, it would open every door of life.

It would be too lengthy a task to follow the mind and conscience of this much-tried lady in their intricate workings upon this difficult problem; for she had a mind as logical as any woman's, and a conscience which she wished to keep void of offense. She had to confront a situation involving the

185

element of race, upon which the moral standards of her people were hopelessly confused. Mrs. Carteret reached the conclusion, ere daylight dawned, that she would be silent upon the subject of her father's second marriage. Neither party had wished it known— neither Julia nor her father—and she would respect her father's wishes. To act otherwise would be to defeat his will, to make known what he had carefully concealed, and to give Janet a claim of title to one half her father's estate, while he had only meant her to have the ten thousand dollars named in the will.

By the same reasoning, she must carry out her father's will in respect to this bequest. Here there was another difficulty. The mining investment into which they had entered shortly after the birth of little Dodie had tied up so much of her property that it would have been difficult to procure ten thousand dollars immediately; while a demand for half the property at once would mean bankruptcy and ruin. Moreover, upon what ground could she offer her sister any sum of money whatever? So sudden a change of heart, after so many years of silence, would raise the presumption of some right on the part of Janet in her father's estate. Suspicion once aroused, it might be possible to trace this hidden marriage, and establish it by legal proof. The marriage once verified, the claim for half the estate could not be denied. She could not plead her father's will to the contrary, for this would be to acknowledge the suppression of the will, in itself a criminal act.

There was, however, a way of escape. This hospital which had recently been opened was the personal property of her sister's husband. Some time in the future, when their investments matured, she would present to the hospital a sum of money equal to the amount her father had meant his colored daughter to have. Thus indirectly both her father's will and her own conscience would be satisfied.

Mrs. Carteret had reached this comfortable conclusion, and was falling asleep, when her attention was again drawn by her child's breathing. She took it in her own arms and soon fell asleep.

"By the way, Olivia," said the major, when leaving the house next morning for the office, "if you have any business down town to-day, transact it this forenoon. Under no circumstances must you or Clara or the baby leave the house after midday."

"Why, what's the matter, Phil?"

"Nothing to alarm you, except that there may be a little political demonstration which may render the streets unsafe. You are not to say anything about it where the servants might hear."

"Will there be any danger for you, Phil?" she demanded with alarm.

"Not the slightest, Olivia dear. No one will be harmed; but it is best for ladies and children to stay indoors."

Mrs. Carteret's nerves were still more or less unstrung from her mental struggles of the night, and the memory of her dream came to her like a dim foreboding of misfortune. As though in sympathy with its mother's feelings, the baby did not seem as well as usual. The new nurse was by no means an ideal nurse—Mammy Jane understood the child much better. If there should be any trouble with the negroes, toward which her husband's remark seemed to point—she knew the general political situation, though not informed in regard to her husband's plans—she would like to have Mammy Jane near her, where the old nurse might be protected from danger or alarm.

With this end in view she dispatched the nurse, shortly after breakfast, to Mammy Jane's in the negro settlement on the other side of the town, with a message asking the old woman to come immediately to Mrs. Carteret's. Unfortunately, Mammy Jane had gone to visit a sick woman in the country, and was not expected to return for several hours.

# XXXII

## The Storm Breaks

THE WELLINGTON RIOT BEGAN AT THREE O'CLOCK in the afternoon of a day as fair as was ever selected for a deed of darkness. The sky was clear, except for a few light clouds that floated, white and feathery, high in air, like distant islands in a sapphire sea. A salt-laden breeze from the ocean a few miles away lent a crisp sparkle to the air.

At three o'clock sharp the streets were filled, as if by magic, with armed white men. The negroes, going about, had noted, with uneasy curiosity, that the stores and places of business, many of which closed at noon, were unduly late in opening for the afternoon, though no one suspected the reason for the delay; but at three o'clock every passing colored man was ordered, by the first white man he met, to throw up his hands. If he complied, he was searched, more or less roughly, for firearms, and then warned to get off the street. When he met another group of white men the scene was repeated. The man thus summarily held up seldom encountered more than two groups before disappearing across lots to his own home or some convenient hiding-place. If he resisted any demand of those who halted him—But the records of the day are historical; they may be found in the newspapers of the following date, but they are more firmly engraved upon the hearts and memories of the people of Wellington. For many months there were negro families in the town whose children screamed with fear and ran to their mothers for protection at the mere sight of a white man.

Dr. Miller had received a call, about one o'clock, to attend a case at the house of a well-to-do colored farmer, who lived

188

some three or four miles from the town, upon the very road, by the way, along which Miller had driven so furiously a few weeks before, in the few hours that intervened before Sandy Campbell would probably have been burned at the stake. The drive to his patient's home, the necessary inquiries, the filling of the prescription from his own medicine-case, which he carried along with him, the little friendly conversation about the weather and the crops, and, the farmer being an intelligent and thinking man, the inevitable subject of the future of their race—these, added to the return journey, occupied at least two hours of Miller's time.

As he neared the town on his way back, he saw ahead of him half a dozen men and women approaching, with fear written in their faces, in every degree from apprehension to terror. Women were weeping and children crying, and all were going as fast as seemingly lay in their power, looking behind now and then as if pursued by some deadly enemy. At sight of Miller's buggy they made a dash for cover, disappearing, like a covey of frightened partridges, in the underbrush along the road.

Miller pulled up his horse and looked after them in startled wonder.

"What on earth can be the matter?" he muttered, struck with a vague feeling of alarm. A psychologist, seeking to trace the effects of slavery upon the human mind, might find in the South many a curious illustration of this curse, abiding long after the actual physical bondage had terminated. In the olden time the white South labored under the constant fear of negro insurrections. Knowing that they themselves, if in the negroes' place would have risen in the effort to throw off the yoke, all their reiterated theories of negro subordination and inferiority could not remove that lurking fear, founded upon the obscure consciousness that the slaves ought to have risen. Conscience, it has been said, makes cowards of us all. There was never, on the continent of America, a successful slave revolt, nor one which lasted more than a few hours, or resulted in the loss of more than a few white lives; yet never was the planter quite free from the fear that there might be one.

On the other hand, the slave had before his eyes always the fear of the master. There were good men, according to their lights—according to their training and environment— among the Southern slaveholders, who treated their slaves kindly, as slaves, from principle, because they recognized the claims of humanity, even under the dark skin of a human chattel. There was many a one who protected or pampered his negroes, as the case might be, just as a man fondles his dog—because they were his; they were a part of his estate, an integral part of the entity of property and person which made up the aristocrat; but with all this kindness, there was always present, in the consciousness of the lowest slave, the knowledge that he was in his master's power, and that he could make no effectual protest against the abuse of that authority. There was also the knowledge, among those who could think at all, that the best of masters was himself a slave to a system, which hampered his movements but scarcely less than those of his bondmen.

When, therefore, Miller saw these men and women scampering into the bushes, he divined, with this slumbering race consciousness which years of culture had not obliterated, that there was some race trouble on foot. His intuition did not long remain unsupported. A black head was cautiously protruded from the shrubbery, and a black voice— if such a description be allowable—addressed him:—

"Is dat you, Doctor Miller?"

"Yes. Who are you, and what's the trouble?"

"What's de trouble, suh? Why, all hell's broke loose in town yonder. De white folks is rise 'gins' de niggers, an' say they 're gwine to kill every nigger they can lay hands on."

Miller's heart leaped to his throat, as he thought of his wife and child. This story was preposterous; it could not be true, and yet there must be something in it. He tried to question his informant, but the man was so overcome with excitement and fear that Miller saw clearly that he must go farther for information. He had read in the Morning Chronicle, a few days before, the obnoxious editorial quoted from the Afro-American

190

Banner, and had noted the comment upon it by the white editor. He had felt, as at the time of its first publication, that the editorial was ill-advised. It could do no good, and was calculated to arouse the animosity of those whose friendship, whose tolerance, at least, was necessary and almost indispensable to the colored people. They were living at the best, in a sort of armed neutrality with the whites; such a publication, however serviceable elsewhere, could have no other effect in Wellington than to endanger this truce and defeat the hope of a possible future friendship. The right of free speech entitled Barber to publish it; a larger measure of common-sense would have made him withhold it. Whether it was the republication of this article that had stirred up anew the sleeping dogs of race prejudice and whetted their thirst for blood, he could not yet tell; but at any rate, there was mischief on foot.

"For God's sake, doctor, don't go no closer to dat town," pleaded his informant, "or you'll be killed sho'. Come on wid us, suh, an' tek care of yo'self. We're gwine to hide in de swamps till dis thing is over!"

"God, man!" exclaimed Miller, urging his horse forward, "my wife and child are in the town!"

Fortunately, there were no patients in the hospital—if there should be anything in this story. To one unfamiliar with Southern life, it might have seemed impossible that these good Christian people, who thronged the churches on Sunday, and wept over the sufferings of the lowly Nazarene, could be hungering and thirsting for the blood of their fellow men; but Miller cherished no such delusion. He knew the history of his country; he had the threatened lynching of Sandy Campbell vividly in mind; and he was fully persuaded that to race prejudice, once roused, any horror was possible.

As he neared the town, dashing forward at the top of his horse's speed, he heard his voice called in a loud and agitated tone, and, glancing around him, saw a familiar form standing by the roadside, gesticulating vehemently.

He drew up the horse suddenly. The colored lawyer,

191

Watson, came up to the buggy. That he was laboring under great and unusual excitement was quite apparent from his pale face and frightened air.

"What's the matter, Watson?" demanded Miller, hoping now to obtain some reliable information.

"Matter!" exclaimed the other. "Everything's the matter! The white people are up in arms. They have disarmed the colored people, killing half a dozen in the process, and wounding as many more. They have forced the mayor and aldermen to resign, have formed a provisional city government and have ordered me and half a dozen other fellows to leave town in forty-eight hours, under pain of sudden death. As they seem to mean it, I shall not stay so long. Fortunately, my wife and children are away. I knew you were out here, however, and I thought I'd come out and wait for you, so that we might talk the matter over. I don't imagine they mean you any harm, personally, because you tread on nobody's toes; but you're too valuable a man for the race to lose, so I thought I'd give you warning. I shall want to sell you my property, too, at a bargain. For I'm worth too much to my family to dream of ever attempting to live here again."

"Have you seen anything of my wife and child?" asked Miller, intent upon the danger to which they might be exposed.

"No; I didn't go to the house. I inquired at the drugstore and found out where you had gone. You needn't fear for them—it is not a war on women and children."

"War of any kind is always hardest on the women and children," returned Miller; "I must hurry on and see that mine are safe."

"They'll not carry the war so far into Africa as that," returned Watson; "but I never saw anything like it. Yesterday I had a hundred white friends in the town, or thought I had— men who spoke pleasantly to me on the street, and sometimes gave me their hands to shake. Not one of them said to me to-day: 'Watson, stay at home this afternoon.' I might have been killed, like any one of half a dozen others who have bit the dust, for any word that one of my 'friends' had said to warn

192

me. When the race cry is started in this neck of the woods, friendship, religion, humanity, reason, all shrivel up like dry leaves in a raging furnace."

The buggy, into which Watson had climbed, was meanwhile rapidly nearing the town.

"I think I'll leave you here, Miller," said Watson, as they approached the outskirts, "and make my way home by a roundabout path, as I should like to get there unmolested. Home!—a beautiful word that, isn't it, for an exiled wanderer? It might not be well, either, for us to be seen together. If you put the hood of your buggy down, and sit well back in the shadow, you may be able to reach home without interruption; but avoid the main streets. I'll see you again this evening, if we're both alive, and I can reach you; for my time is short. A committee are to call in the morning to escort me to the train. I am to be dismissed from the community with public honors."

Watson was climbing down from the buggy, when a small party of men were seen approaching, and big Josh Green, followed by several other resolute-looking colored men, came up and addressed them.

"Dr. Miller," cried Green, "Mr. Watson—we're lookin' for a leader. De white folks are killin' de niggers, an' we ain't gwine to stan' up an' be shot down like dogs. We're gwine to defen' you' lives, an' we ain't gwine to run away from no place where we've got a right to be; an' woe be to de white man what lays hands on us! There's two niggers in dis town to every white man, an' if we've got to be killed, we'll take some white folks 'long wid us, as sho' as there's a God in heaven—as I s'pose there is, though He must be asleep, or busy somewhere else to-day. Will you-all come an' lead us?"

"Gentlemen," said Watson, "what is the use? The negroes will not back you up. They haven't the arms, nor the moral courage, nor the leadership."

"We'll git de arms, an' we'll git de courage, if you'll come an' lead us! We wants leaders—dat's why we come to you!"

"What's the use?" returned Watson despairingly. "The odds are too heavy. I've been ordered out of town; if I stayed, I'd be shot on sight, unless I had a body-guard around me."

"We'll be yo' body-guard!" shouted half a dozen voices.

"And when my bodyguard was shot, what then? I have a wife and children. It is my duty to live for them. If I died, I should get no glory and no reward, and my family would be reduced to beggary—to which they'll soon be near enough as it is. This affair will blow over in a day or two. The white people will be ashamed of themselves to-morrow, and apprehensive of the consequences for some time to come. Keep quiet, boys, and trust in God. You won't gain anything by resistance."

" 'God helps dem dat helps demselves,' " returned Josh stoutly. "If Mr. Watson won't lead us, will you, Dr. Miller?" said the spokesman, turning to the doctor.

For Miller it was an agonizing moment. He was no coward. Every manly instinct urged him to go forward and take up the cause of these leaderless people, and if need be, to defend their lives and their rights with his own—but to what end?

"Listen, men," he said. "We would only be throwing our lives away. Suppose we made a determined stand and won a temporary victory. By morning every train every boat, every road leading into Wellington, would be crowded with white men—as they probably will be any way—with arms in their hands, curses on their lips, and vengeance in their hearts. In the minds of those who make and administer the laws, we have no standing in the court of conscience. They would kill us in the fight, or they would hang us afterwards—one way or another, we should be doomed. I should like to lead you; I should like to arm every colored man in this town, and have them stand firmly in line, not for attack, but for defense; but if I attempted it, and they should stand by me, which is questionable—for I have met them fleeing from the town—my life would pay the forfeit. Alive, I may be of some use to you, and you are welcome to my life in that way—I am giving it freely. Dead, I should be a mere lump of carrion. Who remembers even the names of those who have been done to death in the Southern States for the past twenty years?"

"I 'members de name of one of 'em," said Josh, "an' I

194

'members de name of de man dat killed him, an' I s'pec' his time is mighty nigh come."

"My advice is not heroic, but I think it is wise. In this riot we are placed as we should be in a war: we have no territory, no base of supplies, no organization, no outside sympathy—we stand in the position of a race, in a case like this, without money and without friends. Our time will come—the time when we can command respect for our rights; but it is not yet in sight. Give it up, boys, and wait. Good may come of this, after all."

Several of the men wavered, and looked irresolute.

"I reckon that's all so, doctor," returned Josh, "an', de way you put it, I don't blame you nor Mr. Watson; but all dem reasons ain't got no weight wid me. I'm gwine in dat town, an' if any white man 'sturbs me, dere'll be trouble—dere'll be double trouble—I feels it in my bones!"

"Remember your old mother, Josh," said Miller.

"Yes, suh, I'll 'member her; dat's all I can do now. I don't need to wait for her no mo', for she died dis mornin'. I'd like to see her buried, suh, but I may not have de chance. If I gits killed, will you do me a favor?"

"Yes, Josh; what is it?"

"If I should git laid out in dis commotion dat's gwine on, will you collect my wages from yo' brother, and see dat de ole 'oman is put away right?"

"Yes, of course."

"Wid a nice coffin, an' a nice funeral?"

"Yes."

"All right, suh! If I don't live to do it, I'll know it'll be 'tended to right. Now we're gwine out to de cotton compress, an' git a lot of colored men together, an' if de white folks disturbs me, I shouldn't be surprised if there'd be a mix-up—an' if there is me an one white man I'll stan' before de judgment throne of God dis day; an' it won't be me what'll be 'feared of de judgment. Come along, boys! These gentlemen may have somethin' to live for; but as for my part, I'd rather be a dead nigger any day than a live dog!"

195

# XXXIII

# Into the Lion's Jaws

THE PARTY UNDER JOSH'S LEADERSHIP MOVED OFF down the road. Miller, while entirely convinced that he had acted wisely in declining to accompany them, was yet conscious of a distinct feeling of shame and envy that he, too, did not feel impelled to throw away his life in a hopeless struggle.

Watson left the buggy and disappeared by a path at the roadside. Miller drove rapidly forward. After entering the town, he passed several small parties of white men, but escaped scrutiny by sitting well back in his buggy, the presumption being that a well-dressed man with a good horse and buggy was white. Torn with anxiety, he reached home at about four o'clock. Driving the horse into the yard, he sprang down from the buggy and hastened to the house, which he found locked, front and rear.

A repeated rapping brought no response. At length he broke a window, and entered the house like a thief.

"Janet, Janet!" he called in alarm, "where are you? It is only I—Will!"

There was no reply. He ran from room to room, only to find them all empty. Again he called his wife's name, and was about rushing from the house, when a muffled voice came faintly to his ear—

"Is dat you, Doctor Miller?"

"Yes. Who are you, and where are my wife and child?"

He was looking around in perplexity, when the door of a low closet under the kitchen sink was opened from within, and a woolly head was cautiously protruded.

"Are you sho' dat's you, doctor?"

"Yes, Sally; where are"—

"An' not some white man come to burn down de house an' kill all de niggers?"

"No, Sally, it's me all right. Where is my wife? Where is my child?"

"They went over to see Miss Butler 'long 'bout two o'clock, befo' dis fuss broke out, suh. Oh, Lawdy, Lawdy, suh! Is all de cullud folks been killed 'cep'n' me an' you, suh? For de Lawd's sake, suh, you won' let 'em kill me, will you, suh? I'll work for you for nothin', suh, all my born days, if you'll save my life, suh!"

"Calm yourself, Sally. You'll be safe enough if you stay right here, I've no doubt. They'll not harm women—of that I'm sure enough, although I haven't yet got the bearings of this deplorable affair. Stay here and look after the house. I must find my wife and child!"

The distance across the city to the home of the Mrs. Butler whom his wife had gone to visit was exactly one mile. Though Miller had a good horse in front of him, he was two hours in reaching his destination. Never will the picture of that ride fade from his memory. In his dreams he repeats it night after night, and sees the sights that wounded his eyes, and feels the thoughts—the haunting spirits of the thoughts—that tore his heart as he rode through hell to find those whom he was seeking.

For a short distance he saw nothing, and made rapid progress. As he turned the first corner, his horse shied at the dead body of a negro, lying huddled up in the collapse which marks sudden death. What Miller shuddered at was not so much the thought of death, to the sight of which his profession had accustomed him, as the suggestion of what it signified. He had taken with allowance the wild statement of the fleeing fugitives. Watson, too, had been greatly excited, and Josh Green's group were desperate men, as much liable to be misled by their courage as the others by their fears; but here was proof that murder had been done—and his wife and children were in the town. Distant shouts, and the sound of firearms, increased his alarm. He struck his horse with the whip, and dashed on toward the heart of the city, which he must traverse in order to reach Janet and the child.

At the next corner lay the body of another man, with the red blood oozing from a ghastly wound in the forehead. The negroes seemed to have been killed, as the band plays in circus parades, at the street intersections, where the example would be most effective. Miller, with a wild leap of the heart, had barely passed this gruesome spectacle, when a sharp voice commanded him to halt, and emphasized the order by covering him with a revolver. Forgetting the prudence he had preached to others, he had raised his whip to strike the horse, when several hands seized the bridle.

"Come down, you damn fool," growled an authoritative voice. "don't you see we're in earnest? Do you want to get killed?"

"Why should I come down?" asked Miller.

"Because we've ordered you to come down! This is the white people's day, and when they order, a nigger must obey. We're going to search you for weapons."

"Search away. You'll find nothing but a case of surgeon's tools, which I'm more than likely to need before this day is over, from all indications."

"No matter; we'll make sure of it! That's what we're here for. Come down, if you don't want to be pulled down!"

Miller stepped down from his buggy. His interlocutor, who made no effort at disguise, was a clerk in a drygoods store where Miller bought most of his family and hospital supplies. He made no sign of recognition, however, and Miller claimed no acquaintance. This man, who had for several years emptied Miller's pockets in the course of more or less legitimate trade, now went through them, aided by another man, more rapidly than ever before, the searchers convincing themselves that Miller carried no deadly weapon upon his person. Meanwhile, a third ransacked the buggy with like result. Miller recognized several others of the party, who made not the slightest attempt at disguise, though no names were called by any one.

"Where are you going?" demanded the leader.

"I am looking for my wife and child," replied Miller.

"Well, run along, and keep them out of the streets when you find them; and keep your hands out of this affair, if you wish to live in this town, which from now on will be a white man's town, as you niggers will be pretty firmly convinced before night."

Miller drove on as swiftly as might be.

At the next corner he was stopped again. In the white man who held him up, Miller recognized a neighbor of his own. After a short detention and a perfunctory search, the white man remarked apologetically:—

"Sorry to have had to trouble you, doctor, but them's the orders. It ain't men like you that we're after, but the vicious and criminal class of niggers."

Miller smiled bitterly as he urged his horse forward. He was quite well aware that the virtuous citizen who had stopped him had only a few weeks before finished a term in the penitentiary, to which he had been sentenced for stealing. Miller knew that he could have bought all the man owned for fifty dollars, and his soul for as much more.

A few rods farther on, he came near running over the body of a wounded man who lay groaning by the wayside. Every professional instinct urged him to stop and offer aid to the sufferer; but the uncertainty concerning his wife and child proved a stronger motive and urged him resistlessly forward. Here and there the ominous sound of firearms was audible. He might have thought this merely a part of the show, like the "powder play" of the Arabs, but for the bloody confirmation of its earnestness which had already assailed his vision. Somewhere in this seething caldron of unrestrained passions were his wife and child, and he must hurry on.

His progress was painfully slow. Three times he was stopped and searched. More than once his way was barred, and he was ordered to turn back, each such occasion requiring a detour which consumed many minutes. The man who last stopped him was a well-known Jewish merchant. A Jew— God of Moses!—had so far forgotten twenty centuries of history as to join in the persecution of another oppressed race! When almost reduced to despair by these innumerable delays, he perceived, coming toward him, Mr. Ellis, the sub-editor of the Morning Chronicle. Miller had just been stopped and questioned again, and Ellis came up as he was starting once more upon his endless ride.

"Dr. Miller," said Ellis kindly, "it is dangerous for you on the streets. Why tempt the danger?"

"I am looking for my wife and child," returned Miller in desperation. "They are somewhere in this town—I don't know where—and I must find them."

Ellis had been horror-stricken by the tragedy of the afternoon, the wholly superfluous slaughter of a harmless people, whom a show of force would have been quite sufficient to overawe. Elaborate explanations were afterwards given for these murders, which were said, perhaps truthfully, not to have been premeditated, and many regrets were expressed. The young man had been surprised, quite as much as the negroes themselves, at the ferocity displayed. His own thoughts and feelings were attuned to anything but slaughter. Only that morning he had received a perfumed note, calling his attention to what the writer described as a very noble deed of his, and requesting him to call that evening and receive the writer's thanks. Had he known that Miss Pemberton, several weeks after their visit to the Sound, had driven out again to the hotel and made some inquiries among the servants, he might have understood better the meaning of this missive. When Miller spoke of his wife and child, some subtle thread of suggestion coupled the note with Miller's plight.

"I'll go with you, Dr. Miller," he said, "if you'll permit me. In my company you will not be disturbed."

He took a seat in Miller's buggy, after which it was not molested.

Neither of them spoke. Miller was sick at heart; he could have wept with grief, even had the welfare of his own dear

200

ones not been involved in this regrettable affair. With prophetic instinct he foresaw the hatreds to which this day would give birth; the long years of constraint and distrust which would still further widen the breach between two peoples whom fate had thrown together in one community.

There was nothing for Ellis to say. In his heart he could not defend the deeds of this day. The petty annoyances which the whites had felt at the spectacle of a few negroes in office; the not unnatural resentment of a proud people at what had seemed to them a presumptuous freedom of speech and lack of deference on the part of their inferiors—these things, which he knew were to be made the excuse for overturning the city government, he realized full well were no sort of justification for the wholesale murder or other horrors which might well ensue before the day was done. He could not approve the acts of his own people; neither could he, to a negro, condemn them. Hence he was silent.

"Thank you, Mr. Ellis," exclaimed Miller, when they had reached the house where he expected to find his wife. "This is the place where I was going. I am—under a great obligation to you."

"Not at all, Dr. Miller. I need not tell you how much I regret this deplorable affair."

Ellis went back down the street. Fastening his horse to the fence, Miller sprang forward to find his wife and child. They would certainly be there, for no colored woman would be foolhardy enough to venture on the streets after the riot had broken out.

As he drew nearer, he felt a sudden apprehension. The house seemed strangely silent and deserted. The doors were closed, and the venetian blinds shut tightly. Even a dog which had appeared slunk timidly back under the house, instead of barking vociferously according to the usual habit of his kind.

201

# XXXIV

# The Valley of the Shadow

MILLER KNOCKED AT THE DOOR. THERE WAS NO response. He went round to the rear of the house. The dog had slunk behind the woodpile. Miller knocked again, at the back door, and, receiving no reply, called aloud.

"Mrs. Butler! It is I, Dr. Miller. Is my wife here?"

The slats of a near-by blind opened cautiously.

"Is it really you, Dr. Miller?"

"Yes, Mrs. Butler. I am looking for my wife and child— are they here?"

"No, sir; she became alarmed about you, soon after the shooting commenced, and I could not keep her. She left for home half an hour ago. It is coming on dusk, and she and the child are so near white that she did not expect to be molested."

"Which way did she go?"

"She meant to go by the main street. She thought it would be less dangerous than the back streets. I tried to get her to stay here, but she was frantic about you, and nothing I could say would keep her. Is the riot almost over, Dr. Miller? Do you think they will murder us all, and burn down our houses?"

"God knows," replied Miller, with a groan. "But I must find her, if I lose my own life in the attempt."

Surely, he thought, Janet would be safe. The white people of Wellington were not savages; or at least their temporary reversion to savagery would not go as far as to include violence to delicate women and children. Then there flashed into his mind Josh Green's story of his "silly" mother, who for twenty years had walked the earth as a child, as the result of one night's terror, and his heart sank within him.

Miller realized that his buggy, by attracting attention, had been a hindrance rather than a help in his progress across the city. In order to follow his wife, he must practically retrace his steps over the very route he had come. Night was falling. It would be easier to cross the town on foot. In the dusk his own color, slight in the daytime, would not attract attention, and by dodging in the shadows he might avoid those who might wish to intercept him. But he must reach Janet and the boy at any risk. He had not been willing to throw his life away hopelessly, but he would cheerfully have sacrificed it for those whom he loved.

He had gone but a short distance, and had not yet reached the centre of mob activity, when he intercepted a band of negro laborers from the cotton compress, with big Josh Green at their head.

"Hello, doctor!" cried Josh, "does you wan' to join us?"

"I'm looking for my wife and child, Josh. They're somewhere in this den of murderers. Have any of you seen them?"

No one had seen them.

"You men are running a great risk," said Miller. "You are rushing on to certain death."

"Well, suh, maybe we is; but we're gwine to die fightin'. They say de white folks is gwine to burn all de cullud schools an' churches, an' kill all de niggers they can ketch. Dey're gwine to burn yo' new hospital, if somebody don't stop 'em."

"Josh—men—you are throwing your lives away. It is a fever; it will wear off to-morrow, or to-night. They'll not burn the schoolhouses, nor the hospital—they are not such fools, for they benefit the community; and they'll only kill the colored people who resist them. Every one of you with a gun or a pistol carries his death warrant in his own hand. I'd rather see the hospital burn than have one of you lose his life. Resistance only makes the matter worse—the odds against you are too long."

"Things can't be any worse, doctor," replied one of the crowd sturdily. "A gun is mo' dangerous to de man in front of it dan to de man behin' it. Dey're gwine to kill us anyhow; an' we're tired—we read de newspapers— an' we're tired of being shot down like dogs, widout judge or jury. We'd rather die fightin' dan be stuck like pigs in a pen!"

"God help you!" said Miller. "As for me, I must find my wife and child."

"Good-by, doctor," cried Josh, brandishing a huge knife. " 'Member 'bout de ole woman, if you lives thru dis. Don't forget de headboard an' de footboard, an' a silver plate on de coffin, if There's money enough."

They went their way, and Miller hurried on. They might resist attack; he thought it extremely unlikely that they would begin it; but he knew perfectly well that the mere knowledge that some of the negroes contemplated resistance would only further inflame the infuriated whites. The colored men might win a momentary victory, though it was extremely doubtful; and they would as surely reap the harvest later on. The qualities which in a white man would win the applause of the world would in a negro be taken as the marks of savagery. So thoroughly diseased was public opinion in matters of race that the negro who died for the common rights of humanity might look for no need of admiration or glory. At such a time, in the white man's eyes, a negro's courage would be mere desperation; his love of liberty, a mere animal dislike of restraint. Every finer human instinct would be interpreted in terms of savagery. Or, if forced to admire, they would none the less repress. They would applaud his courage while they stretched his neck, or carried off the fragments of his mangled body as souvenirs, in much the same way that savages preserve the scalps or eat the hearts of their enemies.

But concern for the fate of Josh and his friends occupied only a secondary place in Miller's mind for the moment. His wife and child were somewhere ahead of him. He pushed on. He had covered about a quarter of a mile more, and far down the street could see the signs of greater animation, when he came upon the body of a woman Lying upon the sidewalk. In the dusk he had almost stumbled over it, and his heart came up in his mouth. A second glance revealed that it could not be his

204

wife. It was a fearful portent, however, of what her fate might be. The "war" had reached the women and children. Yielding to a professional instinct, he stooped, and saw that the prostrate form was that of old Aunt Jane Letlow. She was not yet quite dead, and as Miller, with a tender touch, placed her head in a more comfortable position, her lips moved with a last lingering flicker of consciousness:—

"Comin', missis, comin'!"

Mammy Jane had gone to join the old mistress upon whose memory her heart was fixed; and yet not all her reverence for her old mistress, nor all her deference to the whites, nor all their friendship for her, had been able to save her from this raging devil of race hatred which momentarily possessed the town.

Perceiving that he could do no good, Miller hastened onward, sick at heart. Whenever he saw a party of white men approaching—these brave reformers never went singly—he sought concealment in the shadow of a tree or the shrubbery in some yard until they had passed. He had covered about two thirds of the distance homeward when his eyes fell upon a group beneath a lamp-post, at sight of which he turned pale with horror, and rushed forward with a terrible cry.

# XXXV

# "Mine Enemy, Oh Mine Enemy!"

THE PROCEEDINGS OF THE DAY—PLANNED originally as a "demonstration," dignified subsequently as a "revolution," under any name the culmination of the conspiracy formed by Carteret and his colleagues—had by seven o'clock in the afternoon developed into a murderous riot. Crowds of white men and half-grown boys, drunk with whiskey or with license, raged through the streets, beating, chasing, or killing any negro so unfortunate as to fall into their hands. Why any particular negro was assailed, no one stopped to inquire; it was merely a white mob thirsting for black blood, with no more conscience or discrimination than would be exercised by a wolf in a sheepfold. It was race against race, the whites against the negroes; and it was a one-sided affair, for until Josh Green got together his body of armed men, no effective resistance had been made by any colored person, and the individuals who had been killed had so far left no marks upon the enemy by which they might be remembered.

"Kill the niggers!" rang out now and then through the dusk, and far down the street and along the intersecting thoroughfares distant voices took up the ominous refrain—"Kill the niggers! Kill the damned niggers!"

Now, not a dark face had been seen on the street for half an hour, until the group of men headed by Josh made their appearance in the negro quarter. Armed with guns and axes, they presented quite a formidable appearance as they made their way toward the new hospital, near which stood a schoolhouse and a large church, both used by the colored people. They did not reach their destination without having

206

met a number of white men, singly or in twos or threes; and the rumor spread with incredible swiftness that the negroes in turn were up in arms, determined to massacre all the whites and burn the town. Some of the whites became alarmed, and recognizing the power of the negroes, if armed and conscious of their strength, were impressed by the immediate necessity of overpowering and overawing them. Others, with appetites already whetted by slaughter, saw a chance, welcome rather than not, of shedding more black blood. Spontaneously the white mob flocked toward the hospital, where rumor had it that a large body of desperate negroes, breathing threats of blood and fire, had taken a determined stand.

It had been Josh's plan merely to remain quietly and peaceably in the neighborhood of the little group of public institutions, molesting no one, unless first attacked, and merely letting the white people see that they meant to protect their own; but so rapidly did the rumor spread, and so promptly did the white people act, that by the time Josh and his supporters had reached the top of the rising ground where the hospital stood, a crowd of white men much more numerous than their own party were following them at a short distance.

Josh, with the eye of a general, perceived that some of his party were becoming a little nervous, and decided that they would feel safer behind shelter.

"I reckon we better go inside the hospital, boys," he exclaimed. "Then we'll be behind brick walls, an' dem other fellows'll be outside, an' if there's any fightin', we'll have de bes' show. We ain't gwine to do no shootin' till we're pestered, an' dey'll be less likely to pester us if they can't git at us widout runnin' some risk. Come along in! Be men! De govenor or de President is gwine to send soldiers to stop these gwines-on, an' meantime we can keep dem white devils from burnin' down our hospitals an' church-houses. When they comes an' finds out dat we jes' means to protect you' property, dey'll go 'long 'bout their own business. Or, if they wants a scrap, they can have it! Come along, boys!"

Jerry Letlow, who had kept out of sight during the day, had started out, after night had set in, to find Major Carteret. Jerry was very much afraid. The events of the day had filled him with terror. Whatever the limitations of Jerry's mind or character may have been, Jerry had a keen appreciation of the danger to the negroes when they came in conflict with the whites, and he had no desire to imperil his own skin. He valued his life for his own sake, and not for any altruistic theory that it might be of service to others. In other words, Jerry was something of a coward. He had kept in hiding all day, but finding, toward evening, that the riot did not abate, and fearing, from the rumors which came to his ears, that all the negroes would be exterminated, he had set out, somewhat desperately, to try to find his white patron and protector. He had been cautious to avoid meeting any white men, and, anticipating no danger from those of his own race, went toward the party which he saw approaching, whose path would cross his own. When they were only a few yards apart, Josh took a step forward and caught Jerry by the arm.

"Come along, Jerry, we need you! Here's another man, boys. Come on now, and fight for yo' race!"

In vain Jerry protested. "I don't wan' to fight," he howled. "De white folks ain't gwine to pester me; dey're my friends. Turn me loose—Turn me loose, or we all gwine to git killed!"

The party paid no attention to Jerry's protestations. Indeed, with the crowd of whites following behind, they were simply considering the question of a position from which they could most effectively defend themselves and the building which they imagined to be threatened. If Josh had released his grip of Jerry, that worthy could easily have escaped from the crowd; but Josh maintained his hold almost mechanically, and, in the confusion, Jerry found himself swept with the rest into the hospital, the doors of which were promptly barricaded with the heavier pieces of furniture, and the windows manned by several men each, Josh, with the instinct of a born commander, posting his forces so that they could cover with their guns all the approaches to the building. Jerry still continuing to make

208

himself troublesome, Josh, in a moment of impatience, gave him a terrific box on the ear, which stretched him out upon the floor unconscious.

"Shut up," he said; "if you can't stan' up like a man keep still, and don't interfere wid men what will fight!"

The hospital, when Josh and his men took possession, had been found deserted. Fortunately there were no patients for that day, except one or two convalescents, and these, with the attendants, had joined the exodus of the colored people from the town.

A white man advanced from the crowd without toward the main entrance to the hospital. Big Josh, looking out from a window, grasped his gun more firmly, as his eyes fell upon the man who had murdered his father and darkened his mother's life. Mechanically he raised his rifle, but lowered it as the white man lifted up his hand as a sign that he wished to speak.

"You niggers," called Captain McBane loudly—it was that worthy—"you niggers are courtin' death, an' you won't have to court her but a minute or two mo' befo' she'll have you. If you surrender and give up your arms, you'll be dealt with leniently—you may get off with the chain-gang or the penitentiary. If you resist, you'll be shot like dogs."

"Dat's no news, Mr. White Man," replied Josh, appearing boldly at the window. "We're used to being treated like dogs by men like you. If you white people will go 'long an' tend to yo' own business an' let us alone, we'll tend to our'n. You've got guns, an' we've got jest as much right to carry 'em as you have. Lay down yours, an' we'll lay down our'n— we didn't take 'em up first; but we ain't gwine to let you burn down you' churches an' schoolhouses, or dis hospital, an' we ain't comin' out of dis house, where we ain't disturbin' nobody, for you to shoot us down or send us to jail. You hear me!"

"All right," responded McBane. "You've had fair warning. Your blood be on your"—

His speech was interrupted by a shot from the crowd, which splintered the window-casing close to Josh's head. This was followed by half a dozen other shots, which were replied

209

to, almost simultaneously, by a volley from within, by which one of the attacking party was killed and another wounded.

This roused the mob to frenzy.

"Vengeance! vengeance!" they yelled. "Kill the niggers!"

A negro had killed a white man—the unpardonable sin, admitting neither excuse, justification, nor extenuation. From time immemorial it had been bred in the Southern white consciousness, and in the negro consciousness also, for that matter, that the person of a white man was sacred from the touch of a negro, no matter what the provocation. A dozen colored men lay dead in the streets of Wellington, inoffensive people, slain in cold blood because they had been bold enough to question the authority of those who had assailed them or frightened enough to flee when they had been ordered to stand still; but their lives counted nothing against that of a riotous white man, who had courted death by attacking a body of armed men.

The crowd, too, surrounding the hospital, had changed somewhat in character. The men who had acted as leaders in the early afternoon, having accomplished their purpose of overturning the local administration and establishing a provisional government of their own, had withdrawn from active participation in the rioting, deeming the negroes already sufficiently overawed to render unlikely any further trouble from that source. Several of the ringleaders had indeed begun to exert themselves to prevent further disorder, or any loss of property, the possibility of which had become apparent; but those who set in motion the forces of evil cannot always control them afterwards. The baser element of the white population, recruited from the wharves and the saloons, was now predominant.

Captain McBane was the only one of the revolutionary committee who had remained with the mob, not with any purpose to restore or preserve order, but because he found the company and the occasion entirely congenial. He had had no opportunity, at least no tenable excuse, to kill or maim a negro since the termination of his contract with the state for convicts,

210

and this occasion had awakened a dormant appetite for these diversions. We are all puppets in the hands of Fate, and seldom see the strings that move us. McBane had lived a life of violence and cruelty. As a man sows, so shall he reap. In works of fiction, such men are sometimes converted. More often, in real life, they do not change their natures until they are converted into dust. One does well to distrust a tamed tiger.

On the outskirts of the crowd a few of the better class, or at least of the better clad, were looking on. The double volley described had already been fired, when the number of these was augmented by the arrival of Major Carteret and Mr. Ellis, who had just come from the Chronicle office, where the next day's paper had been in hasty preparation. They pushed their way towards the front of the crowd.

"This must be stopped, Ellis," said Carteret. "They are burning houses and killing women and children. Old Jane, good old Mammy Jane, who nursed my wife at her bosom, and has waited on her and my child within a few weeks, was killed only a few rods from my house, to which she was evidently fleeing for protection. It must have been by accident—I cannot believe that any white man in town would be dastard enough to commit such a deed intentionally! I would have defended her with my own life! We must try to stop this thing!"

"Easier said than done," returned Ellis. "It is in the fever stage, and must burn itself out. We shall be lucky if it does not burn the town out. Suppose the negroes should also take a hand at the burning? We have advised the people to put the negroes down, and they are doing the job thoroughly."

"My God!" replied the other, with a gesture of impatience, as he continued to elbow his way through the crowd; "I meant to keep them in their places—I did not intend wholesale murder and arson."

Carteret, having reached the front of the mob, made an effort to gain their attention.

"Gentlemen!" he cried in his loudest tones. His voice, unfortunately, was neither loud nor piercing.

"Kill the niggers!" clamored the mob.

211

"Gentlemen, I implore you"—

The crash of a dozen windows, broken by stones and pistol shots, drowned his voice.

"Gentlemen!" he shouted; "this is murder, it is madness; it is a disgrace to our city, to our state, to our civilization!"

"That's right!" replied several voices. The mob had recognized the speaker. "It is a disgrace, and we'll not put up with it a moment longer. Burn 'em out! Hurrah for Major Carteret, the champion of 'white supremacy'! Three cheers for the Morning Chronicle and 'no nigger domination'!"

"Hurrah, hurrah, hurrah!" yelled the crowd.

In vain the baffled orator gesticulated and shrieked in the effort to correct the misapprehension. Their oracle had spoken; not hearing what he said, they assumed it to mean encouragement and cooperation. Their present course was but the logical outcome of the crusade which the Morning Chronicle had preached, in season and out of season, for many months. When Carteret had spoken, and the crowd had cheered him, they felt that they had done all that courtesy required, and he was good-naturedly elbowed aside while they proceeded with the work in hand, which was now to drive out the negroes from the hospital and avenge the killing of their comrade.

Some brought hay, some kerosene, and others wood from a pile which had been thrown into a vacant lot near by. Several safe ways of approach to the building were discovered, and the combustibles placed and fired. The flames, soon gaining a foothold, leaped upward, catching here and there at the exposed woodwork, and licking the walls hungrily with long tongues of flame.

Meanwhile a desultory firing was kept up from the outside, which was replied to scatteringly from within the hospital. Those inside were either not good marksmen, or excitement had spoiled their aim. If a face appeared at a window, a dozen pistol shots from the crowd sought the spot immediately.

Higher and higher leaped the flames. Suddenly from one of the windows sprang a black figure, waving a white

212

handkerchief. It was Jerry Letlow. Regaining consciousness after the effect of Josh's blow had subsided, Jerry had kept quiet and watched his opportunity. From a safe vantage ground he had scanned the crowd without, in search of some white friend. When he saw Major Carteret moving disconsolately away after his futile effort to stem the torrent, Jerry made a dash for the window. He sprang forth, and, waving his handkerchief as a flag of truce, ran toward Major Carteret, shouting frantically:—

"Major Carteret—O major! It's me, suh, Jerry, suh! I didn't go in there myself, suh—I was drag' in there! I wouldn't do nothin' 'gainst de white folks, suh—no, 'ndeed, I wouldn', suh!"

Jerry's cries were drowned in a roar of rage and a volley of shots from the mob. Carteret, who had turned away with Ellis, did not even hear his servant's voice. Jerry's poor flag of truce, his explanations, his reliance upon his white friends, all failed him in the moment of supreme need. In that hour, as in any hour when the depths of race hatred are stirred, a negro was no more than a brute beast, set upon by other brute beasts whose only instinct was to kill and destroy.

"Let us leave this inferno, Ellis," said Carteret, sick with anger and disgust. He had just become aware that a negro was being killed, though he did not know whom. "We can do nothing. The negroes have themselves to blame—they tempted us beyond endurance. I counseled firmness, and firm measures were taken, and our purpose was accomplished. I am not responsible for these subsequent horrors—I wash my hands of them. Let us go!"

The flames gained headway and gradually enveloped the burning building, until it became evident to those within as well as those without that the position of the defenders was no longer tenable. Would they die in the flames, or would they be driven out? The uncertainty soon came to an end.

The besieged had been willing to fight, so long as there seemed a hope of successfully defending themselves and their property; for their purpose was purely one of defense. When they saw the case was hopeless, inspired by Josh Green's reckless courage, they were still willing to sell their lives dearly. One or two of them had already been killed, and as many more disabled. The fate of Jerry Letlow had struck terror to the hearts of several others who could scarcely hide their fear. After the building had been fired, Josh's exhortations were no longer able to keep them in the hospital. They preferred to fight and be killed in the open, rather than to be smothered like rats in a hole.

"Boys!" exclaimed Josh—"I mean men—for nobody but men would do what you have done—the day has gone 'gainst us. We can see you' finish; but for my part, I ain't gwine to leave dis world widout takin' a white man 'long wid me, an' I sees my man right out yonder waitin'—I been waitin' for him twenty years, but he won' have to wait for me mo' 'n 'bout twenty seconds. every one of you pick yo' man! We'll open de do', an' we'll give some white men a chance to be sorry they ever started dis fuss!"

The door was thrown open suddenly, and through it rushed a dozen or more black figures, armed with knives, pistols, or clubbed muskets. Taken by sudden surprise, the white people stood motionless for a moment, but the approaching negroes had scarcely covered half the distance to which the heat of the flames had driven back the mob, before they were greeted with a volley that laid them all low but two. One of these, dazed by the fate of his companions, turned instinctively to flee, but had scarcely faced around before he fell, pierced in the back by a dozen bullets.

Josh Green, the tallest and biggest of them all, had not apparently been touched. Some of the crowd paused in involuntary admiration of this black giant, famed on the wharves for his strength, sweeping down upon them, a smile upon his face, his eyes lit up with a rapt expression which seemed to take him out of mortal ken. This impression was heightened by his apparent immunity from the shower of lead which less susceptible persons had continued to pour at him.

Armed with a huge bowie-knife, a relic of the civil war,

214

which he had carried on his person for many years for a definite purpose, and which he had kept sharpened to a razor edge, he reached the line of the crowd. All but the bravest shrank back. Like a wedge he dashed through the mob, which parted instinctively before him, and all oblivious of the rain of lead which fell around him, reached the point where Captain McBane, the bravest man in the party, stood waiting to meet him. A pistol-flame flashed in his face, but he went on, and raising his powerful right arm, buried his knife to the hilt in the heart of his enemy. When the crowd dashed forward to wreak vengeance on his dead body, they found him with a smile still upon his face.

One of the two died as the fool dies. Which was it, or was it both? "Vengeance is mine," saith the Lord, and it had not been left to Him. But they that do violence must expect to suffer violence. McBane's death was merciful, compared with the nameless horrors he had heaped upon the hundreds of helpless mortals who had fallen into his hands during his career as a contractor of convict labor.

Sobered by this culminating tragedy, the mob shortly afterwards dispersed. The flames soon completed their work, and this handsome structure, the fruit of old Adam Miller's industry, the monument of his son's philanthropy, a promise of good things for the future of the city, lay smouldering in ruins, a melancholy witness to the fact that our boasted civilization is but a thin veneer, which cracks and scales off at the first impact of primal passions.

215

# XXXVI

## Fiat Justitia

BY THE LIGHT OF THE BURNING BUILDING, WHICH
illuminated the street for several blocks, Major Carteret and
Ellis made their way rapidly until they turned into the street
where the major lived. Reaching the house, Carteret tried the
door and found it locked. A vigorous ring at the bell brought
no immediate response. Carteret had begun to pound
impatiently upon the door, when it was cautiously opened by
Miss Pemberton, who was pale, and trembled with excitement.

"Where is Olivia?" asked the major.

"She is upstairs, with Dodie and Mrs. Albright's hospital
nurse. Dodie has the croup. Virgie ran away after the riot broke
out. Sister Olivia had sent for Mammy Jane, but she did not
come. Mrs. Albright let her white nurse come over."

"I'll go up at once," said the major anxiously. "Wait for me,
Ellis—I'll be down in a few minutes."

"Oh, Mr. Ellis," exclaimed Clara, coming toward him with
both hands extended, "can nothing be done to stop this terrible
affair?"

"I wish I could do something," he murmured fervently,
taking both her trembling hands in his own broad palms,
where they rested with a surrendering trustfulness which he
has never since had occasion to doubt. "It has gone too far,
already, and the end, I fear, is not yet; but it cannot grow much
worse."

The editor hurried upstairs. Mrs. Carteret, wearing a
worried and haggard look, met him at the threshold of the
nursery.

"Dodie is ill," she said. "At three o'clock, when the trouble

216

began, I was over at Mrs. Albright's—I had left Virgie with the baby. When I came back, she and all the other servants had gone. They had heard that the white people were going to kill all the negroes, and fled to seek safety. I found Dodie lying in a draught, before an open window, gasping for breath. I ran back to Mrs. Albright's— I had found her much better to-day—and she let her nurse come over. The nurse says that Dodie is threatened with membranous croup."

"Have you sent for Dr. Price?"

"There was no one to send—the servants were gone, and the nurse was afraid to venture out into the street. I telephoned for Dr. Price, and found that he was out of town; that he had gone up the river this morning to attend a patient, and would not be back until tomorrow. Mrs. Price thought that he had anticipated some kind of trouble in the town to-day, and had preferred to be where he could not be called upon to assume any responsibility. "

"I suppose you tried Dr. Ashe?"

"I could not get him, nor any one else, after that first call. The telephone service is disorganized on account of the riot. We need medicine and ice. The drugstores are all closed on account of the riot, and for the same reason we couldn't get any ice."

Major Carteret stood beside the brass bedstead upon which his child was lying—his only child, around whose curly head clustered all his hopes; upon whom all his life for the past year had been centred. He stooped over the bed, beside which the nurse had stationed herself. She was wiping the child's face, which was red and swollen and covered with moisture, the nostrils working rapidly, and the little patient vainly endeavoring at intervals to cough up the obstruction to his breathing.

"Is it serious?" he inquired anxiously. He had always thought of the croup as a childish ailment, that yielded readily to proper treatment; but the child's evident distress impressed him with sudden fear.

"Dangerous," replied the young woman laconically. "You

217

came none too soon. If a doctor isn't got at once, the child will die—and it must be a good doctor."

"Whom can I call?" he asked. "You know them all, I suppose. Dr. Price, our family physician, is out of town."

"Dr. Ashe has charge of his cases when he is away," replied the nurse. "If you can't find him, try Dr. Hooper.

The child is growing worse every minute. On your way back you'd better get some ice, if possible."

The major hastened downstairs.

"Don't wait for me, Ellis," he said. "I shall be needed here for a while. I'll get to the office as soon as possible. Make up the paper, and leave another stick out for me to the last minute, but fill it up in case I'm not on hand by twelve. We must get the paper out early in the morning."

Nothing but a matter of the most vital importance would have kept Major Carteret away from his office this night. Upon the presentation to the outer world of the story of this riot would depend the attitude of the great civilized public toward the events of the last ten hours. The Chronicle was the source from which the first word would be expected; it would give the people of Wellington their cue as to the position which they must take in regard to this distressful affair, which had so far transcended in ferocity the most extreme measures which the conspirators had anticipated. The burden of his own responsibility weighed heavily upon him, and could not be shaken off; but he must do first the duty nearest to him—he must first attend to his child.

Carteret hastened from the house, and traversed rapidly the short distance to Dr. Ashe's office. Far down the street he could see the glow of the burning hospital, and he had scarcely left his own house when the fusillade of shots, fired when the colored men emerged from the burning building, was audible. Carteret would have hastened back to the scene of the riot, to see what was now going on, and to make another effort to stem the tide of bloodshed; but before the dread of losing his child, all other interests fell into the background. Not all the negroes in Wellington could weigh in the balance for one instant against the life of the feeble child now gasping for breath in the house behind him.

Reaching the house, a vigorous ring brought the doctor's wife to the door.

"Good-evening, Mrs. Ashe. Is the doctor at home?"

"No, Major Carteret. He was called to attend Mrs. Wells, who was taken suddenly ill, as a result of the trouble this afternoon. He will be there all night, no doubt. "

"My child is very ill and I must find some one."

"Try Dr. Yates. His house is only four doors away."

A ring at Dr. Yates' door brought out a young man.

"Is Dr. Yates in?"

"Yes, sir."

"Can I see him?"

"You might see him, sir, but that would-be all. His horse was frightened by the shooting on the streets, and ran away and threw the doctor, and broke his right arm. I have just set it; he will not be able to attend any patients for several weeks. He is old and nervous, and the shock was great."

"Are you not a physician?" asked Carteret, looking at the young man keenly. He was a serious, gentlemanly looking young fellow, whose word might probably be trusted.

"Yes, I am Dr. Evans, Dr. Yates' assistant. I'm really little more than a student, but I'll do what I can."

"My only child is sick with the croup, and requires immediate attention."

"I ought to be able to handle a case of the croup," answered Dr. Evans, "at least in the first stages. I'll go with you, and stay by the child, and if the case is beyond me, I may keep it in check until another physician comes."

He stepped back into another room, and returning immediately with his hat, accompanied Carteret homeward. The riot had subsided, even the glow from the smouldering hospital was no longer visible. It seemed that the city, appalled at the tragedy, had suddenly awakened to a sense of its own crime. Here and there a dark face, emerging cautiously from some hiding-place, peered from behind fence or tree, but shrank hastily away at the sight of a white face. The negroes of Wellington, with the exception of Josh Green and his party, had not behaved bravely on this critical day in their history; but those who had fought were dead, to the last man; those who had sought safety in flight or concealment were alive to tell the tale.

"We pass right by Dr. Thompson's," said Dr. Evans. "If you haven't spoken to him, it might be well to call him for consultation, in case the child should be very bad."

"Go on ahead," said Carteret, "and I'll get him."

Evans hastened on, while Carteret sounded the old-fashioned knocker upon the doctor's door. A gray-haired negro servant, clad in a dress suit and wearing a white tie, came to the door.

"De doctor, suh," he replied politely to Carteret's question, "has gone to amputate de arm of a gentleman who got one of his bones smashed wid a pistol bullet in de— fightin' dis afternoon, suh. He's jes' gone, suh, an' lef' word dat he'd be gone a' hour or mo', suh."

Carteret hastened homeward. He could think of no other available physician. Perhaps no other would be needed, but if so, he could find out from Evans whom it was best to call.

When he reached the child's room, the young doctor was bending anxiously over the little frame. The little lips had become livid, the little nails, lying against the white sheet, were blue. The child's efforts to breathe were most distressing, and each gasp cut the father like a knife. Mrs. Carteret was weeping hysterically.

"How is he, doctor?" asked the major.

"He is very low," replied the young man. "Nothing short of tracheotomy—an operation to open the windpipe—will relieve him. Without it, in half or three quarters of an hour he will be unable to breathe. It is a delicate operation, a mistake in which would be as fatal as the disease. I have neither the knowledge nor the experience to attempt it, and your child's life is too valuable for a student to practice upon. Neither have I the instruments here."

"What shall we do?" demanded Carteret. "We have called all the best doctors, and none are available."

The young doctor's brow was wrinkled with thought. He knew a doctor who could perform the operation. He had heard, also, of a certain event at Carteret's house some months before, when an unwelcome physician had been excluded from a consultation—but it was the last chance.

"There is but one other doctor in town who has performed the operation, so far as I know," he declared, "and that is Dr. Miller. If you can get him, he can save your child's life."

Carteret hesitated involuntarily. All the incidents, all the arguments, of the occasion when he had refused to admit the colored doctor to his house, came up vividly before his memory. He had acted in accordance with his lifelong beliefs, and had carried his point; but the present situation was different—this was a case of imperative necessity, and every other interest or consideration must give way before the imminence of his child's peril. That the doctor would refuse the call, he did not imagine: it would be too great an honor for a negro to decline— unless some bitterness might have grown out of the proceedings of the afternoon. That this doctor was a man of some education he knew; and he had been told that he was a man of fine feeling—for a negro—and might easily have taken to heart the day's events. Nevertheless, he could hardly refuse a professional call—professional ethics would require him to respond. Carteret had no reason to suppose that Miller had ever learned of what had occurred at the house during Dr. Burns' visit to Wellington. The major himself had never mentioned the controversy, and no doubt the other gentlemen had been equally silent.

"I'll go for him myself," said Dr. Evans, noting Carteret's hesitation and suspecting its cause. "I can do nothing here alone, for a little while, and I may be able to bring the doctor back with me. He likes a difficult operation."

It seemed an age ere the young doctor returned, though it was really only a few minutes. The nurse did what she could to

221

relieve the child's sufferings, which grew visibly more and more acute. The mother, upon the other side of the bed, held one of the baby's hands in her own, and controlled her feelings as best she might. Carteret paced the floor anxiously, going every few seconds to the head of the stairs to listen for Evans' footsteps on the piazza without. At last the welcome sound was audible, and a few strides took him to the door.

"Dr. Miller is at home, sir," reported Evans, as he came in. "He says that he was called to your house once before, by a third person who claimed authority to act, and that he was refused admittance. He declares that he will not consider such a call unless it comes from you personally."

"That is true, quite true," replied Carteret. "His position is a just one. I will go at once. Will—will—my child live until I can get Miller here?"

"He can live for half an hour without an operation. Beyond that I could give you little hope."

Seizing his hat, Carteret dashed out of the yard and ran rapidly to Miller's house; ordinarily a walk of six or seven minutes, Carteret covered it in three, and was almost out of breath when he rang the bell of Miller's front door.

The ring was answered by the doctor in person.

"Dr. Miller, I believe?" asked Carteret.

"Yes, sir."

"I am Major Carteret. My child is seriously ill, and you are the only available doctor who can perform the necessary operation."

"Ah! You have tried all the others—and then you come to me!"

"Yes, I do not deny it," admitted the major, biting his lip. He had not counted on professional jealousy as an obstacle to be met. "But I have come to you, as a physician, to engage your professional services for my child— my only child. I have confidence in your skill, or I should not have come to you. I request—nay, I implore you to lose no more time, but come with me at once! My child's life is hanging by a thread, and you can save it!"

222

"Ah!" replied the other, "as a father whose only child's life is in danger, you implore me, of all men in the world, to come and save it!"

There was a strained intensity in the doctor's low voice that struck Carteret, in spite of his own preoccupation. He thought he heard, too, from the adjoining room, the sound of some one sobbing softly. There was some mystery here which he could not fathom unaided.

Miller turned to the door behind him and threw it open. On the white cover of a low cot lay a childish form in the rigidity of death, and by it knelt, with her back to the door, a woman whose shoulders were shaken by the violence of her sobs. Absorbed in her grief, she did not turn, or give any sign that she had recognized the intrusion.

"There, Major Carteret!" exclaimed Miller, with the tragic eloquence of despair, "there lies a specimen of your handiwork! There lies my only child, laid low by a stray bullet in this riot which you and your paper have fermented; struck down as much by your hand as though you had held the weapon with which his life was taken!"

"My God!" exclaimed Carteret, struck with horror. "Is the child dead?"

"There he lies," continued the other, "an innocent child— there he lies dead, his little life snuffed out like a candle, because you and a handful of your friends thought you must override the laws and run this town at any cost!—and there kneels his mother, overcome by grief. We are alone in the house. It is not safe to leave her unattended. My duty calls me here, by the side of my dead child and my suffering wife! I cannot go with you. There is a just God in heaven!—as you have sown, so may you reap!"

Carteret possessed a narrow, but a logical mind, and except when confused or blinded by his prejudices, had always tried to be a just man. In the agony of his own predicament—in the horror of the situation at Miller's house—for a moment the veil of race prejudice was rent in twain, and he saw things as they were, in their correct proportions and relations—saw clearly and convincingly that he had no standing here, in the presence of death, in the home of this stricken family. Miller's refusal to go with him was pure, elemental justice; he could not blame the doctor for his stand. He was indeed conscious of a certain involuntary admiration for a man who held in his hands the power of life and death, and could use it, with strict justice, to avenge his own wrongs. In Dr. Miller's place he would have done the same thing. Miller had spoken the truth—as he had sown, so must he reap! He could not expect, could not ask, this father to leave his own household at such a moment.

Pressing his lips together with grim courage, and bowing mechanically, as though to Fate rather than the physician, Carteret turned and left the house. At a rapid pace he soon reached home. There was yet a chance for his child: perhaps some one of the other doctors had come; perhaps, after all, the disease had taken a favorable turn—Evans was but a young doctor, and might have been mistaken. Surely, with doctors all around him, his child would not be permitted to die for lack of medical attention! He found the mother, the doctor, and the nurse still grouped, as he had left them, around the suffering child.

"How is he now?" he asked, in a voice that sounded like a groan.

"No better," replied the doctor; "steadily growing worse. He can go on probably for twenty minutes longer without an operation."

"Where is the doctor?" demanded Mrs. Carteret, looking eagerly toward the door. "You should have brought him right upstairs. There's not a minute to spare! Phil, Phil, our child will die!"

Carteret's heart swelled almost to bursting with an intense pity. Even his own great sorrow became of secondary importance beside the grief which his wife must soon feel at the inevitable loss of her only child. And it was his fault! Would that he could risk his own life to spare her and to save the child!

Briefly, and as gently as might be, he stated the result of his

224

errand. The doctor had refused to come, for a good reason. He could not ask him again.

Young Evans felt the logic of the situation, which Carteret had explained sufficiently. To the nurse it was even clearer. If she or any other woman had been in the doctor's place, she would have given the same answer.

Mrs. Carteret did not stop to reason. In such a crisis a mother's heart usurps the place of intellect. For her at that moment, there were but two facts in all the world. Her child lay dying. There was within the town, and within reach, a man who could save him. With an agonized cry she rushed wildly from the room.

Carteret sought to follow her, but she flew down the long stairs like a wild thing. The least misstep might have precipitated her to the bottom; but ere Carteret, with a remonstrance on his lips, had scarcely reached the uppermost step, she had thrown open the front door and fled precipitately out into the night.

225

# XXXVII

## The Sisters

MILLER'S DOORBELL RANG LOUDLY, INSISTENTLY, as though demanding a response. Absorbed in his own grief, into which he had relapsed upon Carteret's departure, the sound was an unwelcome intrusion. Surely the man could not be coming back! If it were some one else—What else might happen to the doomed town concerned him not. His child was dead—his distracted wife could not be left alone.

The doorbell rang clamorously, appealingly. Through the long hall and the closed door of the room where he sat, he could hear some one knocking, and a faint voice calling.

"Open, for God's sake, open!"

It was a woman's voice—the voice of a woman in distress. Slowly Miller rose and went to the door, which he opened mechanically.

A lady stood there, so near the image of his own wife, whom he had just left, that for a moment he was well-nigh startled. A little older, perhaps, a little fairer of complexion, but with the same form, the same features, marked by the same wild grief. She wore a loose wrapper, which clothed her like the drapery of a statue. Her long dark hair, the counterpart of his wife's, had fallen down, and hung disheveled about her shoulders. There was blood upon her knuckles, where she had beaten with them upon the door.

"Dr. Miller," she panted, breathless from her flight and laying her hand upon his arm appealingly—when he shrank from the contact she still held it there—"Dr. Miller, you will come and save my child? You know what it is to lose a child! I am so sorry about your little boy! You will come to mine!"

"Your sorrow comes too late, madam," he said harshly. "My child is dead. I charged your husband with his murder, and he could not deny it. Why should I save your husband's child?"

"Ah, Dr. Miller!" she cried, with his wife's voice— she never knew how much, in that dark hour, she owed to that resemblance—"it is my child, and I have never injured you. It is my child, Dr. Miller, my only child. I brought it into the world at the risk of my own life! I have nursed it, I have watched over it, I have prayed for it—and it now lies dying! Oh, Dr. Miller, dear Dr. Miller, if you have a heart, come and save my child!"

"Madam," he answered more gently, moved in spite of himself, "my heart is broken. My people lie dead upon the streets, at the hands of yours. The work of my life is in ashes— and, yonder, stretched out in death, lies my own child! God! woman, you ask too much of human nature! Love, duty, sorrow, justice, call me here. I cannot go!"

She rose to her full height. "Then you are a murderer," she cried wildly. "His blood be on your head, and a mother's curse beside!"

The next moment, with a sudden revulsion of feeling, she had thrown herself at his feet—at the feet of a negro, this proud white woman—and was clasping his knees wildly.

"O God!" she prayed, in tones which quivered with anguish, "pardon my husband's sins, and my own, and move this man's hard heart, by the blood of thy Son, who died to save us all!"

It was the last appeal of poor humanity. When the pride of intellect and caste is broken; when we grovel in the dust of humiliation; when sickness and sorrow come, and the shadow of death falls upon us, and there is no hope elsewhere—we turn to God, who sometimes swallows the insult, and answers the appeal.

Miller raised the lady to her feet. He had been deeply moved—but he had been more deeply injured. This was his wife's sister—ah, yes! but a sister who had scorned and

227

slighted and ignored the existence of his wife for all her life. Only Miller, of all the world, could have guessed what this had meant to Janet, and he had merely divined it through the clairvoyant sympathy of love. This woman could have no claim upon him because of this unacknowledged relationship. Yet, after all, she was his wife's sister, his child's kinswoman. She was a fellow creature, too, and in distress.

"Rise, madam," he said, with a sudden inspiration, lifting her gently. "I will listen to you on one condition. My child lies dead in the adjoining room, his mother by his side. Go in there, and make your request of her. I will abide by her decision."

The two women stood confronting each other across the body of the dead child, mute witness of this first meeting between two children of the same father. Standing thus face to face, each under the stress of the deepest emotions, the resemblance between them was even more striking than it had seemed to Miller when he had admitted Mrs. Carteret to the house. But Death, the great leveler, striking upon the one hand and threatening upon the other, had wrought a marvelous transformation in the bearing of the two women. The sad-eyed Janet towered erect, with menacing aspect, like an avenging goddess. The other, whose pride had been her life, stood in the attitude of a trembling suppliant.

"You have come here," cried Janet, pointing with a tragic gesture to the dead child—"you, to gloat over your husband's work. All my life you have hated and scorned and despised me. Your presence here insults me and my dead. What are you doing here?"

"Mrs. Miller," returned Mrs. Carteret tremulously, dazed for a moment by this outburst, and clasping her hands with an imploring gesture, "my child, my only child, is dying, and your husband alone can save his life. Ah, let me have my child," she moaned, heartrendingly. "It is my only one—my sweet child—my ewe lamb!"

"This was my only child!" replied the other mother; "and yours is no better to die than mine!"

228

"You are young," said Mrs. Carteret, "and may yet have many children—this is my only hope! If you have a human heart, tell your husband to come with me. He leaves it to you; he will do as you command."

"Ah," cried Janet, "I have a human heart, and therefore I will not let him go. My child is dead—O God, my child, my child!"

She threw herself down by the bedside, sobbing hysterically. The other woman knelt beside her, and put her arm about her neck. For a moment Janet, absorbed in her grief, did not repulse her.

"Listen," pleaded Mrs. Carteret. "You will not let my baby die? You are my sister;—the child is your own near kin!"

"My child was nearer," returned Janet, rising again to her feet and shaking off the other woman's arm. "He was my son, and I have seen him die. I have been your sister for twenty-five years, and you have only now, for the first time, called me so!"

"Listen—sister," returned Mrs. Carteret. Was there no way to move this woman? Her child lay dying, if he were not dead already. She would tell everything, and leave the rest to God. If it would save her child, she would shrink at no sacrifice. Whether the truth would still further incense Janet, or move her to mercy, she could not tell; she would leave the issue to God.

"Listen, sister!" she said. "I have a confession to make. You are my lawful sister. My father was married to your mother. You are entitled to his name, and to half his estate."

Janet's eyes flashed with bitter scorn.

"And you have robbed me all these years, and now tell me that as a reason why I should forgive the murder of my child?"

"No, no!" cried the other wildly, fearing the worst. "I have known of it only a few weeks—since my Aunt Polly's death. I had not meant to rob you—I had meant to make restitution. Sister! for our father's sake, who did you no wrong, give me my child's life!"

Janet's eyes slowly filled with tears—bitter tears— burning tears. For a moment even her grief at her child's loss dropped

229

to second place in her thoughts. This, then, was the recognition for which, all her life, she had longed in secret. It had come, after many days, and in larger measure than she had dreamed; but it had come, not with frank kindliness and sisterly love, but in a storm of blood and tears; not freely given, from an open heart, but extorted from a reluctant conscience by the agony of a mother's fears. Janet had obtained her heart's desire, and now that it was at her lips, found it but apples of Sodom, filled with dust and ashes!

"Listen!" she cried, dashing her tears aside. "I have but one word for you—one last word—and then I hope never to see your face again! My mother died of want, and I was brought up by the hand of charity. Now, when I have married a man who can supply my needs, you offer me back the money which you and your friends have robbed me of! You imagined that the shame of being a negro swallowed up every other ignominy—and in your eyes I am a negro, though I am your sister, and you are white, and people have taken me for you on the streets—and you, therefore, left me nameless all my life! Now, when an honest man has given me a name of which I can be proud, you offer me the one of which you robbed me, and of which I can make no use. For twenty-five years I, poor, despicable fool, would have kissed your feet for a word, a nod, a smile. Now, when this tardy recognition comes, for which I have waited so long, it is tainted with fraud and crime and blood, and I must pay for it with my child's life!"

"And I must forfeit that of mine, it seems, for withholding it so long," sobbed the other, as, tottering, she turned to go. "It is but just."

"Stay—do not go yet!" commanded Janet imperiously, her pride still keeping back her tears. "I have not done. I throw you back your father's name, your father's wealth, your sisterly recognition. I want none of them— they are bought too dear! ah, God, they are bought too dear! But that you may know that a woman may be foully wronged, and yet may have a heart to feel, even for one who has injured her, you may have your child's life, if my husband can save it! Will," she said, throwing

230

open the door into the next room, "go with her!"

"God will bless you for a noble woman!" exclaimed Mrs. Carteret. "You do not mean all the cruel things you have said— ah, no! I will see you again, and make you take them back; I cannot thank you now! Oh, doctor, let us go! I pray God we may not be too late!"

Together they went out into the night. Mrs. Carteret tottered under the stress of her emotions, and would have fallen, had not Miller caught and sustained her with his arm until they reached the house, where he turned over her fainting form to Carteret at the door.

"Is the child still alive?" asked Miller.

"Yes, thank God," answered the father, "but nearly gone."

"Come on up, Dr. Miller," called Evans from the head of the stairs. "There's time enough, but none to spare."

# NEW! *Black Classics*

NEW from The X Press– an exciting collection of the world's great forgotten black classic novels. Many brilliant black works of writing lie in dusty corners of libraries across the globe. Now thanks to Britain's foremost publisher of black fiction, you can discover some of these fantastic novels. Over the coming months we will be publishing many of these masterpieces which every lover of black fiction will want to collect. The first set of three books are available now!

## TRADITION by Charles W Chesnutt

In the years after the American Civil War, a small town in the Deep South struggles to come to terms with the new order. Ex-slaves are now respected doctors, lawyers and powerbrokers–And the white residents don't like it one bit!

A sinister group of white supremacist businessmen see their opportunity to fan the flames of race-hate when a black man is wrongly accused of murdering a white woman. But the black population, proud and determined, strike back.

For a gifted black doctor, the events happening before him pose a huge dilemma. Should he take on the mantle of leading the black struggle in the town, or does his first responsibility lie with his wife and children?

First published in 1901 Charles W. Chesnutt's brilliantly crafted novel is grounded in the events and climate of post slavery America and the white supremacist movement. It graphically captures the mood of the period and is rightly acclaimed as one of the greats of black classic writing.

# Black Classics

## THE BLACKER THE BERRY
### by Wallace Thurman

Emma Lou was born black. Too black for her own comfort and that of her social-climbing wannabe family. Resented by those closest to her, she runs from her small hometown to Los Angeles and then to Harlem of the 1920's, seeking her identity and an escape from the pressures of the black community.
She drifts from one loveless relationship to another in the search for herself and a place in society where prejudice towards her comes not only from whites, but from her own race!

First published in 1929, The Blacker The Berry, caused a storm when it was released. It dared to say what everyone in black America knew, but didn't want to admit. For many years it has remained a lost classic in the vault of black literature but its "raw and penetrating insight" has as much relevance for the black community today, as it did decades ago.

## IOLA by Frances E.W. Harper

The beautiful Iola Leroy is duped into slavery after the death of her father but the chaos caused by the bloody American Civil War gives her the chance to snatch her freedom and start the long search for the mother whom she was separated from on the slave trader's block.
With the war unfolding around her, Iola endures her hardships with a growing pride in her race. Twice she rejects the advances of a white doctor, who offers to relieve her from the "burden of blackness" by marrying her, and chooses instead to devote herself to the upliftment of her people. It's here that she eventually finds the true love she has been seeking all her life.

Iola was the most widely read black novel of the 19th century and was hugely influential in high-lighting the plight of black American slaves. It was also the first novel which featured a black woman as heroine and was an inspiration for many later black writers.